Shadow Dwellers

Book Two in the Shadows Series

Trish Moran

Shadow Dwellers

Published by Accent Press Ltd 2015

ISBN 9781783759422

Copyright © Trish Moran 2015

Chapter One

'Really, Abel, I'm not ill at all! Just pregnant!' Ruby protested as her partner helped her out of bed that morning. 'The midwife told me it's quite normal to feel tired at this stage.'

'I'm sure the midwife is correct,' Abel replied, 'but I would like Dr Jensen to take a look at you. It's a good idea to have a second opinion.'

'I never thought you would end up fussing over me like a mother hen!' Ruby complained.

'Another of your quaint Non-Lab sayings!' Abel kissed her brow. 'He'll be here in an hour. Oh, and he's bringing a colleague with him. Dr Amanda Harrison, a psychologist.'

He saw a dark look pass across Ruby's face and took her hands in his.

'Dr Jensen has promised us there will be no publicity. He fully understands our desire for privacy. Beth and Frank have always found his advice and help invaluable with Frankie and Grace.'

'Well, as long as this new doctor understands that, too. It's time we Lab/Non-Lab couples were given some peace now! We're not that unusual anymore. There are many couples like us, with Hybrid children,' Ruby said.

'I know, I know,' Abel nodded, 'but we do need to be sure all is well with our child. We still don't know enough about Lab development yet, let alone Hybrid development. Maybe people like Dr Jensen and Dr Harrison can help us.'

Ruby gave him a smile. 'OK, Abel. Perhaps Dr Jensen and Dr Harrison will show you that I'm absolutely fine and that our baby is, too!'

Patrick Jensen turned to his female companion as they drew up outside the office building.

'Well, Amanda. Here we are at The Compound.'

'The admin building is part of the old Centre, isn't it?' she said, getting out of the car.

'Yes. The research rooms have all been closed down now,' he replied. 'The Nursery and Children wards are empty and there are only a handful of the capsules in use in the Adolescent Ward. Most of the Labs there will be moved into the Mature Ward by the end of this year.'

'Soon there'll be no need of any of the wards, will there? Looks like there are still quite a few people living in the Compound though,' Amanda said, looking at the rows of small houses on their right. 'Are they all Labs?'

'Some of them are single Labs and there are quite a few mixed couples here, too, now. The majority of the couples have a young child or a baby on the way!'

'Ah, yes, the Hybrids. How did they get that name?' his companion asked.

'One of the national newspapers coined the term first when Beth and Frank had Frankie, the first mixed-background child, and it stuck.' Jensen looked up, 'Here's Abel now.'

A tall, broad-shouldered, olive-skinned man was walking towards them, accompanied by a slender black woman almost as tall as he was.

'Abel, Celia!' Jensen said, holding out his hand, 'Let me introduce you to the new psychologist on our team, Amanda Harrison.'

'I'm so pleased to meet you. It was very good of you to let me come along!' Amanda smiled and shook hands with them both.

'You'd like me to take a look at Ruby, Abel?' Jensen continued.

'Yes. As I said, she insists she is fine, but my mind would be more at ease if you can check all is well,' Abel said.

Celia turned to Amanda as the two men walked towards one of the small houses.

'Would you like to wait over here while Abel and Ruby speak to the doctor? Abel will let us know when they are ready.'

'Of course,' Amanda replied, as she followed Celia into a spacious reception area in the office building.

'Would you like tea or coffee?' Celia asked as Amanda settled herself into a large comfortable sofa.

'A coffee would be lovely, thank you,' Amanda smiled.

She looked around the room. There were several other sofas and a coffee table with a neat pile of newspapers and magazines. A notebook with a picture of a dinosaur on the cover was lying on the table. She flicked through it. There were pages of mathematical formulae. She looked up as a small boy ran into the room.

'Oh, can I have my book, please?' he held out his hand for the notebook.

'Is this yours?' Amanda raised her eyebrows, 'Has someone being writing in it for you?'

The boy frowned and flicked through it.

'No!' He breathed a sigh of relief. 'Sometimes Grace tries to scribble in it. I have to hide it!'

'Frankie! We'll be late if we don't leave now!' a voice called.

'Coming, Mummy!' he shouted. He had climbed on to another sofa and was pulling something from under the cushion.

A woman appeared in the doorway.

'Frankie! Have you been taking the nursery toys again?'

'Helen and I *need* these cars!' he said, clutching two toy cars to his chest.

'But you can't keep taking them!' his mother said, 'That's almost stealing!'

'It's nothing like stealing, Mummy! It's only borrowing. I have every intention of returning them to their rightful owner,' he replied indignantly.

'Why do you have to take them home anyway? You can always play with them when you get to nursery,' his mother continued.

Frankie scowled. 'On Thursdays they let the red room children choose first and they take the best ones that we need!'

'Well, they should have a chance to go first sometimes.'

'They're just babies! It doesn't matter which ones *they* play with! They play silly games! *And* they put them in their mouths! Then they're all *wet* when we get a chance to use them.'

'Well, you were a baby once!' his mother said.

'That was ages ago! I'm four now!' Frankie pulled himself up to his full height.

'You're only four?' Amanda blurted out.

Frankie's mother spun around.

'I'm sorry! I didn't notice you there,' she said.

'No, I must apologise,' Amanda replied. 'I didn't mean to startle you.'

Frankie glared at her. 'You said I was *only* four!'

Amanda patted his mother's arm as she opened her mouth to speak.

'I was just surprised at how bright and articulate you are, Frankie! And the work you have done in your book ...' She took a deep breath, 'Oh, but you must be ...'

'A Hybrid! Yes that's right!' he nodded. 'There are quite a lot of Hybrids now, like my sister, but the ones here are quite young; so I can't play with them yet.'

Amanda looked at his mother.

'So you must be Beth,' she held out her hand. 'What an amazing child you have!'

'Thank you!' Beth smiled. She glanced at the clock. 'We have to go now, Frankie, we'll be late!'

'OK, Mummy.' Frankie pushed the cars into her hands and ran to the coffee table, 'Just let me get that magazine about the turbo engine. I can read it while the others have their afternoon nap.'

Amanda sank back onto the sofa as the two hurried out.

'Are you OK?' Celia asked as she came in holding a tray.

'I've just met Frankie,' she replied, shaking her head. 'Are all … Hybrids … so bright?'

'There are only a handful of Hybrids around Frankie's age and they do tend to be more advanced than Non-Lab children, though we haven't made a full assessment up to now.'

'How many Hybrids are there now?' Amanda leaned forward.

Celia's brow creased. 'Around a hundred would be a safe estimate. Most mixed-couple families prefer to get on with their own lives the same as Non-Labs.'

'Of course!' Amanda held up her hands. 'I'm just so amazed! That little boy! His mother is Lab and his father is … Non-Lab, isn't he?'

Celia nodded.

'Are there any children with two Lab parents?' Amanda asked.

'No,' Celia shook her head. 'No Lab has chosen another Lab as a partner.'

'There must be a reason for this,' Amanda continued. 'Has any research been done on Lab relationships?'

'Some of our people have started some investigations; but we don't publicise our findings,' Celia answered.

'It would be fascinating to be involved in such research!' Amanda sighed.

Celia turned to say something as the phone rang.

'I'll take you over to speak to Ruby now. She insists it is a short interview as she is feeling quite tired.'

'Oh, I won't take up too much of her time, I promise! Just a couple of questions.'

Ruby was seated in a large comfortable armchair when

Amanda and Celia entered their home. Outside on the balcony Patrick Jensen and Abel were talking.

'Well, Dr Jensen says I'm absolutely fine!' Ruby said. 'Now Abel has got to believe me!'

'You look to me as if you are growing by the minute, Ruby!' Celia joked.

'I feel it! Dr Jensen thinks, like all Hybrids, our baby will be here at least a month early. I must admit, that was good news for me!' Ruby groaned.

Amanda sat down beside her as Celia went out. 'How much longer have you to go, Ruby?'

'I'm five months pregnant, so probably two or three more months,' she replied, 'going by other Hybrid pregnancies. Hybrid babies seem to develop quicker than Non-Lab babies.'

'I met young Frankie. What an amazing child! Celia tells me all Hybrids are like him. So we have a generation of highly talented youngsters growing up here. Think of what they can offer to society in the future!' The doctor's eyes shone.

'As long as our baby is healthy, that's our main concern,' Ruby pointed out gently.

'Of course,' Amanda quickly agreed. 'Anyway, what I really wanted to talk about was about your life in a mixed relationship; any concerns you may have for your child. What about special educational arrangements? Frankie, for example – are his obvious talents being nurtured?'

'He seems happy enough at the nursery, and at home here on the Compound,' Ruby said.

'I hardly think a local nursery will be sufficient to meet his needs! I would be quite happy to put into place some alternative arrangements for his education, and the same of course for any other Hybrid children,' the doctor continued.

'Thank you, but I think the arrangements we have in mind for our baby will be fine,' Ruby said.

'Well, you could give it some thought,' Amanda gave a

rather brittle smile. 'Now, I'd just like to ask you one or two questions about your life here. You all seem to get on well together, Labs and Non-Labs. What would you say your common interests are?'

'Most of the couples here are parents with young children, or soon to be parents.' Ruby smiled. 'This is our first child, and it's so reassuring to have other parents to talk to!'

'And I expect all of you are thinking about the best future for your children?'

'Of course we want the best for our children!' Ruby said.

Amanda looked around as Abel entered. 'Ruby and I were just talking about the future of your son or daughter. It's so exciting, isn't it?'

Abel smiled and nodded. 'It certainly is! And of course, our little one will have plenty of companions of his or her age; there are five other Hybrid babies due around the same date!'

'Could I perhaps speak to some of the other expectant mothers, Abel? Just a few questions?'

'Dr Jensen is with three of the other mothers-to-be now. I will ask them if they would like to speak with you. I'm sure they won't object,' he replied.

Amanda stood up and shook Ruby's hand. 'I look forward to seeing you again, Ruby. It's been such a pleasure to meet you!'

She looked up at Abel as she walked beside him.

'You know, I'd really like to get to know more about Labs, about your way of thinking – the differences and similarities with us ordinary humans, Non-Labs. And of course how Hybrids develop. From what Celia was telling me, Hybrids are far more advanced than Non-Lab children. Would you be willing to spare me some of your time, Abel?' she asked. She noticed his hesitation. 'It would be for the best, for all Labs and their children.'

'Yes, you're right,' Abel finally nodded.

Chapter Two

'Thank you so much for coming today, Abel,' Amanda said. 'Ali is just going to attach a few monitors to record your heart rate, lung capacity, muscle density and a few other things as you exercise. We can then compare the results with a typical Non-Lab male of what we'd judge to be your age. Dr Jensen told me that Labs also have a rapid healing rate. He told me about your own recovery rate after you were shot five years ago by an anti-Lab supporter.'

Abel smiled. 'Lab age is difficult to establish – we were awakened when we were Mature. As to the rapid healing rate, it was programmed into us when we were created as spare parts for the Non-Lab subscribers. The healing process after the transplant was accelerated.'

Amanda patted his arm, 'Luckily those dark days are behind us now, Abel. The Labs and their Hybrid children can look forward to a promising future.'

Nearly two hours later Amanda smiled as Ali handed her a sheet of results.

'Thank you, Ali,' she said as she sat down at a desk with Abel.

She raised her eyebrows, 'The Labs have a much higher level of fitness in all the areas we looked at today.'

'All Labs are very aware of the benefits of keeping healthy. Fitness has been high on our priorities from our time in The Caves. We also encourage Non-Labs of our acquaintance to follow a strict fitness regime,' Abel replied.

Amanda smiled, 'I couldn't agree more! Without making time for exercise and the gym, I feel very sluggish. Most of my friends would agree with you, too!'

Abel nodded appreciatively as Amanda stood up and walked to get a folder from the far side of the room.

'I can see you do prioritise your physical well-being.'

Amanda gave him a coy glance as she sat down opposite him again. 'I must confess, a little vanity does play a part in my fitness regime!' She opened a notebook and looked up at him. 'I've done some research since I last saw you and it seems there has been a rise in Hybrid births all over the UK and America in the past six months.'

'Yes, our Lab research has already established this fact. And the probable reason for it,' Abel agreed.

His companion looked at him. 'It's directly related to the closing of the Nursery Ward, isn't it?' She continued as he nodded. 'Soon all the Labs will have been released from the Centre wards. The Labs are now feeling driven to … procreate … to ensure the future of the Lab species. Is this the conclusion your research team came to?'

He nodded again. 'Many Labs are in relationships and have started or are planning on having young soon.'

'And a Lab always chooses a Non-Lab partner. Have your researchers any views on this?' she continued.

'Yes, we believe that Labs are not attracted to Labs as partners as this may lead to the same problems that cloning a clone instead of the original would mean. It would increase the chance of magnifying any defects in the programming. Much the same as many Non-Labs do not partner close relatives,' he told her.

Amanda nodded, 'This is very much what our own researchers came up with. You say "in relationships". Aren't some of the young Labs, at least some of the male Labs, considering having young with more than one female? Wouldn't that make sense? They are capable of fathering more than one child with different mothers. Female Labs of course are more limited as they are restricted by the gestation period.'

Abel looked abashed. 'I don't know if our research

factored in the length of the relationship between the Lab and Non-Lab.'

'It would be worth considering for many of your young men, if you are seriously concerned about Lab numbers. The Labs should, of course, be assessing their potential Non-Lab partners carefully, to ensure the young are of the best quality. The male Labs should ensure the women they choose should be of a high standard, physically and mentally. And a woman who would appreciate the honour it is to be chosen to bear a Hybrid child.'

Her hand moved across the desk and touched his lightly. 'I know of one woman who fits all categories; if you are willing, Abel … perhaps it is almost a duty of suitable male Labs to ensure the future of their race …'

He raised his hands, 'I can see the logic in your ideas, Amanda, but I …'

She stood up, 'Think about it, Abel! I will see you this time next week, OK? I've also got a meeting with Joel Harvey, the head of the top performing primary school in the UK. I want his advice on planning a suitable education programme for the Hybrids. Frankie's talents are been wasted in the local nursery, good though it may be. And what about your own child?'

Abel shrugged. 'Well, Ruby and I must discuss this, and you will have to see what Beth and Frank think of your idea. They are happy that they are finally settling down to a more normal family life.'

'We are quite happy with the local nursery …' Ruby began a few days later as she sat opposite Amanda.

'Don't you think you should be putting your child's interests first?' Amanda persisted. 'Don't you realise what an honour has been bestowed on you? You have been chosen to have a Hybrid child! Surely you are going to do all you can to nurture and encourage this child to fulfil his or her full potential?'

Ruby shifted in her chair, 'Well, of course, we'll give our child the best opportunities we can …'

'Can I just ask, what qualifications do you yourself have, Ruby? What was your career previously?'

Ruby shifted uneasily again under the other woman's scrutiny.

'Well, I didn't actually … I thought I might apply for college … maybe when the baby is …' she stammered.

Amanda shook her head sadly, 'Ruby, you are a lovely person; I am sure you will be a caring mother; but you are certainly not equipped to educate a child with the IQ levels of the Hybrids we have interviewed! At two years old they are capable of carrying out tasks that many ordinary children would find well beyond them at five or six years of age. How will you answer the questions your son or daughter will be posing then?'

Ruby gave a sigh of relief as Abel and Frank came in.

'Ah, Amanda, Celia told me I would find you here. Frank is interested in hearing about your plans for educating our youngsters.'

Frank nodded as he pulled up a chair and sat down with them.

'Yes, I know our Frankie is bright, *really* bright. And I want him to have all the chances we can give him. I don't want him messing about at school like I did!'

Amanda nodded and gave a little smile to Ruby, 'I'm sure we all want the best for our children, those born and yet to be born!'

Ruby sat back as the other three sat earnestly discussing schooling ideas.

'Of course, Joel Harvey is highly qualified and has much experience in nurturing the potential of many generations of children,' Amanda was telling the two men.

Ruby quietly sighed. She watched Frank's intense expression as he hung on to Amanda Harrison's every word. Abel's expression was more guarded, but she could see he was also impressed with Amanda's ideas.

The psychologist brushed Abel's arm lightly as he opened the car door for her later that morning.

'And have you considered my offer, Abel?'

He cleared his throat, 'I must admit it is very flattering to be propositioned by such an intelligent and beautiful woman. I am sure that you would make a fine mother,' he gave a smile, 'but I must refuse you, Amanda. I have commitments and responsibilities ...'

Amanda squeezed his arm. 'You also have commitments and responsibilities to the Labs, Abel, to the future of your own race!'

Abel gently patted her hand and removed it, 'I am sure that there plenty of men – Lab or Non-Lab – who would be honoured to have a child with you, Amanda.'

A brittle smile froze on her face as she climbed into the car.

'I'll be in touch with you, and the other couples interested in Joel Harvey's plans.'

'I'd be happy never to see that woman again!' Ruby groaned as Abel returned to the house.

'We will need to discuss Harvey's education plans. They are sound,' he replied.

'She makes having a baby sound like being part of a production line!' Ruby scowled.

'She is right about many things, Ruby. And she cares deeply about the future of our Hybrid children.'

'Don't I know it! Amanda keeps telling me how honoured I should be to be chosen to have a Hybrid child! I wouldn't be surprised to find she has her eyes on a male Lab to provide her with such a wonderful child!'

'Well, she is intelligent and physically attractive; I don't think it will be long before she does find somebody willing! Actually ... Amanda thinks all male Labs have a duty to father as many children as they can as the last of the Labs are awakened. To ensure the future of our species.'

'And did she ask *you* to …?' Ruby's voice trailed off as she saw his expression. 'Just wait till I see her! I'll …'

'Ruby! Calm down! I can see the logic in her thinking, but I did tell her that I would not be interested personally.'

'You can see the logic? You think it would be a good thing for Lab males to impregnate women and then abandon their children?' Ruby cried.

Abel put his arms around her and pulled her close to him, 'No, Ruby. It is better if they have a stable family background, as we plan for our children.'

Ruby nestled into his shoulder.

'Abel?'

'Mmmm?' he replied.

'Were you tempted by her offer? Even slightly?'

'Well, she is an attractive woman, with a convincing argument …' He grinned as she looked up suddenly, horrified, 'but no, not in the least!'

Chapter Three

'Over four years have passed since the Centre was shut down. We all realise that the creation of humans as spare parts is totally unacceptable, but we have to recognise that the technology that enabled this to happen can be used for the good of everyone,' Dr Stoney, the Non-Lab head of the Ministry of Health insisted. 'We can't let it go to waste!'

Abel gave a long sigh. 'I agree with you, Dr Stoney. Over the past three years we have seen some of the benefits of the Centre's research used to help many Non-Labs in countries all over the world. There may be Labs who will be grateful for these developments in their later years. But I am not convinced by the arguments to build a new Centre producing Labs.'

'We have modified the Ministry's proposals seven times in the last two years to accommodate your concerns, Abel,' Stoney continued. 'You rejected the idea of a government-controlled centre to create highly intelligent Labs to fill the gaps in the job market: doctors and nursing staff, and the police force.'

Putting his hands on his knees, Abel leaned forward and faced the minister. 'You have a daughter, don't you, a barrister working in London?' The other man nodded. 'You must be very proud of her.'

Stoney nodded again. 'Yes, very much so, but what does this have to do with our discussion?'

'What would you have said if you were told at her birth that she was destined to be, let me see, a supervisor for London public transport, as there was a great shortage in this area?'

'OK. OK. I take your point,' Stoney spread his hands, 'but this latest proposal is very reasonable.' He took a sheet of paper handed to him by his secretary. 'A government-controlled centre for the creation of Labs for Non-Labs – and who knows, maybe even for Labs – who are unable to conceive in the natural way. The Labs will be programmed with the donor's talents and interests, largely as you and the other Labs were. It's just an extension of IVF really. You surely can't find fault with this.'

Abel held out his hand as the secretary handed him a duplicate sheet. He read it through for several minutes. The two others waited silently.

'This is a good base to start from,' Abel began. 'We would need to clarify which talents and interests donors were allowed to include. Also, how many Labs would each donor be permitted to have created? Would there be certain criteria the donors would have to meet? How could we ensure that the Labs were not being created to be a donor for a sick child? Then there would be the price; would there be a range according to the programmes selected? I must admit, though, that it could be feasible. I assume that there will be Labs working alongside Non-Labs at such a centre?'

'Yes, of course.' Stoney released a long breath. 'Did you take all that down, Sandra? Good, type it up and email it to the relevant committee members, with a copy to myself and Abel.'

The two men stood up and shook hands.

'Keep me updated on any developments, Dr Stoney. I hope we can work together for the benefit of all members of our society,' Abel said.

'I sincerely hope so, Abel.'

Later that week Abel sat down to a meal with Ruby, Celia, Isaac, Johnny, Leon, and Dette. Frank, Beth, and Frankie had joined them, too. He explained the plans that Dr Stoney had outlined for a government-controlled centre to create more Labs.

'It will be carefully monitored and regulated, won't it?' Celia asked.

Abel nodded. 'Yes, there will be a committee of both Labs and Non-Labs to ensure this.'

'It sounds OK, but when I have kids I want normal Hybrid ones,' Leon said.

'Me, too,' his brother agreed.

'What exactly does "normal" mean, Mummy?' Frankie asked. 'What is a normal person like? Are we all normal?'

They all looked around the table at each other.

'Well, whatever is the usual thing, I suppose. Different people see different things as being normal.' Beth smiled. 'Yes, I would say all of us are normal.'

Chapter Four

A short while later Amanda Harrison and Joel Harvey appeared on a television documentary with the outline of their plan for a school for gifted and talented children.

'Well, from the research you have been involved in lately, Dr Harrison, I think we can take it to mean a school for the Hybrid children?' the commentator said.

'Oh, not just for Hybrids!' Harvey waved a hand, 'It will be open for any child who demonstrates an IQ level well above their chronological age.'

'And, as I have discovered from my work with the Hybrids, that will definitely include all Hybrids of nursery age,' Amanda added.

'But our school is not exclusively for Hybrids!' Harvey quickly pointed out. 'It is open to all children, whatever their background.'

Amanda leaned forward, her eyes shining.

'There is no getting away from the fact that the Hybrids are exceptionally clever! We cannot waste such talents for the sake of political correctness. These children, if carefully nurtured, are the key to our future. Not just this country – I mean globally!'

'She's a bit too intense for me!' Ruby remarked as Amanda started to explain her vision of their new school.

'I agree,' Isaac nodded. 'When I interviewed her earlier this month I could feel her passion on the subject, but I also think she's not going to make friends with many ordinary people with her attitude. And I don't think she's really doing the Labs and Hybrids much good either.'

'But she is right, we *know* the Hybrids have a much

higher level of intelligence compared to Non-Lab children, Ruby. And compared to many Labs, too,' Celia pointed out.

'Yes, we have to give them the chance to realise their full potential,' Frank nodded. 'We want Frankie to go far, don't we, love?'

Beth gave a wry shrug. 'As long as he is happy, Frank.'

'And that is what we want, too, isn't it, Ruby?' Abel smiled.

'Why are the Hybrids more intelligent than the Labs?' Leon asked.

'I don't know, but I'm glad they are,' his brother Johnny said with a grin, 'otherwise *our* future kids will have trouble keeping up in school!'

'But they'll be excellent sport players!' his brother added.

'And will end up playing in the England squad, like their fathers!' Ruby smiled.

'I hope so!' Leon smiled.

'Yeah! Nothing could beat the feeling of helping England to bring home the World Cup last year!' Johnny added. Leon grinned and gave him a high five.

'According to the research done by our own Lab team, we Labs were programmed to develop at a greatly accelerated rate compared to our donors, and also to be talented in the areas selected by our donors,' Celia explained. 'The Hybrids seem to have inherited the accelerated growth from the Lab parent, though not such rapid development as Labs, but their brains seem able to acquire knowledge from a wide variety of topics and at an accelerated rate. The findings so far demonstrate that they seem to be able to pick up facts and understanding of any topic they take an interest in from a young age.'

'Then a special education is really necessary for Hybrids, isn't it?' Frank looked at Celia.

'I agree,' she replied.

'One thing that does worry me,' Ruby interjected, 'is that not enough attention has been paid to the emotional and social development of our children.'

'Ruby is right,' Beth nodded. 'We want children who are happy and who can socialise with both Labs and Non-Labs.'

'Don't you agree with that, too, Celia?' Isaac asked her. 'Aren't you worried about your own future children?'

Celia shrugged. 'A hypothetical question!'

'Is she still seeing that footballer friend of yours, boys?' Isaac asked casually as Celia left the room.

'He's still as keen as ever, but …' Johnny began.

'… I don't think he's the one for her!' Leon finished his sentence.

Ruby noticed the smile that flickered over Isaac's face.

'And what about you, two? Any truth in the rumours about the lovely twins you have been seen escorting around town?' Beth asked them.

The boys looked at each other.

'Yes,' Johnny said. 'In fact …'

'… we'd like you all to meet them soon!' Leon smiled.

As everyone prepared to leave later that evening, Ruby walked beside Isaac.

'You're very fond of Celia,' she said.

'Oh, she's up there with the famous names now! She wouldn't be interested in me!' he sighed, 'It's funny, so many Labs are busy having families – that was one thing I discussed with Amanda during the interview – but Celia still seems to distance herself.'

'I think she still has to sort out her own feelings about how she came to be here, Isaac,' Ruby said.

'But she gets on really well with her subscriber, Vincent Craig. He's come to terms with Celia being here and the loss of Marissa, his daughter. He even spoke to me about it.'

'Celia was so excited about meeting his ex-wife, Vanessa,' Ruby explained, 'but it didn't happen. At the last minute Vanessa backed out and told Vincent that she couldn't face a living replica of Marissa. Until Vanessa comes to terms with it, I don't think Celia can move on.'

Chapter Five

Another person was watching the television programme with interest. 'I have always imagined interbreeding with Non-Labs would contaminate our blood; but looking at the findings of your team has made me have a change of heart, Dr Amanda Harrison!'

Adam Palmer leaned back in his seat, smiling.

'I really must get to meet you!'

Not everyone was as impressed with Amanda Harrison's plan for a school for the gifted Hybrids. The next morning most of the tabloids voiced many people's fears.

School for the gifted and privileged!

Ordinary folk won't have a chance competing for university places or in the job market against this pampered new breed of superkids!

School for Scandal!
Hybrids to be coached for places at the best universities

We know who'll be running the country in the next generation ... and what their priorities will be!

'We're not *Non-Labs*! We are *humans*! We are the race that civilised this planet in the first place!' the Minister of Education led a heated debate in the House of Commons later that week. 'We refuse to be treated like second-class citizens in our own country!'

Dr Jensen sat in his office and looked at his colleague sitting opposite him.

'I know you're passionate about this, Amanda, but your proposals have certainly made things difficult for Labs and Hybrids who have just started to settle down and enjoy a more normal life alongside the rest of the population. The Prime Minister made his views quite clear to Abel and myself this morning.'

'I cannot believe that people can be so narrow-minded!' she answered angrily. 'Even Joel Harvey, who fully understands the potential of these children, has backed off completely! We have the chance to do something spectacular with the next generation and everyone flees in fear for the sake of political correctness! No wonder the world is in the state it is in today!'

'Still,' the doctor spread his hands, 'I think it will be better for everyone if we put this proposal on hold for the moment. It would be better if you share your ideas about education for the Hybrids quietly with the parents interested.'

'I will certainly be speaking to Abel and the other more enlightened people who are interested!' she retorted. 'I'll start with special classes for the Hybrids on the Compound. Once people realise the potential of these special children they'll be banging on my door, Patrick, mark my words!'

A week later a coach came through the gates of the Compound. Ten children aged from three to five years old stepped down, each holding a schoolbag and an iPad.

'Good morning, Frankie. Can you, Hugo, Ethan, and Mariella organise the class for the first lesson, as you are the eldest? The little ones can set up their computers,' Amanda turned to Abel, a broad smile on her face. 'It didn't take much persuading for many parents of the Hybrid children to realise the great opportunity our Compound School would offer their gifted children. Joel Harvey may be running scared, but I'll manage this school without his help!'

'How many children are enrolled now?' Abel asked her.

'Twenty, so far. Twelve day children and eight weekly boarders,' Amanda smiled. 'And I think there will be others ready to join us once we show them what we can really do!'

'Most of the teachers are our own Labs from the Compound, aren't they?' Abel continued.

She nodded, 'And as the children progress I can call upon several Labs and Non-Labs working at both Cambridge and Oxford Universities. We are going to do great things!'

'You are certainly a champion for Hybrid education, Amanda!' Abel said admiringly.

His words went through her head that evening as she arrived home. It was a pity that he had turned down her offer of having a child with him. He was wasted on that Ruby! A nice enough girl, but uneducated and without any ambition. She sighed as she thought of two other Labs she had made an approach to on the Compound. They obviously found her intimidating.

She slipped off her shoes and poured herself a glass of wine. The letters she had picked up at the entrance lay on her lap, mainly bills except for a handwritten envelope. Tearing open the envelope, she smiled as she read the letter.

My dear Dr Harrison,

I was greatly impressed with your uplifting ideas on the value of harnessing the exceptional talents of the Hybrid children and your confidence in voicing your views against such opposition. As a Lab myself, albeit single at present ...

The writer ended by leaving his phone number and requesting a meeting with her. Amanda frowned. She didn't recognise the name, Adam Palmer; but eventually she decided she would phone him.

'I was delighted that you agreed to meet with me, Dr Harrison,' Adam said as they sat down in an exclusive

French restaurant later that week.

'Please, call me Amanda,' she replied. 'After the press and internet coverage I've received for daring to air my views, your letter came as a welcome surprise, Adam.'

'Too many people fear the unknown. They quite happily let golden opportunities pass them by, wasted.'

'I agree! And I'm not going to let that happen,' Amanda nodded. 'Tell me, have you a personal interest in the education we are providing at the Compound?'

Adam gave a slow smile. 'Well, not just yet. To be honest, I have been looking for the perfect partner, mentally, physically ... And what about yourself, Amanda? Have you any plans of your own?'

'With my present knowledge, the only child I would be willing to bear is a Hybrid – that's if I also meet my perfect partner, Adam ...' Amanda returned his smile.

Chapter Six

'Have you noticed anything ... well ... unusual about me? I thought you two might have realised ...' Amanda said to Beth and Ruby a few weeks later.

Beth looked at her face. 'You ... you're pregnant, aren't you, Amanda?' she cried.

The older woman nodded, smiling happily. 'Five weeks, to be precise!'

'And, the father, he's a Lab, I take it?' said Ruby.

Again Amanda nodded. 'Of course! I'm carrying a Hybrid child!'

'What's his name?' Beth asked. 'If he is a Lab, surely we know him?'

'Adam Palmer.'

'I don't recognise the name, but Labs often choose a new name once they leave the Compound,' Ruby said.

'Congratulations to both of you!' Beth smiled and kissed her cheek.

'Yes, congratulations!' Ruby said. 'Will you be setting up home together now?'

'Oh, we're not planning on living together, though we will be both involved in bringing up our child. The child will live with me, of course,' Amanda told them.

'Well, I have plenty of maternity clothes I'm rapidly growing out of,' Ruby offered.

'And between us we have enough toys to open a toyshop!' Beth added. 'So if you want anything, just let us know.'

'That's very kind of you,' Amanda smiled. 'But Adam and I have made a list of acceptable educational toys we will allow our child to play with. And of course I'm following a very strict diet to ensure baby is given the best possible start in life! No chocolate like I've seen you nibbling on, Ruby!'

'Oh, I ate like a horse during both my pregnancies!' Beth quickly interjected. 'And I'm planning on doing the same for any future babies, too.'

Ruby groaned as Amanda walked away. 'She always makes me feel so inadequate! I've no education worth talking about, and now we've got to put up with the perfect pregnancy too.'

Beth patted Ruby's arm, 'Don't let her bother you, Ruby.'

But as the days went on, Ruby felt more and more vulnerable around Amanda. 'She seems to know the best way to do everything – even being pregnant! Abel has actually started to quote her,' she complained.

'Just be yourself, Ruby,' Beth said. 'Here comes Frankie! She's right about the school though, he's thriving.'

As Beth went to join Frankie and his father, Ruby sighed.

'Be myself? But who am I? I've been Ruby for nearly five years now. What happened to Stella, the girl I used to be?'

Early the next morning she rose and dressed. Abel stirred slightly as she kissed him and whispered, 'I'm going out for a few hours, Abel. I'll be back early afternoon.'

He sleepily muttered a reply before rolling over and closing his eyes again.

Two hours later Ruby was getting off the train in Hambleton. She strolled along the main street past the small shopping centre and stopped as she neared the supermarket. She vividly remembered standing in the same spot with Mrs Gardiner and seeing Ket, the first Lab she encountered, held by two security officers. The tell-tale tattoo on the inside of his wrist had given him away as being one of the 'Ferals', as people had called the Labs back then. She could picture the look of desolation and fear in his eyes clearly. Her own life had been at such a low point then, too – orphaned, then losing her grandmother. No one had wanted her. Impulsively, she had screamed and caused a disturbance so he could escape. That was the last full day in her life as 'Stella'. Little did she know then what the future held in store for her and for Ket.

She sighed and walked on towards the house she had shared with her grandmother. A young family was living there now; two little girls were playing happily in the garden while a line of bright children's clothes fluttered in the breeze behind them. She stopped and looked at the neighbouring house and wondered if Mrs Gardiner still lived there. An old black cat appeared from the back garden and made its way towards her, purring and twining itself around her legs.

She smiled. 'Sooty? You still remember me?'

'It was a long time before he stopped looking out for you on your way home from school, Stella.'

The voice made her look up sharply.

'I … I …' she stuttered.

'Don't worry, love,' the old woman smiled. 'It's Ruby now, isn't it? Come inside and let's have a cup of tea, shall we?'

Mrs Gardiner seemed frailer than when Ruby had last seen her, but her gentle smile and kind eyes were unchanged.

'Sit yourself down,' she said. 'You look as if you need to take the weight off your feet! Not long to go, I imagine?'

Ruby shook her head. 'Do many people know about me, Mrs Gardiner?'

'I think it's time you called me Eve, now you're a grown woman yourself, Ruby,' she said as she laid out the cups on the table, 'Nobody, as far as I know. I knew it was you the first time I saw you on the television with the Labs, when the whole story was new! It was such a relief to see you, and looking so happy too. Especially after all the speculation around when you went missing. I kept my ideas to myself, mind. Didn't want them to think I was a batty old woman. And anyway, you weren't in a hurry to say who you were. Couldn't blame you really, love. You had a tough time of it all as a child.'

'Nearly five years have gone by since I was here. I was just thinking about the last day I was Stella. The day we saw the feral boy at the supermarket,' Ruby said. 'Ket. He's known as Keith these days.'

'What happened to you? How did you get to meet the Ferals, or should I say Labs? Me and Delia, your old schoolfriend, we were so worried about you. Delia would often phone me to chat about you. There were three reports of a young girl spotted near here, but none of them came to anything,' said Mrs Gardiner.

Ruby sat back and told her old friend about her life since she ran away that night, setting up homes for the Labs that Abel and his group had helped to escape from the wards in the Centre, and the difficulties they'd had getting it closed down and finally getting the Labs recognised as a race in their own right.

Ruby shook her head. 'I hardly remember what it was like to be Stella. It's as if she was somebody else. Though some days I feel nothing has changed that much ...'

Eve squeezed her hand. 'Something bothering you, love? You always used to come around here and have a cup of tea and a slice of my cake when things got too much for you. Not that you said much. You were such a tough little girl, always looking out for your gran. I used to think you spent so much time making sure she was all right you didn't always have time to enjoy being a child.'

'I let her down at school, didn't I?' Ruby said. 'She had high hopes of me being a real scholar. I was useless. I'd have been completely stuck if it wasn't for Delia back in those days!'

'Don't undervalue yourself, love. You could have done very well at school if you weren't always busy looking after your gran. You had different priorities, that's all,' she replied firmly. She looked at the younger woman's face. 'And now you're scared you're not going to be a good mother, aren't you? Who's been putting ideas into your head? If you give that young one as much care and attention as you gave your gran, it'll be the happiest child ever!'

'Oh, Eve! You always knew how to cheer me up!' Ruby smiled. She looked at her watch, 'Is that the time? Where have the hours gone? I'd better be getting back home now!'

'And keep in touch, young lady!' the older woman hugged her close, 'I don't want to wait another five years to see this young one of yours!'

'I promise I'll be in touch again soon, Eve. You'll have to come and meet my new family!' As Ruby made her way to the door she rubbed her stomach. 'Ooh, I think I've eaten too much of your delicious cake!'

Suddenly she stopped and took a deep breath, 'Oh, I don't think this is your cake! I think – the baby –'

Half an hour later two paramedics were in Eve's front room. Ruby cried out as she doubled with pain again.

'It's no use, Ruby. The baby isn't going to wait to get to hospital!' one of them said.

'Abel …' Ruby began.

'On his way, love. You hold on to my hand and just concentrate on your baby!' Eve murmured.

The next time Ruby opened her eyes, Abel was stroking her face.

'Our little one is impatient to come into the world!'

'She's beautiful. Perfect!' Abel repeated for the umpteenth time as he showed his daughter to Celia, Beth, and Frank at the Compound the next day.

'After lining up Dr Jensen and a team of medical experts, you chose to have her on someone's lounge floor!' Celia laughed as Amanda Harrison entered.

Amanda shook her head. 'What were you thinking of,

Ruby? Your baby's health and safety is of paramount importance!'

'Ruby was wonderful!' Abel countered.

'I hadn't realised baby Agnes was planning on making such an early appearance,' Ruby smiled.

'Hybrids aren't like Lab babies; they don't indicate when they are ready for their next stage of development,' Beth quipped. 'You'll find that out for yourself before too long, Amanda!'

'I certainly won't be taking any risks! I shall monitor my pregnancy carefully and be fully prepared for any eventuality!'

Grace leaned over and kissed the tiny baby's head. 'Hello, baby Ness.'

'Let's go and leave Ruby and our daughter to have a well-deserved rest!' Abel said, gently laying the child in a cot by her mother's bedside and leading the others from the room. Celia stayed behind for a few moments as the others left.

'She's beautiful, Ruby,' she whispered. 'Sometimes, I wish … If I could …'

'I know what you're thinking, Celia,' Ruby said. 'Maybe it is time to move on.'

Celia laughed. 'What am I thinking of? You must be exhausted. Sleep well, the pair of you.'

Ruby watched as she pulled the door closed behind her and sighed. She leaned over the sleeping infant.

'I'm going to be a really good mother for you, Agnes, my precious one. And Abel will be the best father ever. You don't need to worry about anything!' she whispered.

Chapter Seven

A few months later, in a private hospital with gentle classical music playing in the background, a nurse held up the tiny squalling child, wrapped her in a blanket, and passed her to Amanda Harrison.

'A fine baby girl! With a fine set of lungs, too!'

'Perfect! Just as I knew you would be!' her mother murmured. She looked up at Adam and smiled. 'She's going to have such a good future! Our beautiful Virginia.'

'She's wonderful!' Adam whispered as he stroked her soft, downy head.

Chapter Eight

Celia picked up the phone for the third time and dialled the number again. She took a deep breath and gripped the handset tightly in her hand as she heard the dialling tone.

'Hello?' a young man's voice said suddenly.

'I …' Celia cleared her throat, 'I … would like to speak to Vanessa Drew, please.'

'Sure. Who shall I say it is?' Celia heard the sound of footsteps and a door being opened.

'It's … Celia … from the Compound … I spoke to Vince last week. I told him I'd like to speak to Vanessa again. And he said, maybe, well, maybe she'd be ready to talk to me … again. Are you her son? Maybe this is not such a good idea,' Celia stumbled over her words.

'Hey, slow down! You're Celia? Yeah, I'm Tom. Look, I know the meeting between you and Mom didn't, well, get going, last time but look, time's gone by. Maybe Vince is right; maybe she will want to talk to you. I think it might be a good idea if I speak to her first. I'm not trying to put you off, Celia, really. If you give me your number, I'll speak to Mom first. And the others. Mom will ring you back. Or I will,' he said.

Celia nodded, then realized she had to speak. 'Yes, that's great. Thank you so much, Tom!'

'I'll call tomorrow, at about this time, OK, Celia?' he continued. 'And I really hope Mom and you, well, that you do get to know each other. And get to know us, too! We're family really, aren't we?'

'Thank you so much,' Celia whispered. 'I really would like to get to know you all … as family.'

Her hands trembled as she picked up the phone and dialled another number, 'Isaac? I did it!'

Her words tumbled over each other as she explained the phone call to Vanessa's home.

'Well done, Celia!' Isaac's voice was warm. 'I'm sure Vanessa will come around to you. A long time has gone by since your last meeting. Phone me as soon as you've spoken to him tomorrow, OK?'

They continued to talk, but Isaac was aware that Celia's mind was really on the phone call to Florida.

The expected call was foremost on her mind all through the next day. 'I'm sorry, Ruby. What were you saying?' she asked, looking up.

'I said you really aren't with us today, Celia!' Ruby smiled. 'You're not going to get anything done until you've heard from Tom or Vanessa, are you?'

Celia sighed and turned away from the computer.

'You're right, Ruby. I really can't concentrate. What if he doesn't call? What if Vanessa doesn't want to speak to me? What if …'

'Celia! You'll drive yourself crazy!' Ruby held up her hands. 'Come on! We're going out. We'll drive up to Peak View with a picnic.'

For the rest of the day Celia had little time to think about the phone call. They walked for miles along the hillside paths with Ruby chattering on about life on the Compound, the children, the newcomers – everything except the awaited phone call. Celia laughed as they finally arrived back at the Compound.

'You've worn me out, Ruby! I don't know if I can stay awake for the phone call!' She hugged Ruby to her before she turned off at her own front door. 'You're such a good friend.'

'Let me know what happens, won't you?' Ruby looked serious. Celia nodded and went through the doorway.

It was nearly midnight when Ruby picked up the phone. Abel appeared at her side as she heard Celia's voice on the line.

'Tom rang! And I spoke to Vanessa. It was a bit … strange. I don't know if she only agreed to speak to me because of Tom; but, anyway, the whole family are going to come to London to meet me. Vince is coming, too. He phoned me just after Tom did. He's really excited about it. He said he'd book us all in at the same hotel.

'That's great, Celia!' Ruby said. 'You're going to meet up with Vanessa and all her family. Are you going to get someone to go with you for moral support?'

'Yes,' she replied. 'I'm going to ask Isaac. He actually did offer earlier.'

Abel pulled Ruby to him as she switched off the phone.

'I hope it works out OK this time,' he said quietly. 'Celia needs to move on with her life; have her own family.' He had a distant expression on his face. Ruby wondered if, despite his earlier protests, Abel would like to know his own background too.

Chapter Nine

'One week to go!' Celia spread a dress and a pair of trousers on the bed. 'What do you think I should wear to meet her? Something not too formal, nor too casual. Definitely not the black suit! What do you think, Ruby?'

She stood and held a pink sweater against herself. 'I must make a good impression!'

Ruby hugged her. 'You'll be fine. Even her son thinks she's coming around to you, doesn't he?'

'But last time … last time we were only in the same room for two minutes before she left. She could hardly look at me!' Celia almost whispered.

'But that was nearly five years ago, Celia. People change,' her friend replied.

'I hope you are right, Ruby.'

Chapter Ten

Celia stood outside the hotel entrance, smoothed her pink angora sweater over her hips, and pushed her hair back out of her face. 'I should have put on something else. She'll think I'm frivolous; all girly!'

'Don't worry, Celia!' Isaac pulled her arm through his. 'You look fine. She's not going to be thinking anything like that about your appearance.'

'You're right, Isaac. It's about *who* I look like, isn't it?'

'Hey, she wants to meet *you*. They all do.'

As they entered the foyer a group of people seated in a window alcove stood up. The woman looked directly at Celia as the man beside her steadied her elbow. Two teenage boys were on the other side of her.

Celia stood frozen in the middle of the floor.

Vanessa raised her hand to her mouth and closed her eyes for a moment.

'Those big brown eyes! They are just the same! I never could resist Marissa's big brown eyes, neither could her daddy! You've certainly got her eyes, Celia!' she said quietly and then stepped forward slowly. Celia felt a tremor as they shook hands.

'I'm … I'm so glad you came! That you all came!' she whispered.

'Hey, we've been looking forward to meeting you!' the older boy said, holding his hand out. 'I'm Tom. We spoke on the phone.'

'Eddy; pleased to meet you. And you too, sir,' the second boy said.

'Bill; pleased to make your acquaintance!' Vanessa's

husband held out his hand.

'Well, if we're done with all the introductions,' Vince said, moving forward and smiling at Celia, 'let's adjourn to our rooms. My suite is the biggest – that's the one good thing about being stuck in a wheelchair, you get the best suites! Maybe we could wait in there while you two ladies have a bit of a chat in your suite, Vanessa?'

'Honey, you OK with that?' Bill gave her a questioning look.

Isaac squeezed Celia's arm as both women nodded.

Vince swivelled his chair around and headed to the lifts with the others following him.

Soon the two women sat facing each other. 'Do you fancy some coffee? I could ring for room service.' Vanessa suggested. Celia nodded.

They both remained silent as a young woman placed a tray with two coffee cups on the table between them.

Celia watched as Vanessa picked up the pot with trembling hands and poured two cups. Taking a deep breath she said, 'Thank you so much for coming to see me. And I must say again, I'm just *so* sorry you lost your little girl! So, so sorry!'

Vanessa swallowed hard and looked down. 'Thank you. But you mustn't apologise! None of this, any of it, was your fault! It's just taken me longer than I thought it would to come to terms with it all.' She held out her hand and pressed Celia's. 'You poor thing! It's taken me a long time realise how unfair I have been to ... resent you when I lost my little girl.'

'It must have been very hard for you to ... to know I was still here when the news of the Centre became known ...' Celia faltered.

Vanessa stood up and came to sit next to her. Putting her arms around her she hugged the younger woman. 'I'm so sorry! Sorry for not being here for you sooner. But I'm here now. And we can all be a family, if you like the idea. Your two, well … your brothers, really, are very keen on getting to know you!'

'I have a family,' Celia said softly.

'Yes, you have! You'll have to tell me all about yourself. What work do you do? Vince said you're even better with computers than he is!'

Celia smiled and told her about some of the work she did, 'It's mainly with the Labs. Sorting things out for them.'

'You still live on the Compound, don't you? Maybe on our next trip I could get to know some of your friends at the Compound. Vince said they're like family to you.'

'They would all love to meet you, too!' Celia smiled. 'On your next trip.'

She asked Vanessa about her life in America and they compared photos of homes and friends.

After an hour had passed, Vanessa squeezed her arm, smiling as she stood up. 'Let's go and join the others, shall we? We can all get to know each other a little bit better this weekend.

She linked her arm through Celia's as they made their way to the larger suite.

Isaac was pleased to see Celia visibly relax over the next few days. The two women chatted easily, seeming so much like mother and daughter.

As they said their goodbyes at the airport, Vanessa hugged Celia and looked across at him. 'You look after our girl now, Isaac.'

'There's nothing I'd like to do better!' he smiled.

There was a companionable silence as they drove back to the Compound later that day.

'The weekend went really well,' Isaac said.

Celia looked at him, a smile on her lips. 'Yes. I never thought I would feel like this! I have a family!'

'I meant what I said when I promised Vanessa that I'd look after you,' Isaac told her.

She smiled again and squeezed his hand. 'I know, Isaac.'

Chapter Eleven

Ness ran across the stage and gave a lopsided curtsey as she accepted the certificate from the dance teacher, followed by Ginny, and gave a little wave to her mother, father, and baby brother Zac as she ran back to her seat clutching her certificate. After the speeches and prize giving, both girls hurried to show their parents.

'My little Sugar Plum Fairy!' Abel scooped up the delighted Ness.

'Look, Mummy! I passed my exam,' she cried excitedly, holding out her certificate.

'You danced beautifully! You too, Ginny!' Ruby told her.

'Look, Mummy!' Ginny pushed the certificate into her mother's hands.

The ballet teacher stood beside her, 'Yes, she's done so well, ninety-two per cent for her first exam! Not many other four-year-olds do so well! You must be proud of her, Mum!'

Amanda frowned. 'Only ninety-two? In which areas does she need to improve?'

The ballet teacher looked taken aback. 'But … but she's really done well, for such a little one … Of course, all the children find the timing and smooth transition of movements difficult at first, but with practice …'

'So that's what we'll work on, Ginny. Well, we had better get off; we'll be late for your tennis lesson.'

'But Ms Harrison …' the teacher began.

Abel and Ruby exchanged glances as they watched Ginny's shoulders slump as she followed her mother.

Two hours later Amanda flung open the front door as Adam arrived.

45

'Adam! Thank God you're here! Just take your daughter out of my sight!'

'What has happened?' he asked.

'Well, not only does she let herself down at the ballet exam, but she wastes *my* time and that of her tennis coach for the next hour!'

Adam stepped into the lounge to see a stony-faced Ginny sitting on the sofa.

'Why don't you let us have a little chat, Amanda,' he said. Adam and his daughter both listened as Amanda stamped up the stairs and the sound of her bedroom door slamming.

Adam picked up the ballet certificate and looked at his daughter, 'Did you try your best for this exam?'

Ginny nodded.

'And the tennis?'

'No! *She* said I was as useless as any old Non-Lab child, so I showed her *how* useless I could be!' Suddenly she burst into tears. 'And now *you'll* think I'm as useless as any old Non-Lab child, too!'

Adam sat down beside her and pulled her to him.

'No, I don't, love. I know how clever you are, after all, I'm a Lab. We know things your mother doesn't know, don't we? After all, *she's* only a Non-Lab at the end of the day.' He gave her a wink. 'How about I arrange for us to spend a whole weekend together, instead of just Saturday afternoon? We could relax, be ourselves.'

Ginny looked up. 'Oh, Daddy! I'd love that!'

'But you are going to have to work really hard for your mother for the next few weeks. Make sure you keep her happy, then I'll see what I can do, OK?'

Ginny nodded her head solemnly.

'And, Daddy …' she frowned, 'I do love Mummy, even though she's a Non-Lab.'

'Of course you do, love. I chose the best Non-Lab woman to be your mother!' He smiled, 'Now see how good you can be for her for the next two weeks!'

Two weeks later she ran down to let her father into the house.

'I've been really good!' she shouted.

'Yes, she has,' Amanda appeared behind her. 'She was quicker than Ness and Martha in Maths today and she has been completing her homework and dance practice every evening without complaining once!'

Adam ruffled his daughter's hair.

'A father's influence is certainly worth having, Adam! I don't know what you said to her, but she's been the perfect child these last two weeks!'

Adam smiled back. 'She really has been working hard. And you, too – rushing around, taking her here and there! You could do with a break yourself, Amanda. A bit of "me time"! How about I take Ginny for the whole weekend instead of just Saturday and you catch up with some friends, pamper yourself?'

After some hesitation, Amanda agreed to Adam's plans.

Ginny bounced up and down with excitement as she waited by the window for her father's car to appear on the Friday evening.

'He's here!' she shouted, running to open the front door.

Amanda handed a bag to Adam.

'She has her maths to finish and she must practice her new ballet steps for Monday,' she said.

'I'll make sure she does everything, Amanda!' he promised.

With a brief wave to her mother, Ginny turned to her father and asked him what he had planned for the weekend.

'Well, first of all we're going to a beautiful house in the country instead of my flat. I think you'll like it!' He smiled at her.

'Is it *your* house?' she asked.

'Mine and yours, if you like it,' he replied.

'I will *love* it!' she replied eagerly.

'Wait until you see it!' her father chuckled.

'Is it big? Does it have lots of books in, like Mummy's house? Is the garden big? Can we play hide and seek in it?' The questions tumbled out of her mouth.

'All I will say is that it's a very special house!' he laughed in reply.

After an hour the car headed up a steep, tree-lined hillside and turned into a winding track. The track ended at a pair of tall metal gates which opened automatically. Inside there was an expanse of lawn bordered by tall pampas grasses. Adam followed a long driveway and stopped beside a marble staircase.

'This is no ordinary house!' he said as he helped Ginny out of the car. 'Wait until I show you around!'

He smiled at her excitement in each room of the computer-controlled house. Ginny screamed with delight as she waved a hand to turn on and off the lights and control the music and TV systems. She drew a deep breath as doors silently opened and closed as they walked through them.

'They're like magic!' she whispered, slipping her hand in to her father's.

'No, just modern technology!' he answered.

In the ultra-modern kitchen, she watched in amazement as Adam placed the items for lunch in a container and a voice analysed the food and gave the cooking time required. A cooking hood came down from the ceiling and covered the dish.

'It will signal when it's ready,' Adam said, 'Let's go downstairs, shall we?'

He led them down to the basement to a large, well-furnished gymnasium. Through the doorway they came to an indoor swimming pool linked by a glass tunnel to an outdoor pool.

'As you know, exercising your body is as important as exercising your mind!' Adam told her.

'This looks like a fun place!' Ginny squealed.

As they walked back to the house she pointed to a large conservatory.

'What's in there?' she asked.

'We'll take a look around there after lunch,' Adam told her.

After finishing her meal, Ginny sat back with a satisfied sigh, 'That was the *best* meal I have *ever* had! And a pudding, too! We only have puddings as a special treat at home!'

Adam looked at Ginny and smiled. 'Your mother is right to keep you healthy. She knows you're a special child.'

'Because I'm a Hybrid,' his daughter nodded. 'And I have to work *really* hard at everything! Mummy says I have to work harder than ordinary children because I'm talented. I should be really proud of my Lab blood!'

'She's right, Ginny. People of our race can do great things!' Adam nodded.

'What can we do?' she asked.

'We can learn more about Labs and Hybrids and find out how to produce the best people so we can prepare for a great future for our kind!'

'What about the Non-Labs? People like Mummy and our friends?' she asked.

'The Non-Labs have been looking after themselves for long enough! They don't need any help! We must concentrate on our own kind now!' he answered.

He stood up. 'Come with me!'

He led her to the conservatory. 'Inside this room are the latest developments in technology to help me with my research on our future people,' he told her as he opened the door. 'Perhaps you will want to join me here later?'

'Wow!' Ginny said as she gazed around at the equipment set up around the room.

Her father smiled, touching a screen which immediately jumped to life. With a few touches it displayed an array of data.

'A few facts about our brains, Labs, and Hybrids and a comparison chart with Non-Labs!' He touched the screen to bring up a series of graphs.

'Non-Labs don't compare too well, do they?' he said with a wry smile.

'Mummy is clever,' Ginny insisted.

Adam brought a 3D image of a head onto the screen, 'Yes, she comes out pretty favourably compared to data on the other Non-Labs I collected.

'That's Mummy?' Ginny's eyes widened.

'A virtual version of your mother, yes!' Adam smiled.

'I wish I could come and work here with you now, Daddy!' Ginny sighed.

'I don't think it will be that long before you can, young lady, if you work your hardest at your school subjects,' he replied.

'I will, I promise!' she said eagerly. 'And I'm going to start to do some extra work now! I'm going to find out all I can about brains. If we're going to make great future Hybrids and Labs we need to know a lot about brains.'

'That's a great idea, Ginny! How about we make a start today?' He smiled as he saw her face fall. 'With a trip to the zoo to observe the animals there – and the people!'

'I'm going to love working here with you, Daddy!' Ginny jumped up and hugged her father. 'I'm going to work hard so I can come soon!'

'Shh! I'm trying to concentrate!' Ginny frowned at Frankie during lunch break later that week.

'What are you reading, Ginny?' he asked, closing the book over to see its cover. '*Research on the Human Brain.* Wow, Ginny, that's pretty heavy stuff for a kid!'

'I'm not a kid!' she said snatching the book back, 'I'm a Hybrid! We have to think about our future!'

'So you're going to be a brain surgeon, are you?' Frankie

grinned.

Ginny turned her back on him as she sat down beside her.

'No, I'm going to do research and … stuff!'

'*By analysing the molecular structure of the average adult brain as demonstrated by the above statistics …*' he read aloud, 'Phew! A little light reading! Let's go and play basketball. Grace and Ryan are there now!' He stood up and headed for the court, 'Come on, let's challenge them!'

Ginny hesitated for a few moments then looked around as Hugo, a Hybrid a few months younger than Frankie, sat down beside her. He took the book from her hands.

'Hey, I'm impressed! You don't waste your free time, do you? Are you planning on university early, too?'

'My mum says I should go as soon as I can. Frankie and Ness say we should enjoy being kids as long as we can.'

'Yes, but we're not just kids, are we? We're Hybrids. We need to think about the future!' Hugo said.

'That's what my dad says!' Ginny told him excitedly. 'He has a big house and lots of rooms for research and …' she put her hand to her mouth. 'But I'm not supposed to tell anyone! Not even Mummy!'

'Your mum's Amanda Harrison, isn't she?' Hugo asked.

Ginny nodded.

'It must be great having parents so interested in your future!' Hugo looked wistful.

'Your dad's a Lab, isn't he?' Ginny asked.

'Yeah, an architect, more interested in buildings than people. I hardly ever see him.'

'And your mother?'

Hugo shrugged his shoulders disdainfully. 'Just a regular Non-Lab!'

Chapter Twelve

'I had hoped I could take you with me on this trip to New York and Washington, with Suzette to care for you while I was lecturing, but my schedule is too hectic,' Amanda told her daughter. 'So your father said he was quite willing for you to stay with him while I am away.'

'So I can stay with Daddy for *all* the holiday?' Ginny beamed.

'Yes. Adam has promised to get you to your ballet and tennis lessons and to make sure you keep up with your homework. You'll have extra over the holiday, of course,' Amanda continued.

'A whole two weeks with Daddy!' Ginny repeated. 'I must try to finish reading my book by Friday!'

That night as she tucked her daughter into bed Amanda removed the book which had fallen from Ginny's hand. She smiled as she read the title *Research on the Human Brain.* How proud she was of her wonderful Hybrid child.

'How about tonight we chill out and have a pizza and watch a film?' Adam suggested as they drove away from Amanda's house at the start of the holiday.

Ginny glanced back guiltily, 'Mummy has a very low opinion of pizza and she doesn't think many films are suitable for children; most of them are mind-numbing rubbish.'

'Oh, don't worry. We all need a bit of junk food now and again and I'm sure we can find you a film that isn't *absolutely* mind-numbing rubbish!' Adam assured her. 'Later in the week I thought we could spend the day in

London. There is an exhibition at the Science Museum that I think you'll find interesting, one I'm sure your mother would approve of!'

Ginny took a deep breath as they stepped into the DVD rental shop. She ran and picked up a copy of the latest Disney animated film.

'Grace said this film was *really* good! Not mind-numbing at all! Can I watch it, Daddy?' she asked.

'Of course you can – though we might not share this with your mother, eh?' he smiled. 'Now I want to find a *totally* mind-numbing film I can watch later this evening when you're asleep.'

Ginny wandered amongst the shelves, occasionally picking up a DVD. She was grimacing at the lurid cover of a horror film when she heard several DVDs clatter to the floor. Looking up she saw a teenage boy leaning against a shelf, clutching his chest. A girl about his age, dark curly hair tied back into a loose ponytail, was pushing something into his mouth as he struggled to breathe. One of her eyes was covered with a patch and her face was decorated with several piercings. Ginny gave a gasp as the boy's eyes met hers. She quickly turned and sprinted to her father.

'Daddy! Come quickly! Come quickly! There's a pirate trying to kill a Lab!' she whispered urgently, pulling her father's sleeve.

'What are you talking about, Ginny?' Adam looked up in surprise.

'Please, Daddy! Just come now before it's too late!' Ginny urged, dragging him by the sleeve after her. 'They're down here by the scary films!'

The young couple looked up as Ginny and her father came around the corner. The boy was leaning against the girl's shoulder. He glanced up and his eyes widened.

'You've been letting your imagination carry you away, Ginny …' Adam began, and then stopped as he caught the boy's eye. 'But you *are* a Lab, aren't you?'

He smiled and walked towards them. Ginny followed half-hidden behind his back, looking warily at the girl who had stepped defensively in front of the boy, a mean expression on her face.

'Hold it right there!' she snarled. 'Maybe Angus doesn't want to talk to you!'

'It's OK, Zig,' Angus said, patting her arm. He held out his hand and shook Adam's. 'You're a Lab, too, aren't you?'

Adam nodded, rubbing the plastic strip on his wrist. 'Yeah. I don't always advertise it, though!'

He flicked Angus's right hand over and frowned at the unblemished skin.

'You're not from the Compound?'

'No. I'm not,' he replied glancing around him nervously.

'Perhaps we could go somewhere a bit more comfortable for a chat?' Adam said.

'There's a coffee bar just across the square,' Angus suggested. 'Let's meet up there in ten minutes.'

'Do you think that pirate girl is dangerous?' Ginny whispered a short while later as they settled themselves at a quiet corner table in the cafe.

'She's not a pirate, Ginny. She must have injured her eye,' her father replied. 'What kind of Lab can Angus be, if he's not from the Compound?'

'I *still* think she looks really dangerous!' Ginny shuddered as the young couple came into the café.

'If he's a Compound Lab, he may be able to help you ...' Zig said softly as the couple made their way towards them.

'Shh! We'll keep my problems out of the conversation for the moment!' Angus retorted.

They slid into the seats opposite; all exchanging wary smiles.

Adam introduced himself and Ginny.

'Zig and Angus,' the young man nodded.

'So you're a Lab?' Adam asked. 'It's funny we haven't seen you around here before.'

'We're just staying here for a few weeks. We live in Edinburgh,' Angus replied. 'What brings you to this area?'

'I'm researching future Lab development. Just setting up a new laboratory in the area,' Adam told him. 'You're not originally from the Compound then?'

'No,' Angus replied slowly. 'I'm one of the Independent Labs.'

'The Independents?' Adam raised an eyebrow. 'I've not heard anything about this group before.'

'They …we … keep ourselves to ourselves,' Angus replied. He noticed Adam glance at Zig.

'Yeah, Zig's a Non-Lab, but she's been a great help to me. She's entirely trustworthy,' he added.

'How many Independents are there altogether?' Adam asked.

'Oh, three in our group,' he said, 'We're from Scotland. We've met another group from Cornwall, four girls and two guys from London. They told us about a group they've been in touch with in New York. We were originally hoping to work together, pool our findings.'

Adam frowned, 'Originally?'

Angus gave a short laugh, 'Yes, things didn't work out quite as we had hoped; so I'm on my own at the moment.'

'Have you your own laboratory?'

'Yeah. In Edinburgh …' Angus said.

'I'd love to see it! Find out what you've been working on! We could perhaps share our research?' Adam said enthusiastically.

Zig looked at Angus, 'That would be great, wouldn't it? Help each other?'

Angus cracked his fingers, 'That depends on, well, several things …'

'Of course!' Adam nodded, 'You're wondering if I am just going to take off with your ideas! Believe me, you can trust me! Look, why don't you come around to our place? I can show you my laboratory. I've not much data set up; it's in the early stages at the moment …'

'And I'm going to do my own research on brains!' Ginny chipped in.

Zig laughed. 'But you're a kid? What are you? About four?'

'Nearly five! But a *Hybrid* nearly five!' Ginny sat up to her full height.

Adam turned to Angus. 'Are you free to come now?'

'It's a bit too late today,' the younger man stood up. He seemed agitated, 'We'd better get going, Zig.'

'Wait a minute,' Adam stood up too, 'We'll drop you off. Come on, Ginny.'

Despite Angus's protests Adam led the way to the car.

'Look, this may be the help you need, Angus! You can't turn it down!' Zig whispered.

She directed Adam to a B&B nearby.

Angus quickly climbed out of the car and headed for the front door, fumbling with his keys.

'We could meet up tomorrow,' Adam suggested. 'I can pick you up in the morning.'

'Yeah, we'd like that,' Zig nodded at Angus, 'He's just a bit nervous with strangers; but I trust you. We'll be ready at nine, OK?'

Inside their room Angus was clutching his chest again.

Zig handed him two tablets and a glass of water. A few minutes later she gave a sigh of relief as the colour returned to his face.

'Angus, *please*, let this guy help you! He's like you, he'd *understand*!' she pleaded.' I bet they could sort out your heart problem at the Compound!'

He shook his head. 'What if he's with *them*?'

'No. Not with a kid in tow!' She shook her head. 'At least *ask* him about the ID. There was something in the papers before about the Compound Labs using fake IDs, that's why they were able to live like … ordinary people.'

Adam stopped the car outside the terraced house the next morning and both the young people appeared. Angus gave a tentative smile as they climbed into the car.

'Who created you? Lab or Non-Lab?' Adam asked as they drove towards his own house.

'Non-Lab, he passed me off as his son. He died just over eight weeks ago.' Angus locked and unlocked his fingers.

'Anyone else in the family?' the older man continued.

Angus shook his head.

'Let's see how we get on today. I'm happy to share my findings so far with you. When are you planning to go back to your laboratory in Edinburgh?'

'There are a few complications …' Angus once again was nervously locking his fingers. Zig cleared her throat, but looked down as he shot her a look.

'If there's anything I can do …?' Adam said.

The two men went straight to the research room while Zig followed Ginny around the house open-mouthed. She laughed as doors silently opened and closed as they walked through them.

'It's like something from a sci-fi film!' she breathed.

Ginny was in her element.

'Just look at this!' she pulled down a transparent screen and keyed in a few numbers. A metallic voice gave the temperature and humidity of both inside and outside the house.

'Come and see downstairs!' Ginny hurried ahead of Zig and led her to the basement gymnasium and swimming pools.

'As everyone knows, exercising your body is as important as exercising your mind!' the younger girl told her solemnly.

In the conservatory, Adam was showing Angus around. 'I'm only at the early stages, basic research. I'm aiming eventually to develop the *elite* in Labs and Hybrids.'

'That's what our vision is, too,' Angus nodded. He felt

more relaxed as he discussed Lab research with his new acquaintance.

Adam looked at him thoughtfully, 'The development of the Compound Labs is common knowledge now. How was your group … brought into existence?'

'Well,' Angus began, 'I am a clone of Professor Angus McBride. He was a retired lecturer from Edinburgh University and he was extremely interested in what had taken place in the Centre. He created me six years ago.' He nodded at Angus's surprised expression. 'Using a programme of accelerated development I reached maturity after two years. We were working with a friend of his, Dr Rajid Pounamar. Pounamar created a clone of himself a few months after I was created – Takir. The four of us worked on a cloning programme until two years ago Pounamar was killed in a car crash. The following year McBride's health began to deteriorate. For the next six months we continued the research he had started under his guidance. Then Takir became impatient. He said McBride was losing his sharpness, was too conservative with his ideas. He had his own plans!

'Unknown to either of us, he had already created a clone of himself – Sanjit! Shortly after McBride died things came to a head. Takir and I … disagreed over something. He and Sanjit left to join the girls down south, and in the hope of making contact with other groups, too.'

Angus sighed, 'A few weeks later Zig and I left the house, too. As I'm the supposed son of McBride I should be his sole heir. Unfortunately, when I was asked to produce ID to verify my claim. I couldn't, so I said I was too distressed and planned to spend time with some relatives in England. If I can get my ID sorted out I will be able to lay claim to it all.'

'Didn't McBride or Pounamar supply you with acceptable IDs?' Adam raised his eyebrows as Angus shook his head. 'Well, luckily it's a problem easily remedied!'

He pulled a notebook from his pocket. 'Write down your name and supposed date and place of birth and I will arrange things for you – if we're going to be working together as partners?'

Angus smiled and held out his hand.

'Partners!'

'Does your mum ever come here?' Zig asked Ginny the next day as they swam in the pool.

'No. She doesn't know about this house. Just about Dad's flat,' she replied.

'You seem to keep a lot of secrets from her,' the older girl continued.

'Well, yes, but that's OK, 'cos she's only a Non – oops!' Ginny looked guilty.

'Yeah, just a dumb Non-Lab like me, hey?' Zig pulled herself on to the side of the pool.

'No, she's not dumb! She's clever! Like you!' Ginny said brightly. 'It's just … Mum doesn't let me do lots of normal things. It makes her cross. Dad lets me do normal things, as long as I work hard, too. Were your parents strict?'

'My mum was lovely. Soft as anything. Maybe it would have been better if she had been stricter with me!' Zig suddenly stood up, dived into the water, and swam several lengths.

'Hey, you're really fast, I bet you could beat Frankie! Or even Hugo!' Ginny said admiringly.

Later that day, Adam smiled at Angus and held out a birth certificate, a driving licence, and a letter informing him of his National Insurance number.

'Now you've got your ID you can sort out the legalities in Edinburgh and show me around your laboratory!' he beamed. 'We could fly up there tomorrow morning. Why don't you give your solicitor a call?'

'I'd love to go to another country!' Ginny joined in excitedly. 'What is Scotland like, Zig?'

'Pretty much like England, except the people talk properly!' Zig said in a thick Scottish accent.

The next morning Zig laughed as Ginny stood with her mouth open as they climbed into a taxi outside Edinburgh airport.

'What did the man say? Is he really speaking English?'

'You'll soon get used to it!' she told her.

Half an hour later the taxi drew up outside a tall detached house on a quiet, tree-lined road. Adam put their suitcases down in the hallway and turned to Angus.

'Let's take a look at your laboratory, shall we?' The two men disappeared down the cellar steps.

Zig made her way to the kitchen, followed by Ginny. She opened the fridge door and wrinkled her nose in disgust as she viewed the mouldering contents.

'This'll have to go in the bin and I'll have to make a trip to the supermarket. There's nothing at all to eat in the house.' She grabbed her bag and made for the door.

'Can I come with you?' Ginny hurried after her.

Meanwhile. the two men were peering at a screen.

'So this is the programme McBride used? At what points can you input or edit features?' Adam was asking.

'It was a straight-forward clone. Nothing was changed except for the speed of development. Look, that is shown here,' Angus told him.

'From McBride's data, there was a flaw in the composition of his heart,' Adam said. 'Surely there must have been some alterations made to the blueprint to prevent the clone – yourself – being similarly afflicted?'

'I suppose I'm lucky not to have been affected, or not yet, anyway.' Angus gave a slight shrug, 'We did a complete copy. We had no knowledge of altering the blueprint. I would like to learn more about this from you.'

'I can upload the details that I have onto your computer. I must admit that, due to a fall out with some of my colleagues, I do not have the full information I need to answer this. I have some details of the original format of my donor. Perhaps we could compare the two to throw some light on this.'

Several hours later Zig and Ginny appeared in the laboratory.

'Here, we've brought you some pizza,' Zig said.

'What have you been doing, Daddy?' Ginny looked at the screen.

Adam spread his hands. 'Well, we've only being comparing notes so far. But by pooling our knowledge we have so much potential!'

'If you are going to be working here all day tomorrow I'll catch up with some friends of mine,' Zig said.

'What about Ginny?' Adam asked. The older girl rolled her eyes at the ceiling.

Ginny smiled, 'I can stay and help you, Daddy!'

'Maybe when you're a bit older, Ginny.' He pulled a wad of notes from his wallet and gave it to Zig. 'Look, how about you two go out and have a bit of fun tomorrow. I promise tomorrow evening we'll all spend some time together!'

Zig gave a whistle at the amount of cash in her hands.

'Well, I suppose we could find something to do for a few hours …'

'There's the theme park up on the coast, Zig. It's pretty good,' Angus suggested.

'And the new shopping centre is over that way, too. Mmm, I suppose we could kill a few hours,' she conceded.

Chapter Thirteen

'This is sooo good!' Ginny said for the tenth time that day as they picked their way through the crowds in the theme park. 'Can we go on the ghost train again?'

Zig groaned. 'Again? Let's try something else. How about I watch you on that little train?'

'That's for babies!' Ginny snorted. She looked longingly at the Devil's Vengeance, where a group of teenagers were hanging upside down with loud shrieks and cries.

'You're just too short for those rides yet. Maybe in a few years' time.' Zig caught her glance. 'Hey, do you want me to win you one of those giant teddies on the shooting range?'

Ginny watched in awe as Zig picked off every target.

'You were incredible! Even the man on the stall thought so!' she said she walked away clutching a huge pink teddy. 'Do you practise a lot?'

'Most kids round my way knew how to shoot or use a knife.' Zig shrugged and glanced at her watch, 'One more ride on the ghost train, then we head back home, OK?'

'And one more stick of candyfloss?' Ginny pleaded.

'I can't believe you've never had candyfloss before! Still you've eaten enough today to make up for it!' the older girl shook her head.

'Ginny, go show your daddy the teddy,' Zig said to her as they arrived back at the house to have the door opened by a white-faced Angus. She pulled him into the kitchen and took a bottle of tablets from his pocket.

'I'll be fine! Honest! I just lost track of the time,' Angus said as he sat slumped on a chair in the kitchen. He took the bottle from Zig with trembling hands and sent it tumbling to the floor.

Ginny was returning to the kitchen when she heard the noise. She peeped through the doorway to see Zig ducking down to gather up the tablets. Spotting some on the floor near her, Ginny picked them up and put them into her pocket.

'You're definitely overdoing it, you know! The old guy promised you'd take a break this evening,' Zig was saying, holding a glass of water to Angus's mouth as he swallowed two of the tablets. Slowly the colour returned to his face. He gave her a wan smile.

'I'm fine. And how did you two get on today?'

Zig sighed. 'Yes, that's another thing. I didn't come here to babysit, you know!'

Ginny drew back sharply, tears springing to her eyes. She flung the teddy to the floor and ran upstairs.

The two young people looked at each other in alarm.

'How much did she hear?' Angus said.

His girlfriend groaned. 'I'll go and see!'

She picked up the teddy and ran upstairs. Ginny was lying in bed staring at the ceiling.

'Look, I'm sorry, I didn't mean ...'

'I'm *not* a baby!' Ginny retorted. 'I *don't* need a babysitter!'

'I know. What I meant ...'

'And I thought you enjoyed today, too!' she began to cry.

'Please, Ginny! I did. I just meant, well, sometimes I'd like to be with people my age. I'm sure you want to spend time with kids sometimes, too!'

Ginny stared at the ceiling.

'Anyway, as far as young kids go, you're OK, you know. There are not many young kids I could spend the whole day with without going nuts!'

She sat down on the edge of the bed holding the teddy.

'Did your father like Ted?'

'He's too busy at the moment.'

'Hmmm, like Angus, too busy!' Zig remarked.

Ginny sat up. 'You can't blame them! They're doing really important research! It's the future of the Labs we're talking about!'

'Well, we're not going to have their company this evening. Angus is heading back to the laboratory to continue their important research.'

'Is he sick?' Ginny asked her, fingering the tablets in her pocket.

Zig shook her head. 'No, just a headache! He's fine.' She smiled at Ginny, 'Fancy watching a film? There's a good one on TV tonight. Hey, we could make popcorn too!'

'Popcorn? I've never made popcorn before!' Ginny sprang from the bed.

Zig gave Angus a wink as she brought a plate of sandwiches down to the two men.

'Thought you boys might need some sustenance!'

Adam absently took a sandwich from the plate, 'Which file did you say you stored Sanjit's details on, Angus?'

'Thank you, Zig. I don't know what we'd do without you, Zig!' she said loudly.

'Thanks, love. Is everything all right?' Angus said.

'Sorted,' she replied.

'I can't open this folder. Give me a hand here, Angus. I want to check up on his data,' Adam said.

'See you later,' Angus gave his girlfriend a quick smile before he turned back to the screen and keyed in a password, 'Each file has a separate code, for security.'

Zig sighed and went back upstairs.

'Ah, that's it!' Adam said as Angus opened the file. 'Why do you bother with her?'

'What?' Angus said.

'She's not only inferior in intelligence, she's actually physically flawed! Look at her face! I assume Independent Labs can't interbreed in the same way as us, but for goodness' sake select a Non-Lab higher in intelligence and physical appearance before you consider having young!'

'I'm not thinking about having ... young, not at the moment anyway. Zig'll do for now,' Angus replied. 'She's been useful keeping Ginny occupied, hasn't she?'

'Hmm, she came in handy today,' Adam conceded. 'But now that we've started serious research into future Labs we've no space for her anymore. It's time to think of getting rid of her.'

'Yeah, I'll speak to her, soon,' Angus muttered. He turned back to the computer screen. 'Here's the format for Sanjit – it's a straight clone of Takir himself!'

Adam shook his head, 'Our researchers explained why they were against the cloning of a clone. I didn't look into all the details, something to do with increasing the risk of any flaws in the first clone being magnified. This could be a greater problem with the accelerated development your donors followed.'

'If we download the data we have on to the system you have at your house we should be able to make a more detailed analysis.'

'We could move there at the weekend. Without the girl,' Adam said. 'I'll take Ginny out for the day tomorrow, that'll give you time to get rid of her, OK?'

The younger man looked as if he wanted to say something, but he gave a brief nod.

'That was a great film!' Ginny said after watching *Pirates of the Caribbean*. 'I'd *love* to be a pirate! It would be *so* exciting!'

'Not in real life,' Zig told her. 'Don't forget, this is just a film.'

'I used to think you were a pirate!' Ginny said.

Zig fingered her eye patch. 'No, this just hides a horrible mess! Want to see it?'

Ginny nodded and sat motionless as Zig raised the eye patch to reveal a sunken eye socket with a jagged scar running from top to bottom.

Ginny drew a breath. 'What happened?'

'A fight with a knife. I didn't expect her to fight so dirty!'

The younger girl sat up straight, 'We could find her, get her back!'

Zig put the eye patch back in place, 'Nah! It's not worth it now. I've left those days behind for good. Don't want to end up like my old man!' She noticed Ginny's puzzled frown. 'My dad.'

'Where is he?'

'Prison, on the street … don't know and don't care!'

'Where's your mum?' Ginny asked softly. 'Is she nice?'

Zig bit her lip hard.

'She *was* nice, the best mum ever! Went to hospital for a small operation, caught one of those superbugs, dead within a month!' She pointed to her eye. 'That's why I never let them try to fix *me* up!'

Ginny put her arms around Zig's neck, 'Well you've got us for friends now! We'll look after you. And your eye patch isn't too scary … when you get used to it!'

'You may be one of those clever Hybrids, but you're just a kid underneath. A good kid, though!' Zig smiled.

'Well, I thought today could be our day together, Ginny,' said Adam at breakfast the next morning. 'And we'll leave Angus and Zig to spend some time together. They must have lots to talk about, eh, Angus?'

As she closed the door behind them Zig gave an exaggerated sigh. She put her arms around Angus's neck. 'I know what I plan to do first!'

'Come on!' He laughed and pulled himself free, 'We haven't been in Edinburgh for nearly a month! Let's go and see Ian and Craig. See what's been happening around here.'

'Can't we go to them tomorrow?' Zig pouted, 'Adam said he's taking Ginny back to her mum tomorrow. We'll have all the time we want then.'

'Zig, this work I'm doing with Adam – it's serious, you

know.'

'Oh, I know that! But can't we have a bit of time for us?' she asked. 'Even Adam stops now and then to spend time with Ginny.'

'Yes, but she's a …' Angus stopped and started rubbing his chest. He pulled out the bottle of tablets he always kept in his pocket and swallowed two of them. 'These are nearly gone. Did you order any on the internet?'

Zig pulled a bottle out of her bag and handed them to him. 'The last site has disappeared. I had to find a new one. More expensive, too. Why don't you ask Adam for help? I'm sure …'

'I will, but not just yet!' he pocketed the new bottle and pulled his jacket on. 'Come on, I need some fresh air. Let's go round to see Craig.'

'Do I have to go home tomorrow, Daddy?' Ginny pouted, her arms folded across her chest as they drove back to Angus's house that afternoon.

'I thought you'd be missing your mother by now, Ginny.'

'I do, sort of; but I've had such fun with Zig. She said …'

'I really don't want to hear anything else that Zig said. She's just a Non-Lab. And not very educated, either!' Adam sighed. 'Anyway, love, I think she'll be getting back to her own friends and family soon. Maybe even today.'

'But … we're her friends! She said …' Ginny began.

'It's for the best, love. She needs her Non-Lab people and we have very special work to do,' her father patted her hand. 'I'm looking forward to the future, with you working beside me in the laboratory! Isn't that what you want, too?'

'Yes, of course …'

'How are you getting on with your book about the brain?'

Ginny blushed, she'd hardly opened it in the last week.

'Fine.'

'That's my girl, my Hybrid girl!' Adam turned and smiled at her.

They drove the rest of the way home in silence. When they drew up in front of the house Ginny sprang out and ran up to the front door. She was relieved to see Zig open it.

'Adam, thank God you're back!' Zig cried, grabbing his arm and pulling him into the house.

'What the …?' he began.

'It's Angus!' Zig sobbed, 'It's the latest tablets! They don't work! We've been ripped off with duds! And he won't let me call for an ambulance!'

They were now all in the lounge where an ashen Angus lay on the sofa.

'Has he got a headache?' Ginny asked.

'He's having a heart attack!' Zig cried. 'Help us, Adam!'

A look of disgust passed across the older man's face.

Ginny ran from the room and returned a few minutes later with the handful of tablets she had picked up from the floor. Zig snatched them from her hand and forced two into Angus's mouth.

'Where did you get these?' Zig asked her.

'You dropped them on the floor when Angus had a headache,' she replied. 'Is he OK now?'

'For the moment, but he really needs help, Adam. He didn't want to ask you, but …' Zig said.

'Well, now you know why the other Independents left me behind; I'm flawed!' Angus said softly.

'So you're just a flawed Lab? No wonder you stuck with her!' Adam tossed a look at Zig. He turned and made for the door. 'Come on, Ginny, time to pack our bags.'

'Are we going to take Angus and Zig to the Compound? Abel will find someone to make Angus better,' she said as she followed him.

'Please Adam, we need to hurry' Zig's voice trembled. 'Angus has about another twelve hours of these tablets left!'

Adam turned on his heels and went up to his room.

'Wait here!' Zig said to the other two and ran after Adam, stepping into his room and shutting the door behind her.

'You're wasting your time!' Adam snapped, throwing things into a holdall.

'No!' she retorted. 'We've no time to waste. Angus is running out of time; so this is what we're going to do!'

She stood in front of him with her arms folded.

'You've had some run-in with your Compound Lab friends – that's obvious because Ginny says you never go there nor mix with any of them. Me and Angus are going there today to get their help –'

'They won't help *you*!' Adam interrupted.

'They'll recognise Angus as a Lab, just as you and Ginny did!' she replied, 'And when we show them the stuff Angus has on his memory stick they'll be interested!'

'That's *my* research!' Adam looked furious.

'That's right, I'll tell them where to find you if they want to ask you questions about anything! It might look better if you faced them yourself first, don't you think?' She turned to leave then stopped and looked back at him. 'Oh, and I don't think you'll find Ginny will take it too well if I point out how her loving father is abandoning us, do you?'

A smile spread across Adam's face. 'It might be better if I just got rid of the pair of you.'

'OK, you could get rid of me easily enough. But you get rid of Angus and you've lost any chance to get in touch with the other Independents. You'll still be working alone,' Zig looked defiant.

Adam closed his eyes and took a deep breath. What the girl said was true. He had often thought there would come a time when he would have to face the Compound Labs as his daughter grew up. He'd make out that he persuaded a reluctant Angus to meet the Compound Labs, so they could learn more about Independent Labs. He'd present himself in a stronger position this way. This might be the best time to face them.

He looked up and nodded. 'OK, we'll leave in ten minutes. I'll do the talking with Abel.'

Zig gave a sigh as she raced back down the stairs.

'Angus, Ginny! We're leaving in ten minutes!'

Ginny bounded up the stairs and beamed at her father. 'Daddy! I *knew* you would help!'

Chapter Fourteen

'That's the last of the tablets, Angus.' Zig sounded anxious as she handed them to him in the back seat of the car. 'How much further to go, Adam?'

'About two hours,' he replied.

The rest of the journey passed in silence. Ginny nodded off in the front seat, while Zig kept an anxious eye on Angus.

Ginny was jolted awake as the car turned into the main gates of the Compound and a voice asked them to identify themselves. She noticed her father hesitate and leaned over.

'It's me, Ginny, and my dad. Our Lab friend is sick!'

The gate was opened and they drove in, pulling up in front of the reception.

Abel appeared with Amanda behind him as Ginny and Adam got out of the car.

'Url ...' Abel began, looking at Ginny's father in amazement.

'Ginny!' Amanda rushed forward and grabbed her daughter. 'What's happened, Adam?'

'It's a long story,' Adam held Abel's gaze, 'We've a sick Independent Lab here. He needs help quickly!'

'Independent Lab?' Abel nodded. 'OK, *Adam*. You had better bring him in. But we'll need to talk later.'

Ten minutes later Angus was in the medical room while Zig waited with Ginny in the reception building.

'I think it's time I got you home, young lady! What on earth has your father been getting up to, and what was he thinking of getting you involved with these people?' Amanda said, giving Zig a disparaging look. 'I think we need to have a serious discussion, your father and I!'

'I want to stay here and see how Angus is,' Ginny insisted. 'And I can't leave Zig here on her own!'

At that moment Ruby arrived. 'Let's all go across to our house while we wait for news about Zig's friend.'

Ginny sat with her mother in the lounge, giving her an edited version of the previous two weeks, while Ruby kept Zig busy in the kitchen.

'How did you get to meet Url … Adam?' she asked.

Zig told her how they had met in the DVD shop. 'Labs seem to have an extra sense when they are near each other, don't they? I must admit Adam has never been really keen on me, being a Non-Lab *and* flawed,' she pointed to her eye. 'But Ginny's a great kid.'

Ruby picked up the tray of drinks and sandwiches. 'Come and have a drink. You must be ready for something after that long drive. Abel will phone us and tell us what is happening as soon as he can.'

Twenty minutes later she picked up the phone on its first ring. She nodded and made a few comments then turned to the others.

'They're going to have to operate straight away. It'll take a few hours. Would you like to go and say a few words before he goes in, Zig?'

Zig nodded silently.

Ruby squeezed her arm, 'He's in good hands, you know.'

'Of course he is. They're *Lab* doctors, Zig!' Ginny stood up. 'Can I go too?'

Amanda stood up, 'No, Ginny. I'm taking you home now.'

'But …' she protested.

'Go home with your mother now, Ginny. Zig can stay here with us. We'll call you tomorrow,' Ruby said.

Amanda frowned as she watched Zig hug her daughter.

'See you, Gin.'

Chapter Fifteen

'So, Url.' Abel sat opposite Ginny's father. 'We didn't expect to see you around here again.'

'No. I'm not surprised,' Adam nodded. 'I hadn't planned on it happening like this myself; but maybe what happened is for the best. We might even be able to work together.'

'I can name a few Labs who would not be too keen on working with you!' Abel replied coldly. 'First of all there are the four Labs that you were willing to sacrifice in your last "research project"!'

Adam looked down. 'I know, I know! I was arrogant. I thought I was better than many Labs. But I assure you, things are different now. Why else do you think I have been trying to persuade Angus to come here and tell you what he knows about the Independent Labs, even though I didn't know what reception I myself would get?'

Abel looked sceptical. 'I have arranged for some of the others to come here tomorrow. We will decide together what to do next. They will want to know more about Angus and the Independent Labs. We had no previous knowledge of any other Labs but ourselves.'

'I have a lot to offer the Compound Labs. Angus and I have started a research programme already. Research that will affect Compound Labs and Independent Labs.'

'Whether you will be accepted by the other Compound Labs is not up to me alone,' Abel said, standing up to leave.

They sat opposite each other again the next morning. A knock sounded on the door and several people entered. Adam recognised the Labs Celia, Fiona, and the two sets of twins he had kidnapped as part of his previous research.

Isaac, their Non-Lab friend, was also present.

Adam shuffled in his chair and stood up as Milly approached him with Lily behind her.

'You have the nerve to come here and suggest working with *us*?' she shouted.

Adam spread his hands,' I know you have every reason to mistrust me –'

'You're right! We don't want to see you at all!' she interrupted. 'You tampered with our minds – you risked our lives!

Adam gave a wry grin. 'A fair point – but you wouldn't have been able to stand up to me like this if I hadn't made that slight modification …'

Her face reddened as she stepped forward.

'Milly!' Lily grabbed her arm. 'Let's just sit down and see what he has to say, shall we?'

Milly looked at Leon and Johnny, the twins whose lives had also been put at risk.

Leon nodded. 'Let's give him a chance to explain why he's here.'

Abel looked at Adam as the other Labs sat down. 'Who are the Independent Labs? And how did you get involved with them?'

In the medical block, Angus lay white-faced and still on the bed surrounded by tubes and monitors. In a clear box near his bedside a small, pale pink artificial heart beat gently. It was linked to his chest with thin wires. At each beat a light pulsed on a monitor above Angus's head. Occasionally the pulse flickered before resuming a steady beat.

Zig stood with a look of horror on her face.

'He looks … he doesn't look as if …' her voice trailed away.

Ruby put her arms around her. 'Dr Schultz is the Lab doctor in charge of the operation. Just let him tell you what's happening, Zig.'

Schultz cleared his throat. 'Let me reassure you that Angus has responded favourably so far. He's in an induced coma at present. Perhaps it is better if we adjourn to my office to discuss his progress.'

As they sat down in the adjoining room he continued, 'Let me explain what we are doing. As you know, Angus has a seriously damaged heart. Over the past two years my colleagues and I have been investigating both Non-Lab and Lab hearts. We have been perfecting an artificial heart that could be substituted for defects we found in Non-Lab hearts. We think this is the best option for Angus.' He brought up a 3D model on the computer screen in front of him. 'It's designed to learn to replicate the original heart, which is why the replacement is linked to the patient's heart. At this stage, the first twelve hours, the replacement is learning the original heart's characteristics. This will prevent a rejection at the second stage of the operation, which is when the new heart will be substituted for the original. During the first stage the new organ is also able to automatically detect any flaws and self-correct. This will be carefully analysed before the new heart is substituted.'

'You've never done an operation like this before, have you?' Zig said. 'How do you know it's going to work?'

'No, we haven't operated on any human, Lab or Non-Lab, though similar operations on larger mammals have been successful. The increasing medication Angus has taken has also caused further damage to his heart. Without a new heart he would certainly face a limited life span,' Schultz said quietly.

'I knew he should have asked for help sooner!' Zig sobbed.

'We have every hope that this operation will be successful. We will carefully monitor his progress over the next few days.'

In the meantime Adam was facing the Compound Labs. 'Since our last … encounter … I have continued my interest in future Lab development.' He raised a hand as Milly began to speak. 'I acknowledge that my previous attitude was unacceptable. You can see from the data I have given Abel that I now have the good of all Labs, Compound and Independent, at heart.'

'How do we know this is all the data you have?' Milly asked.

'You are all free, indeed welcome, to visit the laboratory I have set up at my country home. I would appreciate some input on what Angus and I have been working on lately.'

'The future of your laboratory and your role in the research will have to be discussed and decided upon,' Abel said.

Adam's lips tightened but he sighed and shook his head slightly, 'I have to accept that, after previous events ...'

'Let's hear about the Independents,' Leon leaned forward. 'Where do they come from?'

'And why haven't we heard about them before this?' his brother added.

'The only Independent I have met is Angus. He was working with two others, Takir and a clone Takir made of himself, Sanjit. They abandoned Angus when his heart condition became apparent.'

'Well, at least you didn't abandon him!' Lily said.

Adam smiled. 'Well, he's still a Lab.' He continued to tell them all he knew of Independents.

'Angus is aware of three other groups; but I am fairly certain that there are other groups around the world,' he concluded.

'I think we need to discuss our plan of action ourselves before deciding what role, if any, Adam will play,' Milly said.

'If you could wait in the room you were given last night, Adam?' Abel suggested.

Adam faced the others before following Abel to the door. 'I understand your reluctance to include me, but don't forget

I can provide useful information, too. I don't know how I can convince you that I am a changed person. I have a child now; you must know, Abel, just bringing young into the world changes your whole perspective.'

Abel returned to a heated discussion between Milly and Celia. Milly wanted Adam to leave straight away, but Celia felt that he could provide valuable information. Leon, Johnny, Isaac, and Lily sat silently.

'If we send Adam away, how will we know what he is getting up to?' Abel asked. 'At least if he's working with us we can keep an eye of him.'

Milly reluctantly agreed. 'Can we establish Url's – Adam's – role though? I do not trust him in any way! He must not be allowed under *any* circumstances to work unsupervised or to retain any data personally.'

'Or spend time alone with Angus until we know a bit more about *him*,' suggested Celia. 'I think we need to think about the Non-Lab, Zig, too. What does she know about all this?'

'And Adam's daughter, Ginny. Amanda doesn't seem to know much about what she gets up to with her father. She wasn't even aware of his country house,' Abel added. 'I'll get Ruby to talk to them.'

'And we still have the two main issues to deal with,' Isaac said. 'Firstly, the Independents, and secondly Adam's and Angus's research.'

'Angus's work will have had input from the Independents he was associated with earlier,' Lily pointed out.

'Why weren't we aware of the possibility of Independent Lab groups? How could we have been so blind?' Celia shook her head. 'We were so wrapped up in our own lives and the Hybrid children that our eyes have been closed to what was happening around us!'

'How can we find out about the Independents?' Johnny asked. 'Especially if they are not willing to come forward?'

'Why aren't they willing to come forward?' Leon

frowned.

'I imagine for a variety of reasons,' Isaac offered. 'One, their creators do not wish to put their work under scrutiny. Two, they may be afraid, as early Compound Labs were, about what rights they have. And three: they may, of course, have their own agenda.'

There was a moment of silence.

'I think we had better start to make contact with the Independents that Angus already knows of and take it from there,' Abel said eventually. 'I will talk with Adam and gather all the details he can provide; Isaac, you can work with us to decide on how to make contact. Celia and Milly – take a look at the data Adam has given me. And we'll arrange a visit to his home laboratory as soon as possible.'

Celia nodded. 'I would like to be involved in a working party to visit the laboratory.'

Milly nodded. 'Me too.'

'There is just one thing left to consider,' said Abel.

The others looked at him.

'How much should we make this public knowledge?'

'I think we should keep this to ourselves for the moment, until we have a better understanding of what is happening,' Celia said.

The others looked at each other and nodded in agreement.

After Adam had been asked to come back into the room, Abel explained to him what they had decided. He spread his hands in a gesture of acceptance.

'I'm just grateful you are giving me a second chance. I won't let you down.'

He gave a long sigh as he walked from the room, then closed his eyes as he heard a harsh voice call his name. He turned to face Amanda.

'So I'm finally able to track you down! I've been told you were in very important discussions with Abel and some others,' she snapped. 'Now I think you've some explaining to do with me!'

Adam gestured to the small room he had been allocated.

'Certainly, Amanda. Please sit down.'

'Why did you take my daughter to Scotland? Who are these people you have let her associate with? Ginny also mentioned a house she stays in sometimes that I wasn't even aware of!'

'First of all, Amanda, at no time was *our* daughter ever in any danger. Secondly, some very important information regarding Lab research came up during her visit to me. Obviously, I could not ignore it,' Adam told her quietly. 'Hence the trip to Scotland. As for the house, well it's common knowledge now, so feel free to visit any time you wish.'

Amanda bristled. 'I won't be treated like this, Adam! I've a good mind to take out a court order to prevent you seeing Ginny again!'

Adam stood up with both hands on either side of the chair he leaned close to her face.

'Don't *ever* think of keeping me away from my daughter! At the end of the day, you are a Non-Lab, Amanda. Ginny has Lab blood in her veins. If you force her to choose, you know what will happen!'

She flinched as his face came close to hers. He slowly drew back.

'I insist you tell me where you take Ginny and about the company she is keeping,' she said quietly.

Adam nodded. 'OK, I will keep you informed. Don't worry about the company she has been keeping. Angus is a Lab and the girl, well, she won't be around for long.'

Chapter Sixteen

'It's great!' Angus's eyes shone as he walked across the hospital room. 'I'm not waiting for that horrible tight feeling all the time!'

He gave a deep breath and looked down at his chest. Zig fingered the fading scar.

'It's nearly gone already! That's amazing!'

'Lab healing properties!' Dr Jensen smiled. 'I was amazed the first time I met Abel and saw how quickly a gunshot wound to his chest healed.'

Dr Schultz joined them. 'Yes, our patient is making excellent progress! Abel would like to talk to you as soon as you are feeling up to it, Angus.'

'I'm ready to see him now! I just want to thank you, him, and everyone, for all they have done for me,' Angus said enthusiastically.

'I'll arrange for him to speak to you for an hour this afternoon. You may feel well, but we should take things slowly, we don't want to tire you out. A nurse will be on hand if you need any help,' Schultz continued.

'I'd better leave you for the moment, too. I'll call by this evening, if that's OK, Doctor?' Zig said.

The doctor agreed as he led a reluctant Angus back to his bed.

Several hours later Abel found the patient eagerly waiting for him.

'Abel, I'm so glad to meet you!' he smiled. 'You, all of you, you've given me a new life! I can't thank you enough! And Adam, where is he? I haven't seen him yet.'

'Oh, you'll see him later. I'm glad to see you have made

such good progress. Dr Schultz and Dr Jensen said your healing powers are on par with Compound Labs; but you still have to take things easy, we don't want any setbacks,' Abel said, sitting beside the bed. 'I would like you to tell me about the Independents. We were not aware of any other groups of Labs before meeting you and talking to Adam.'

'Yes,' Angus nodded, 'My group and the other groups we came in contact with were not keen on publicity. Not after seeing what you went through.'

'Didn't you think that from our stronger position, we would be able to help you find a place in society?' Abel asked.

'Independents are also afraid of letting our research fall into the wrong hands,' the young man replied.

Abel frowned.

'Non-Labs, who don't understand their goal.'

Abel waited again.

'To produce the perfect Non-Lab or Hybrid!' Angus said in a low voice. 'Even my donor, Professor McBride, felt that Non-Labs weren't getting it right. Preserving life that was so flawed it could be of no benefit to our world.'

He put a hand on his chest. 'That's why I had to work so hard to cover up my own flaw!'

'Tell me about Takir and the work you were doing with him and both your donors,' Abel said.

For the next hour Angus told him about the research they had carried out together. 'McBride was a slave driver! Looking back, though, I think he knew his time was limited. He tried to keep control over myself and Takir; but once Pounamar died Takir began his own investigations in secret.'

'Adam told me that he cloned himself to make Sanjit,' Abel commented.

'Yes. Adam said that cloning from a clone was frowned on by Compound Labs,' Angus said.

'He's right. You'd have to discuss the technicalities with our research team, but it is not something we would consider doing. Compound Labs who are, as we say, twins or triplets, were cloned from the original donor.'

Abel took out a notebook.

'According to Adam, your group was in contact with some other Independent Lab groups?'

'Yes, the girls from Cornwall who introduced us to the two guys from London, and the New York group. We had only contacted the New York group by email at the time Takir and Sanjit moved out of the house in Edinburgh. They may have made contact with them and even others by now.'

Abel jotted down places where they may be able to trace Takir. 'Celia has started an internet search for other groups of Independents. We'd really like to talk to them,' he added.

As Abel was leaving the medical centre two hours later, Zig came to the door.

'Can I go and see him for a few minutes? Is he tired?' she asked.

At the same time Adam and Isaac appeared.

'He can't have too many visitors, I'm afraid,' the nurse said, coming from her office.

'We won't keep him long.' Adam stepped in front of Zig and pushed open the door.

'Adam!' Angus sounded delighted to see him.

Zig stepped back. 'Oh … I'll … I'll call by tomorrow morning.'

Abel smiled at her. 'Why don't you come and eat with us? Ginny was asking about you when she finished her classes. I think she is still here; she could join us, too.'

'I told my friends all about you, Zig!' Ginny said as they sat in Ruby and Abel's lounge a short while later. 'I said that you had earrings in your face and a pirate patch and that you can shoot a gun really well!'

She lowered her voice, 'I didn't tell Mummy, though. I don't think she would approve of me going to a funfair.'

'That must be her now. It's a shame you have to go so quickly,' Zig said as the doorbell rang.

Amanda came into the room and held out her hand to Ginny, 'Come on now. We can't be late for your music lesson. Where's your bag? Do you have all your homework?'

'See you soon, Gin,' Zig said giving her a hug.

'Can you come to the school house at lunchtime and meet my friends?' Ginny asked.

Amanda gave a tight smile and took Ginny's hand. 'I'm sure Zig is far too busy!'

'Not at all! Of course I will,' Zig smiled.

She sighed as she sat down at the table with Ruby and Abel. 'I don't think she approves of me.'

Ruby laughed, 'Don't worry about it! There aren't many Non-Labs she does approve of, even though she is one herself!'

Abel passed Zig her plate. 'So tell us how you got to meet Angus and the other Independents.'

'It seems so long ago now,' she began. 'I was in one of the student pubs in Edinburgh with a couple of friends when Angus came in with Takir. They sat by themselves; they seemed to be talking about something really serious. They didn't take any notice of anyone else in the pub. I'd written them off as pretty boring, actually! Then I went to the Ladies and in the corridor I bumped into Angus. He was leaning against the wall and looking really ill. Most people seemed to think he was drunk, but I knew he hadn't had that much. I stopped and asked him if he wanted me to get his friend, but he was way against that! I helped him to go outside and he wanted me to get something from his pocket; so I thought oh-oh, a druggie! But it turned out to be real medicine stuff. He took a couple of tablets and soon seemed fine again.'

She smiled, 'Takir came out and Angus grabbed me and kissed me like that's what's keeping him! Then he slipped me his number before they both went off.'

'When did he tell you he was a Lab?' Abel asked her.

'Not until after Takir and Sanjit had left, just after

Angus's father died. All the stress of the funeral and everything brought on an attack suddenly. He wasn't able to hide it. He told me about this later. I thought I'd be able to move into the house with him but he said he had to go away for a while; so we went to London. We went to see some girls there, but they told him they weren't interested in working with him anymore. They'd been speaking to Takir. We booked into a bed and breakfast place. By this time I thought he must be in trouble with the police or something – he was worried his money would run out, but he said he couldn't go and claim his father's house and stuff, even though he was the old man's only living relative. I told him to come clean with me or I was off. So finally he told me the whole story. I was amazed. My boyfriend was a Lab! We moved further north, where it was cheaper to live, while we thought what to do next. Then we got to meet Adam and Ginny, and that was a really lucky break!'

'So the girls, they were Independents, I presume?' Abel said.

'Yeah, they must have been, if they knew Takir,' Zig nodded. 'They said they originally came from somewhere in Cornwall.'

'What do you know about the research Angus was involved in?' Abel continued.

'Not much. I'm not really into science and stuff. I knew they wanted to make a sort of super person. Get rid of all the defects normal people have. I'd listen to them talking about it, but it didn't make much sense to me, or the stuff they had on the computer,' Zig shrugged. 'Ginny understood a bit about what they were doing. She's so clever! Labs and Hybrids are so clever!'

Chapter Seventeen

Zig had taken Ruby's younger child, Zac, to the park while Ruby worked with Celia in the office. After playing for an hour he was back in his buggy falling asleep. She decided to walk a different route back to the house.

The Compound was bigger than she had first thought. There were several groups of small houses, the schoolhouse and play area, the community hall, the medical block, the research block, and the vegetable gardens. As she walked past them she saw a young man struggling to tie bamboo canes to runner bean plants. She stopped and smiled.

'You need to make a tripod shape, that means the canes support each other,' she said.

He looked up and shrugged, 'I was trying to follow this diagram, but I don't seem to be ending up with the same shape!'

'Here,' she put the brake on the buggy and went to join him. 'Put the first cane this way, and the next … here … then hold the third as you put the twine … here. There you are!'

'You make it look so easy! Are you a gardener?' the man asked her.

She shook her head, 'No, but I used to work with my granddad on his allotment when I was little. He grew all his own vegetables.'

'You're Zig, aren't you? You came with Angus,' the man said. He held out his hand. 'I'm Bailey.'

She shook his hand. 'Are you the Compound gardener?'

He gave a rueful smile, 'Not really. I'm trying out different species of GM vegetables.' He pointed to a low building bordering the vegetable garden. 'They will be grown in there. The vegetables grown out here are the control version – the ones that have not been modified.' He sighed. 'But I think the sowing season will be over before I get these planted!'

'I can give you a hand!' Zig smiled. She gathered up a handful of canes. 'Do you want these sown in lines along here?'

'Yes, I have a plan,' he answered, holding out a crumpled piece of paper.

'Let's get going then!' Zig said. 'I'll do the runner beans, you start on some of the other plants!'

They worked alongside each other for an hour, talking only to ask for equipment or tools. Finally Zig looked at the buggy as Zac stirred.

'Oh, I'd better get Zac back home. I think he's ready for his lunch!'

Bailey stood up and smiled. 'Thanks so much, Zig. I wouldn't have got this far without you.'

'I've really enjoyed myself. Perhaps I could come tomorrow morning?' she replied.

'Would you?' the young man beamed, 'That would be really useful. At the rate I'm working at, I'm not going to get on to the research side of things at all!'

Over the next few days Zig and Bailey worked together each morning. After planting out the vegetables Bailey showed her around one of the greenhouses.

'In this room they have propagated normal developing plants,' he explained. He led her into the adjoining room. 'This is my team. Here we are developing the same plants but with different characteristics than normal. For example, these plants are resistant to several common insects. Over here Diane is working on a method to accelerate the development of these plants, so we could actually have three crops per year.'

'Wow!' Zig commented. 'But many people are against

GM crops, aren't they? They're afraid that the stuff you do to the plants might not be good for us.'

'No one has died from eating GM crops,' he replied, 'but many people around the world die from lack of food. We need to find ways to increase the world's food production.'

One afternoon Zig explained to Angus how she had been spending her mornings.

'What's up?' she asked him as he sighed.

'Nothing, just a bit tired, that's all,' he said.

'Oh, sorry, love, and here am I chattering on and on.' She got up and bent to kiss him, but her lips landed on his cheek as he turned his head away. 'I … I'll see you tomorrow, OK, love?'

As she walked out of the room Adam and Abel were entering.

'I think he's a bit tired today,' she told them.

Angus sat up. 'Hey, Adam, Abel! I've been thinking about our earlier ideas, Adam, the ones based on Takir's research. If only I could get out of here and get started again! I had a new idea …'

Adam gave her a withering smile. 'Perhaps he's just tired of certain company!'

Zig bit her lip as the door closed behind her. She was back at work in the garden that evening, examining some of the plants and making notes, when she heard someone clearing their throat behind her.

'Ruby told me you were here,' Adam said. He leaned over and read the notes she had made. He gave a short laugh. 'Hmm – size of leaf, texture, colour! Very scientific observations, Zig.'

She blushed and pulled the notebook to her, 'I'm not the scientist, Bailey is! I just tell him what I see.'

'Angus is moving to my house tomorrow. He's joining a team of Labs from the Compound. You won't be seeing him again.' He raised his eyebrows. 'Why don't you face up to things? You're just wasting your time around here. You don't fit in. It's time you moved on!'

'I told you, I can speak to Zig myself!' They both looked up as someone shouted.

'Angus?' Zig stood up, turning her back on Adam.

'Give us a few minutes, please, Adam,' Angus waited for the older man to walk away. 'I'm leaving tomorrow morning, Zig. It's a great opportunity. It's what I've always wanted to do!'

'So … you won't be around much, then?' Zig's throat felt dry as he shook his head. His face was impassive as he turned to look at her.

'Well, we knew this wasn't going to last for ever, didn't we, Zig?'

Zig busied herself with a plant, pulling off the dead leaves, 'Oh, I wasn't planning on anything long-term … in fact, I was thinking I might be moving on myself soon.'

'Yeah, I thought you might be. Well, I'd better go and sort out my things. Bye, Zig,' he patted her shoulder.

She kept her face turned away from him. 'Bye, Angus.'

Ruby found her sitting on the veranda later that evening. She sat down beside her.

'Do you feel like talking?' she asked her gently.

Zig shrugged her shoulders, 'I was thinking it's time I moved out of here. Angus is OK now. And, well, things aren't going any further with … us … so it's probably best if I made a move now. Thanks so much for putting me up.'

'It's lovely having you here, Zig. What were you thinking of doing?'

'Oh, I don't know. Maybe go to Edinburgh, maybe London,' she shrugged again, 'I've a few friends here and there.'

'Wait until you have a clear idea of what you want to do. There's no hurry. Don't go just yet.'

Zig began to cry softly. 'I thought Angus loved me! I loved him, and he really needed me! I've never had anyone depend on me before. Now I'm back to being useless Zig.

No education, no talents, good for nothing!'

'Hey, that's not true! You're really good with the children. And Bailey said he wouldn't have managed the vegetable garden without you!'

She sighed and patted Zig's arm, 'I know a girl who was just like you – she felt she had no one in the world that cared about her, and no real future.'

'What happened to her?'

'Things didn't look too good at first, but she eventually found her way and went on to prove herself to herself.' There was silence for a while. 'Though even now, at times something small can knock her back a bit, well, temporarily.'

'Is she OK now?' Zig asked.

Ruby nodded. 'She is, she's more than OK now!' She looked at the forlorn figure beside her. 'Stay here for a while, Zig. You're just getting to know people and finding your feet. Angus is an ambitious young man. He doesn't know what he's capable of himself yet. And neither do you. Abel and I were talking the other evening. If you want to continue working with Bailey, you could make it into a full-time paid job. You could even go back to college if you wanted. There's room in one of the houses with two Labs, you know Rachel who works in the medical block? She's looking for someone to share the rent with her and her friend. Why don't you think about it for a day or two? And later this week an old friend of ours, Sakura, is coming to stay for a few days. Perhaps you've heard of her? She's a Lab, married to the US president's son.'

'Oh, yes, I saw her on TV playing with those two other Japanese women,' Zig said. 'I'm not really into classical music, but they were great!'

'Yes, they are very good. She's taking a break from music for the moment as she's expecting their first baby soon. She's coming here for a rest. We're planning a picnic with some of my old friends, Non-Labs! You'll enjoy it!'

Zig was relieved to think she didn't have to make a

decision on her future straight away. It was also a huge relief to know she was really welcome – by some people at least – on the Compound. For the next few days she worked hard in the garden. Most afternoons Ginny came to see her after school, always quickly followed by her mother ready to take her to an activity.

'Ginny! Your hands are muddy, and look at your shoes! You know we have to get to ballet in half an hour,' Amanda said one afternoon.

'Oh, Mum! Can't I miss it just once? I want to help Zig plant out these beans,' she said.

'Perhaps you can help me tomorrow, you don't have school on Saturday, do you?' Zig suggested.

'No, that won't be possible, Ginny has lessons all morning and will be with her father for the remainder of the weekend,' Amanda replied crisply.

'Hey, you could come and join me and dad and Angus; like before!' Ginny interjected.

Zig looked down. 'No, Gin; that won't really work anymore. I'll see you next week, OK?'

She watched the two of them walk away, Ginny turning to give a last wave. Zig gave a sigh.

Bailey appeared carrying a tray of small plants and set them down beside her.

'That woman could make problems for herself in the future if she doesn't ease up with Ginny.' He shook his head then looked at Zig. 'And you need to ease up a bit too! Perhaps you'd like to join us this evening? We're going bowling.'

Zig smiled. 'I'd like that, Bailey. Thanks.'

Chapter Eighteen

'Frankie, you spread the tablecloth out on the trestle table in the garden. Ginny, Grace, you carry these plates out, carefully now! Ness, can you manage the salad bowls?' Eve Gardiner was readying everything for the picnic. 'Delia, I think that'll will be enough bread; Ruby, are those sausages about ready?'

'There's enough food here to feed an army, Ruby!' Delia laughed.

'Well, Frankie, Grace, and Hugo all have good appetites, and my two are close behind them! Plus Ginny is staying with us for the weekend as both her parents are busy, and then there are the two girls from next door! That's before we think about the adults!'

'You just sit back, Sakura. You need a bit of spoiling.' Eve handed her a cup and sat down beside her, 'When is your baby due?'

'The doctor thinks in about a month's time,' Sakura smiled, rubbing her swollen stomach.

'How is your final year at uni going, Delia?' Ruby asked her old schoolfriend.

'The MA is really hard work, but I'm enjoying it!' she replied.

'Better than school, then?' Ruby smiled.

'Absolutely!' Delia shook her head, 'And they say they're the best years of your life! It got worse when you left, though the sixth form wasn't so bad. Once the glam girls had left!'

'Rochelle and co!' Ruby nodded.

'We had our group of glam girls, too! They could make

anyone's life a misery.' Zig nodded.

'Those girls weren't so bad at junior school, were they?' Delia said, 'Remember our camping trip in year five?' She shrieked with laughter. 'That canoe trip!'

'And Mr Grogan fell in the river!' Ruby added.

'His face!'

The two young women laughed and reminisced about happier early days.

Sakura looked wistful. 'It must be wonderful to have memories of yourself as a growing person!'

'Yes, memories are important,' Eve said. 'Still, you will have lots of lovely memories of your children as they grow up.'

A sudden shout from the children made them all look up. Ness and Ginny were standing and facing each other.

'You just take that back!' Ness shouted.

'No! It's true!' Ginny shouted back.

Ruby hurried down and stood between the two children.

'What is it?'

'Ginny called Maria from next door a ...' Ness began hesitantly.

'A stupid Non-Lab!' Ginny finished the sentence. 'Well, she is, isn't she?'

'It's OK, Ness; you go back to the others,' Ruby said, taking Ginny to a quiet place in the garden.

'You can't say that, Ginny! First of all it's very rude, and secondly it's not true! Don't forget, *I'm* a Non-Lab, and so are Zig and Mrs Gardiner! You don't judge a person by their race!'

'Yes, I know,' Ginny looked down at the ground. 'She just made me angry. My mum says I'm like a stupid Non-Lab when I make her angry.'

Ruby sighed. 'Look, why don't you forget about who's a Lab or a Non-Lab and just enjoy playing together as children? You might be surprised how much you can all enjoy yourselves!'

'Hey! I could pretend to be a Non-Lab all day. And see what it feels like! That would really help me with my research into brains!'

Ruby shook her head and sighed.

'Well, first of all, you must apologise to Maria.'

'OK.'

'And *mean* it!'

Ginny's brow furrowed as she looked over at Zig chatting happily to Sakura and the other adults, 'OK. I do mean it, Ruby. I know there are a lot of nice Non-Labs. You're really lovely!'

Ruby watched her walk up to the girl and talk to her. Hugo stood by as Ginny apologised, then picked up a ball and followed her.

He glanced around and whispered to her, 'You had to apologise; but you know what you said is true, don't you? We *know* that Labs and Hybrids are superior in intelligence. We are the future! One day we'll show them, Ginny! People like you, me, Ethan, and Mariella. For the moment we have to play along!' He turned back to the others with a smile and soon had a game arranged involving all of them as Ginny stood with a puzzled look on her face.

'Are you three ready for bed?' Ruby called up to Ginny and the other girls. 'Frankie has the story to read to you before you go to sleep.'

'Ready!' Grace called back, climbing into bed. 'Frankie promised to finish the Froggy story tonight!'

Ruby appeared in the doorway, holding a sleepy Zac. Frankie came up behind her with a brightly covered book.

'All ready to see what happens to Froggy?' he smiled.

'He'll get free!' Ness's eyes shone. 'He always does!'

'Don't you want to hear the story, Ginny?' Ruby asked her.

'I have my own book here,' she replied.

'Not the brain one again!' groaned Ness.

Ruby's eyes widened as she looked through Ginny's

book.

'Pretty heavy stuff for bedtime reading, love! Is this what you read with your mum before you sleep?'

'Not always. Sometimes she tests me on my French vocabulary or some maths formulae,' Ginny said.

Ruby tried to hide her astonishment.

'Well, if you want to listen to the story tonight you might enjoy it.'

'Read, Frankie!' Ness urged. 'How does Froggy escape from the wicked Lizard Lords?'

Ruby sat with the baby falling asleep in her arms. She watched as slowly Ginny became more interested in Froggy's adventures and her own heavy book slid from her hands. By the end of the story all three girls were wide-eyed as they heard how the brave-hearted amphibian escaped from the clutches of the tyrant lizards.

'Those lizards were really mean!' Ginny commented as Frankie closed the book.

'But Froggy's *so* clever; he *always* gets away!' smiled Ness.

Ruby leaned down to kiss the girls goodnight.

'Being a Non-Lab can be quite fun sometimes, can't it?' Ginny murmured to her sleepily.

Once all the children were asleep Ruby sat down with Sakura and Zig.

'Tired?' she asked as Sakura rubbed her stomach.

'Yes, but I have enjoyed the day with your friends. They are very kind!' Sakura smiled.

'Are Simon's parents getting used to you?' Ruby asked.

'His father is a bit more relaxed, but his mother still resents me,' Sakura sighed. 'I hoped when we told them I was pregnant that they would be pleased – but sometimes I catch her looking at me as if I am expecting a monster! She still holds me responsible for Simon joining a special department involved with Labs in the New York Police Department, although it was entirely his own decision to work with them. And now Zig has been telling me about the Independent Lab groups! Wait until this becomes public knowledge!'

Ruby nodded. 'Yes, we don't know enough about them yet. Abel thinks it's better if it's kept out of the news for the moment at least. We are trying to get in touch with some of the groups, build up some links with them.'

'I think that is for the best, though I'm sure there must be Independent Labs going through the same ordeal of finding a place to fit in as we did not so long ago,' Sakura sighed. 'Once I found out I was pregnant I had dreams of doting grandparents. I want my baby to have happy childhood memories. All those memories you have. I envy you!'

'Maybe when the baby is born things will get better,' Ruby suggested. 'Everyone loves babies!'

'And not all childhood memories are good ones,' Zig said.

'You must have *some* good ones,' Sakura prompted her.

'Oh, yeah; stuff I did with my mum. But when she died ... nothing good after that. My dad was usually drunk; I bunked off school, got into trouble. It was only when I got a warning from the police that I came to my senses.'

'Well, things are looking better now, Zig!' Ruby smiled at her.

'And what about your own childhood, Ruby?' Zig asked her.

'Remember that girl I told you about with no education, who ran off?'

Zig nodded. Ruby told them the story of her life – finding herself alone when her gran died, running away, meeting the Labs, and making a new life with them.

As Zig climbed into bed much later that night she sighed contentedly. She felt a bond with both the women. She wasn't the only one feeling different in the world.

Chapter Nineteen

Angus was engrossed in studying data on the computer screen when Adam and Celia walked in.

'You know, it's amazing, the differences in our blood samples. I just wish we were in touch with more Independent Labs to make further comparisons,' he told him.

'I've made contact with two other groups, but they are reluctant to arrange a meeting at the moment. I think they are afraid of been taken over by the Compound Labs and having to follow the laws set down for us,' Celia told him.

'No luck contacting Takir?' Adam asked him.

Angus sighed. 'Not so far; but I had the idea of contacting someone who might be able to help me. An old friend in Edinburgh.'

'Perhaps you could chase him up?' Celia suggested. 'He might be more willing to speak to us through you.'

A few days later Angus knocked on the door of a house in Edinburgh. A young girl opened it.

'Oh, it's you,' she said standing in the doorway and blocking his entrance.

'Liz, let me come in for a moment, please,' he said.

She sighed and stood back. 'Not for long. And don't go and get ill here!'

Angus opened his shirt and revealed the faint scar on his chest, 'No chance of that! I've a brand new heart!'

She looked sceptical.

'The Compound Labs did this. A brand new synthetic heart! I'll outlive you all now!'

Liz ran her fingers over the scar. 'Really?'

'You want me to prove it? I'll race you to the top of the

street and back!' Angus laughed.

Liz turned and led him into the lounge where two girls were seated. 'It's Angus and his brand new heart, girls!'

'Jackie! Helen! It's so good to see you!' Angus smiled broadly.

One of them got up and came towards him.

'Is this true? A new heart?'

Angus nodded, laughing. 'You bet, Jackie!'

They sat down together and listened as Angus described his collapse and operation at the Compound.

'So you've joined the Compound Labs?' Helen asked.

Angus nodded. 'It was that or die. Anyway, I'm involved in research with a team of them now.'

'Research funded by the government?' Jackie sneered.

'No, the Labs themselves running the whole thing!' Angus insisted.

'Until the government move in,' Helen added. 'We all know the Compound Labs do as they are told now!'

'And what have you been up to these days? Breaking scientific frontiers?' Angus asked.

The three people looked at each other but said nothing.

'Go on, then!' Angus urged them.

'It's up to Takir, if he wants to tell him,' Liz said. She turned to Angus. 'Give me your number; I'll get Takir to call you, if he decides he wants to get in touch.'

Despite various entreaties, Angus could get no more from them. Finally he rose to leave.

'Make sure you don't bring any Compound Labs around here, OK, Angus?' Jackie warned him as he left.

Angus nodded. 'Don't worry. Just get Takir to call me. We've a lot to talk about.'

It was a week later when he received a phone call.

'Takir! I'd almost given up on you!' he said.

'Are you on your own?'

'Yes,' he replied.

'Good. I'd like to meet up with you. But not with your

new friends, OK?'

'OK.' Angus listened as Takir gave him directions to a small hotel just outside Edinburgh.

'I'll be there, what day is it now? Sunday. I'll be there Tuesday morning. Ask for me at the desk,' Takir told him. 'Remember, Angus, any sign of Compound Labs and the meeting is cancelled. OK?'

Two days later Angus waited nervously at the desk as the receptionist rang through to Takir's room.

'Certainly, sir. I'll get someone to bring him up right now,' she replied as she smiled at Angus.

A young man in the hotel uniform appeared behind Angus and took him to the lift. They alighted at the fifth floor and he was led along a richly decorated corridor to two tall wooden doors. The hotel porter gave a discreet knock and opened the door to an answering voice. Angus stepped into an opulently furnished suite. Takir was seated in a deep armchair set in a bay window overlooking green fields. He gestured for Angus to join him in a similar chair nearby as the hotel porter quietly closed the door behind him.

Angus gave a low whistle and looked around. 'You've certainly been doing well for yourself, Takir.'

The other man nodded. 'We're well looked after in this organisation. That's all I can tell you at the moment.'

'Are you still involved with creating the perfect Lab?' Angus asked.

Takir nodded his head excitedly, 'And you won't believe how far we have come! We have plans to produce a Lab endowed with much greater attributes than we ever thought possible back in our early days, Angus. And we are looking for trusted Labs to join us in our research.'

'You can count me in, you know that, Takir,' Angus answered eagerly.

The other man sighed. 'I think I do know you. But I also know you hid a dark secret from us in the past.'

'How could I tell you about my heart problem when I

knew how you would react? And I was right. Anyway, that's all in the past now. The Compound Labs have given me an invincible new heart!' he continued.

'Yes, your new heart is one of the reasons you are here today. We would like to find out more about this procedure, as it could well be something we can use or adapt for our own use. Before I can tell you anymore about our organisation you'll need to undergo a full medical check-up and a series of lie detector tests to ensure you present no threat to us.'

'I'm more than willing to comply.'

'Good. The car will be at the door for us in five minutes.' Takir smiled.

They travelled for several hours to a small medical centre situated in a remote area.

'Is this where you do your research?' Angus asked.

The other man shook his head. 'No one is allowed near our main centre until we have established their credibility.'

After several more gruelling hours, Angus once again sat opposite his old friend who smiled as he scrolled through a document on his computer screen. 'Well, Angus, as I had hoped we will soon be working together again. Welcome to the group. Our Benefactor is the sole sponsor for the Radicals, which started as a group of New York Independent Labs. It's the strongest group of Independent Labs on any continent and it's expanding every day. Since joining them I've been involved in experiments way beyond what you and I were capable of organising. Tomorrow I will take you to Bramways and you can see just how far we have come with our research!'

The following morning Angus settled himself into Takir's car and they headed once again into the wild highland countryside. Finally they turned into a long driveway that led to an old grey brick mansion and pulled up in front of wide steps. Sanjit was waiting for them and came down the steps as they parked the car.

'Welcome to Bramways Abbey, Angus!' he smiled.

'Impressive building,' he said.

'Wait until you see what goes on inside!' Takir sounded excited. 'Let's take a walk around to the old stable buildings. That's the laboratory block now.'

He nodded to two men in security uniforms at a reception desk.

'You'll have to leave any mobiles or flash drives here, Angus,' Takir told him. Sanjit walked on ahead and unlocked an office door. The two men followed him in.

'Sit down, sit down,' Sanjit urged, pulling a chair up in front of a computer screen. 'In our earlier research to create the perfect Lab, what did we consider?'

Angus frowned. 'Intelligence level, talents, physical fitness.'

'Yes, these are the finest characteristics of a human,' Takir joined in enthusiastically. 'But here at Bramways we are taking things one step further! As we know, humans are often far behind other species when it comes to the senses and physical attributes.' His face lit up. 'We are selecting the most highly developed attributes from other living species – finding out which animals have the best sight, which ones have the keenest sense of smell or hearing. We are also working on a substance similar to steroids used by Non-Labs to enhance physical abilities, but eliminating any harmful side effects. If we can add these abilities to a highly intelligent Lab, just think of the being we can create!'

'So you have created a Lab with these added attributes?' Angus gasped.

'Not yet, we are still in the early stages. We have quite a way to go! Look at this example.' He brought up a series of images on the screen. 'We selected the auditory system of several wild creatures – owl, bat, antelope – and adapted and matched them to our subjects before transplanting them. At the moment we are only using Non-Labs for our investigations. We are at the stage of inserting a separate "enhancement" into each individual. Many have been most successful!'

'Wow! This is really something, Takir!' Angus gave a low whistle as he looked at the images displayed on the screen. 'But this kind of research must cost a fortune! How do you manage it?'

'The Radicals have an American backer. No one knows who he is, or even if he's a Lab or Non-Lab. We deal with his lawyer who refers to him as "Our Benefactor".' Takir gave a proud smile. 'He is very generous. This is just the start. At the moment we are implanting only one enhancement per person. We're aiming eventually to implant several enhancements into one person. These trial runs are on Non-Labs, but hopefully by next year we will be ready to start on Labs.'

'How do you monitor their progress?' Angus continued.

'Well, we have daily and weekly tests we carry out, and ...' he glanced at his watch. 'It's about feeding time. Sanjit will take you. He's monitoring them today.'

Sanjit appeared in the doorway, beckoning a puzzled Angus to follow him as he led the way out of the laboratory and down the corridor.

'I bet your Compound Labs haven't anything like this, eh, Angus?' Sanjit said.

Angus shook his head. 'Nothing! Where do you get the Non-Labs for your trials?'

'City centres, bus stations – you can usually pick up a few youngsters from these places. Some need cleaning up – not just giving them a bath, but getting them over alcohol or drug dependency – before we can use them. That can take some time.'

'What happens to these Non-Labs when you have finished your investigations?' Angus asked.

Sanjit shrugged. 'We tell them we'll wipe their memories clean, give them back their normal eyes, ears, or whatever, and take them back where we found them.'

'But surely …' Angus began.

'No, of course we don't! Though it can be shorter than they expected, they end up with a better life here than they were used to,' he smiled, 'So it's winners all around!'

They entered a small dimly lit room and sat facing a window. He flicked a switch to reveal a view of woodland bordered by a grassy area. There were ropes, nets, and wooden frames set out as an assault course. At intervals in the grassy border were differently coloured wooden platforms.

Sanjit nodded to the top area where a group of people were emerging through a wide set of French windows. Angus recognised one of them as Liz. The others were a mixed group of male and female teenagers.

'Two-way mirror. We can see and hear them; but they can't see or hear us,' Sanjit told him. 'All members of the Zoo, as we call our friends here, get a generous breakfast, then they undergo physical training for two hours. They all have access to a healthy lunch, then there's a further exercise period of one hour followed by free time until six o'clock. Every night they play for their supper. Each boy or girl must use their given enhancement to be the first in their group to locate the box, except for the Muscles who compete to get their wristband on the chosen goal first. The winners form Team A, who have first sitting for supper. This meal is not so generous, meaning there's not always enough left for Team B. So it pays to be a winner! We monitor it to see whose enhancements are not functioning to full capacity.'

Liz's voice sounded through a speaker on the wall.

'We'll start with Eyes.' They watched as two teenage boys stepped forward and each put on a wristband handed to them.

'The colour of the wristband tells them their starting point,' Sanjit explained as the boys took their places on a coloured platform.

Liz blew the whistle and both boys set off, searching

amongst the grassland and woodland. Suddenly one shouted and held up an object.

'Otis, well done. You've improved your timing by 2.3 seconds. You're in A. Tony, you're in B,' Liz said. Otis high-fived a young girl while Tony threw himself on the grass dejectedly.

'Let's have Ears next,' Liz continued. Two girls and one boy stepped forward. They each took a wristband and found their platform. Liz blew the whistle and they began their search. The girls moved their heads slowly from side to side and headed in the same direction, unaware of each other. The boy seemed to struggle, taking a few steps one way and then another, undecided in which direction to go. One of the girls froze, then stealthily ran towards a point. Half a minute later the second girl headed for the same goal, giving a cry of dismay as the first girl held something aloft.

'Jez again! Same timing, but OK. Join Otis. You're B again, Lynne, you, too Simpson. What's the matter with you? You need to concentrate,' Liz said as the two of them joined Tony.

'Noses,' Liz continued. The procedure was repeated with a girl and boy. The boy seemed disorientated, often shaking his head as if to clear it. The girl walked confidently forward, sniffing the air and soon appeared triumphantly holding aloft her prize, taunting the boy who aimed a kick at her legs.

'Don't get any warnings this time, Cam! You know what happened last week! Any violence towards Brit and you don't eat at all tonight!' Liz said firmly as he scowled and threw himself down beside Tony's group.

'So, Muscles, ready?' Liz waited until the two remaining boys stood either side of her, then handed them their wristbands. The others watched as Liz blew her whistle and they set off across the assault course, sprinting, climbing, running, and jumping at amazing speeds. Finally there was a triumphant cry from one of them.

'Rhys is in A, by 0.04 seconds!' Liz smiled. 'OK, As – in you go. Let's hope you're not too hungry and that Cook has been generous tonight, don't you agree, Bs?'

'Entertaining, eh?' Sanjit laughed as he flicked the switch shutting off the view and turned the main light on again. 'Let's go and see Takir. He will have analysed the results by now.'

Takir looked up as they entered an adjoining laboratory. 'Cam is underachieving compared to four weeks ago. We need to take a closer look at him. The two Muscles are not so fast tonight. Jackie can get on to that.'

'Maybe they need a stronger dosage?' Sanjit suggested taking the results. 'I'll go over these with Jackie and Helen, OK?' He left the room as he nodded.

Takir seized Angus by the shoulder. 'Come and have a look at these!' He led him to a small glass-walled room at the back of the laboratory. He gave him a white suit, gloves, and goggles and pulled on the same himself.

'We can't risk any contamination!' he explained. Inside the room he illuminated two small containers. Inside each was an eyeball.

'Look at that!' he said excitedly. 'Wildcat. Adapted, resized, and modified ready for transplant!'

Angus drew a deep breath. 'When will you be transplanting them?'

'Tomorrow, or Tuesday. They won't last longer than a week. We have the subject ready. He was a drug addict, nothing hard, but we needed several weeks to detox him. He should be ready now.'

Takir secured the room and walked with Angus to the door. As they stripped off the protective suits Angus looked at him.

'I'd like to join you here, Takir,' he said.

Takir frowned. 'I'd like to have you here, Angus, now you're fit, but we've decided you might be more useful where you are at the moment. You'll be able to keep us

109

informed of any new developments with the Compound Labs. Of course, you'll be able to join us here as often as you can make it!'

He looked up frowning as a young man hurried towards him.

'What is it, Lee?' he asked.

'It's the new patient, Takir!' the young man answered breathlessly.

'What about him?' his frown deepened. 'He should be ready for operating tomorrow, surely he's not going to take longer to detox?'

'He's … he's …dead! It was probably his heart!'

Takir slammed a hand against his forehead. 'The eyes. They won't last for more than a week! And where are we going to get a suitable person at such short notice?'

'Just for once couldn't we just pick someone up randomly?' the younger man suggested.

'It's too risky. Our Benefactor would not even consider it,' Takir shook his head. 'We're safe as long as we stick to the ones that no one is looking for.'

'Hey, wait a minute!' Angus held up his hand. 'I think I can supply an ideal candidate – no family, no close friends. And she would probably be willing, with a little persuasion …'

Takir looked at his face. 'You are thinking of Zig, aren't you? She doesn't drink or take drugs, does she?'

'No. Not after seeing what they did to her father,' Angus replied, 'And I'm sure I could persuade her …'

Chapter Twenty

'Are you still working, Zig? I thought you went home an hour ago. It's nearly dark!'

Zig looked up at Bailey. 'Oh, hi. I didn't realize the time. I just thought I'd try to map out which plants seem to be performing better than others, the GM ones and the control group. I got some books out of the library about soil conditions and different chemicals plants need. I remember my granddad would say things like "it's too acid" or "it needs potassium".'

'Greg has some soil tester kits. Have a word with him. It'll have to be tomorrow. He's gone home now,' Bailey replied. 'Some of us are going to try out that new Italian restaurant in town this evening. Would you like to join us?'

'That would be great, Bailey. Give me half an hour to clean up and get changed.'

Zig smiled as she listened to Bailey in the restaurant later that evening.

'No, really, Zig, you should think about signing up for a course in horticulture at the college. You're certainly talented. We couldn't do without you now!' Bailey insisted.

'He's right, Zig,' Rachel, her roommate, added, 'We've all been programmed with different talents, but none of us has much of an idea about practical planting and caring for crops.'

'I'm not really a reading and writing person,' she began.

'No excuses! You were doing very well with those books you had out today. Think about it seriously, Zig,' Bailey countered.

'You should go for it!' Ruby told Zig the next morning,

when she came to look after Zac for a few hours. 'You might even inspire me to do something, too! I keep putting it off and making excuses.'

'Having two young children is quite a reasonable excuse, Ruby!' Zig smiled.

'I have lots of offers of help,' Ruby said. 'Tell you what – we'll both go and make enquiries! We'll inspire each other!'

'OK, it's a deal!' Zig agreed.

'I'll arrange for someone to look after the children one afternoon later in the week!' Ruby added.

Zig was humming to herself as she worked that afternoon. Bailey had been delighted that she was taking his advice seriously. Hearing a noise close to her she looked up expecting to see him again. Her heart missed a beat and she stood up slowly.

'Angus …'

'Yes. It's me, Zig. How are you?' he smiled.

'Fine. Fine. What about you?'

'OK. I miss you, though,' he said quietly.

'Well, you're busy now. You and Adam, with your new research.' Zig stooped down and started to pour a soil sample into a container. Her hands shook and most of the soil ended up back on the ground.

Angus knelt next to her, 'Let me help you with that.'

He watched as she pulled a new sample from the soil and held out the container. He felt her tremble as he brushed her hand.

'It's so good to see you again, Zig!' He pushed her hair from her face.

'I'm not going to get involved again!' Zig told Rachel as she put on some clean clothes an hour later. 'We're just going for a drink and a chat. He's still going to be absorbed in this new research he's doing with Adam. He won't always be popping by to see me!'

'You never know! You certainly still seem keen on him!' Rachel laughed.

'I've really enjoyed this evening. I was afraid you'd tell me to get lost when I turned up today,' Angus sighed as he pushed away his plate. 'I treated you badly, Zig, just leaving like that.'

'Oh, well you had … have real important research with Adam and the other Labs,' she said.

'And I still can make time for us, if you want,' he continued. 'Look I really want to make things up to you. How about we go away; just you and me; for a few days? We both could do with a holiday. What do you say, Zig?'

'Well, I don't know! When?' she asked.

'Tomorrow!'

'Tomorrow?' she repeated.

'I want to show you I'm serious! Please say yes! I can pick you up tomorrow afternoon, about five, OK? You don't know how much it would mean to me,' he leaned over and took her hand. 'Please say yes, Zig!'

'I'll only be gone for a few days,' Zig explained to Ruby the next morning. 'And we'll definitely sign up for a college course when I get back!'

'Are you sure he's such a reformed character?' Ruby looked uneasy.

'Yes! We had such a lovely evening together yesterday. It was like old times – no, better than old times!' Zig laughed. 'Bailey said he can manage the garden himself for a few days and Greg can help him out if he needs it.'

She looked up to see Ginny running towards her. She held out her arms and the young girl jumped into them.

'Bailey said you were going away!'

'Yes, just for a short holiday. I'll bring you back a present!' Zig smiled.

'I'll miss you, Zig!'

Ginny clung to her neck. Zig hugged her back. 'I'll miss you, too, but I'll be back soon!'

Ruby watched the car drive away and turned to Abel. 'I

don't trust that man at all, Abel. I wish she hadn't gone with him!'

'She's old enough to do as she wants,' he replied.

Ruby sighed. 'Well, if it all ends in tears, she has us!'

Chapter Twenty-one

It was dark when they pulled up in front of the sprawling country hotel.

'We'll stay here tonight and head off early tomorrow,' Angus said. He glanced at his watch, 'Good timing. I've booked dinner in an hour.'

'Wow! I've never stayed in such a lovely place,' Zig said as she climbed out of the car.

'Wow!' she repeated as the bellboy led them to their room.

'Nothing but the best for my Zig!' Angus put his arms around her and pulled her to him. 'And don't forget I've a new heart now! I never tire!'

Zig was up before Angus the next morning. As she washed her face in the bathroom she ran a finger over her scarred eye. Then she caught a glimpse of Angus in the mirror. She saw him try to hide the look of disgust as he turned away. Quickly she pulled her eye patch into place.

'This holiday is a really good idea, Angus!' Zig leaned over and stroked his arm later at breakfast.

He smiled and looked up from the map in his hand.

'You know, I was thinking; there's a friend I'd like you to meet, quite near here … no, it's not the right time! Forget I said anything!'

'You've got to explain now you've started!' she laughed.

He sighed. 'No, I may offend you, ruin the holiday. And I really, *really* don't want to do that!'

'No, you'll have to tell me now, Angus!' Zig said.

'Forget it. We'll talk about it another time. It was stupid of me to think about it at this moment, stupid!' he smiled and stood up. 'Come on let's get our bags and get moving. We're heading for Scotland, but to the hills this time, not a grimy city!'

As she put the last things in her bag Zig turned to Angus.

'Please tell me what you were thinking of earlier. Why would I be offended?'

He gave a deep sigh, 'You might think I don't appreciate you as you are. To me you'll always be beautiful. It's not about appearances.'

Zig touched her eye patch. 'It's about this, isn't it?'

Angus groaned, 'Look, since I got my new heart, and that was all thanks to you, I've been a new person. I've got confidence I never possessed before! I just want the same for you, Zig.'

She looked at him.

'There's a friend of mine, on our route, we could just go and talk to him. He could tell you what he could do for you. He's brilliant, Zig. I've seen the work he has done. If – and only *if* – you want, we could call by and see him just for a chat.'

Zig moved uneasily, 'I don't know, Angus …'

He pulled her to him and hugged her, 'It's OK, we'll forget about it. I knew I shouldn't have mentioned it. Now I feel so good myself I just want the same for you! You're not offended, are you, Zig?'

He pulled her closer as she shook her head.

They had started their journey and were driving along in silence when Zig turned to him.

'OK, let's go and just talk to your friend. Just talk, no decisions today! It will probably be very expensive anyway. I don't think I'd be able to afford it, Angus.'

'Oh, money isn't a problem. I can take care of all that. My "father" was worth a lot more than anyone ever imagined! And it's all mine! After all you've done for me I want to do this for you.' He smiled. 'But don't worry: no decisions today, Zig!'

He squeezed her hand as they turned into the driveway of Bramways Abbey.

A smartly dressed woman appeared as they reached the front of the building.

'Angus, Dr Neilson was so pleased to hear from you. This must be the young lady.'

She shook hands with them both and led them inside along a high corridor hung with portraits of people from a bygone age. She stopped at a polished mahogany door and knocked. On hearing a voice she pushed open the door and they stepped into a richly furnished room.

Behind a large mahogany desk a man was rising, smiling as he came towards them.

'Angus! And you must be Zig. How lovely to see you!' he said, his eyes twinkling behind rimless glasses as he clasped her hand warmly. He looked like someone's grandfather, she thought.

He sat them down in two large leather armchairs.

'Angus has told me that you'd like more details about the medical procedures we carry out here and the help we can give people like yourself,' he began.

'I … I … I only want to know a bit about it, I'm not thinking of doing anything at the moment!' Zig said hurriedly.

'Of course, my dear!' the doctor smiled. 'Just let me take a look, would you?' His hands felt soft and warm as he pushed the patch up and ran a hand over her damaged eye. 'Ah, yes, it's a quite straight-forward case. We can give you back full vision in both eyes and reconstruct the eye socket completely. Restore you to your former beauty! It's a procedure we've carried out on several patients, usually reconstruction after an injury caused by an accident.'

He walked to a filing cabinet and pulled out a folder which he pushed across the desk to them.

'Here's our brochure. You can see we cover a wide range of corrective and cosmetic surgery. And you'll see we come highly recommended.'

Angus picked up the brochure and flicked through the first two pages with Zig nervously peeping over his shoulder. He cleared his throat and glanced at Zig. 'Well, the first thing we'd have to feel confident about is, are there any dangers that the operation might not be successful?'

'Mmm, in any operation there is always the chance that something could go wrong. But here at Bramways we have a one hundred per cent history of success. That's because we have a team of highly qualified and dedicated surgeons. And excellent after-care treatment.'

'And how long has the hospital been running for?' Angus continued.

'We had our ten-year celebrations last June, for the opening of Bramways and for my decade of service here!' Dr Neilson replied. A phone on his desk rang. 'Excuse me while I take this, would you?'

He turned and spoke into the receiver. 'Thank you; I'll be right down, Jones.'

Angus and Zig looked up as he stood up.

'I've a little matter to attend to. How about I leave you to take a good look through our brochure for a few minutes; then you may have some other questions for me?'

Zig grabbed Angus's arm as the door closed behind him. 'Angus, I'm not really ready for this just yet.'

'Relax; we're just getting some information!' Angus leaned forward and kissed her lips. 'They seem to know what they're doing here. Look at the list of credentials. Hey, I didn't know the drummer from The Divas had been here! Take a look!'

Zig glanced nervously through the brochure he had put in her hands. 'Some famous names all right.'

They continued their conversation until the door opened again.

'Sorry to leave you for so long. Any more questions?' the doctor asked as he sat down again. Zig shook her head.

'Well, just take the brochure and think about it at your leisure. Then if you think it is the right course for you, let us know and we can put your name on our waiting list.'

'Could I just ask how long the waiting list is?' Angus asked.

'For this particular transplant, about two years.'

Once again the phone rang. The doctor apologised again as he picked it up.

'What? The next *three* applicants? This can't be right!' He listened for a few minutes. 'Yes, do! And please ring me straight back!'

He shook his head and frowned. 'This has never happened before in ten years! We have scheduled a transplant, similar to your own, for tomorrow; but the applicant, an elderly patient, unfortunately died this morning. So my colleague rang the next patient on our waiting list, and unfortunately he wasn't available, so he tried the next two on the list and, unbelievably, cannot get in touch with either of those two women either!

'If we don't have a patient by tomorrow the organs will be useless!' He smiled at Zig, 'If you wanted, we could put you right at the top of that two-year waiting list!'

Angus looked at Zig and raised his eyebrows. She got to her feet and held out her hand, 'Oh, no! Thank you but I … I need some time to think things through! Goodbye, Dr Neilson. Thanks for all your advice. I'll go through the brochure very carefully! Thank you so much!'

Angus smiled at the doctor and followed her out. Five minutes later they were seated in the car.

'I'm sorry, Angus!' Zig said.

'Don't apologise, Zig. It's your decision!' Angus gave her a quick smile and reached for the ignition.

An image of the look of disgust on his face that morning came into her mind. She reached forward and stopped his hand, 'No. If the doctor still can do this tomorrow … I will, Angus!'

Angus looked at her. 'Are you sure?'

She nodded.

They both got out of the car and headed back to the main door.

'Perhaps they managed to get in touch with someone on the waiting list by now,' Zig ventured.

'No harm in asking!' Angus smiled.

Chapter Twenty-two

Zig looked small and pale as she lay on the hospital bed the next morning. 'We've changed places!' she whispered.

Angus smiled. He touched her face. 'Don't worry, you're in excellent hands! And I'll be here waiting for you, OK?'

She nodded, unable to say anything else. Her hand slipped from his grasp as the anaesthetic took over.

It seemed only moments later when she felt herself being moved and strong arms lift her onto a different bed. A nurse reorganised her drip and placed her hand on the bedside table.

'There's a bottle of water within reach. And here's the bell if you need anything, love,' she told her.

Zig gingerly touched the bandages over her eyes, 'Why are both my eyes bandaged?'

'They will be for a few days. The doctor will be along in a short time to answer any questions you have, dear,' she continued. 'Get as much rest as you can now.'

Zig smiled as she felt someone slip into a seat beside the bed. 'Angus?'

He squeezed her hand, 'I'm here.'

'Can't I take the bandage off my good eye?' Zig started to pull at the bandage.

'No! You must leave it.' Angus grabbed her hand. 'Ah, Dr Neilson's here. He can explain.'

Zig heard the swish of his coat and the scratch of a pen on paper.

'The operation went extremely well. You are well on the road to recovery, young lady!' he said.

'Why are both my eyes bandaged?' Zig asked.

'There's no need for alarm. We have replaced both eyes. You would have trouble with your vision if we had not done this. It's normal procedure, nothing to cause alarm.'

'No! I wasn't told …' Zig tried to sit up.

The doctor patted her arm. 'Now calm down. I'm going to give you a sedative to help you to rest; that will make your recovery that much quicker!'

Again she felt herself drift away.

'What if I never get out of this blackness, Angus?'

'Tonight's the night!' Zig could hear the smile in Angus's voice. She held out a trembling hand.

'Don't be scared, everything will be fine!'

Zig shivered as she heard the swish of Dr Neilson's coat and the soft pad of the nurse's feet close behind him. She had learnt to identify different people by their own particular sounds.

'Well, let's see how we're doing, shall we? Time to take a look around again, my dear.' The doctor chatted easily as he cut and gently peeled the bandages away.

Zig put her hands to her eyes, feeling her eyelashes fluttering under her fingers. She peeped through them and gave a sob of relief as she could make out the fabric of the bedclothes.

'It's dark!' she whispered.

The doctor chuckled. 'Yes, it's ten o'clock at night, so it *is* dark! We always remove the bandages in dim light. You can gradually build up to bright light. You need to let your new eyes get used to it.'

He moved her face to the left and right, shining a torch into each eye.

'Perfect. Absolutely perfect!' he beamed.

Zig slowly peered around her. Angus was holding out his hand and smiling.

'Come on, time for a walk around, if the doctor says it's OK?'

'An excellent idea! The poor girl has been bedridden for long enough! Why don't you take a stroll in the garden?'

Zig stood up as Angus placed a dressing gown around her shoulders. With her arm tucked into his they made their way to the French windows. She laughed excitedly as they stepped outside.

'Ha, is this what it's like to have two eyes? I can't remember it being this good! I can see everything so clearly! What was that? Ah, a little mouse!'

'A shrew, actually,' Dr Neilson smiled. 'Tell me what else you can see, Zig.'

'A moth just about to fly – there it goes! And that … ah, yes! It's a beetle … look, running under the stone!'

Angus shook his head in amazement. 'I can't see it!'

'It's the little movements that I see the best!' Zig turned around. 'I need a mirror! I need to see my new eyes!'

'Oh, wait for a while,' the doctor suggested, 'They're a bit swollen and bruised looking at the moment. They'll be fine in a couple of days!'

'I don't mind …' Zig began.

'Better do as the doctor orders!' Angus said half-jokingly.

Chapter Twenty-three

'I've been waiting for two days now, Angus. My eyelids feel OK, they don't hurt me. I can even tolerate bright lights now!' Zig complained. 'Why won't someone just give me a mirror?'

'Very soon, don't worry!' he replied.

'I can't wait for people at the Compound to see me! When Ginny sees I'm not a pirate anymore! What did Ruby say when you told them I'd be away for a few more days than planned?' she continued. 'I wish I could have spoken to them myself.'

'Well, you know phones are not allowed on the ward. Dr Neilson is very strict about that,' Angus shrugged. He stood up. 'The medical team will be here to put you through a few more tests soon. I'd better get going. See you later, Zig.'

'I'll be glad when this is all over and we can leave, Angus!'

He gave her a brief kiss on her forehead. 'Be patient!'

Zig sighed as the door closed behind her. More tests! At first it had been amazing to find out what she actually could see. Her eyesight was greatly improved.

After the usual morning examination Dr Neilson smiled at her.

'You're one of our greatest triumphs, Zig. Your eyes are remarkable.'

'Still no mirror? I must see what I look like!' Zig protested. 'And when will I be discharged, doctor? I really feel fine now!'

'A few more days, I would say,' he patted her shoulder and turned away to fill in her chart. He exchanged a few words with the nurse as she came in. Zig watched as the woman placed her handbag on a chair near the bed. She leaned forward and threw the coverlet over the bag.

'Nurse, could I have a jug of cold water please?' she asked smiling. She gave a sigh of relief as the woman picked up the jug and left the room. She sprung from the bed and slipped her hand into the bag and smiled as her hand closed around a compact. A mirror! At last! She opened it slowly and brought it up to her face and gazed at her reflection. The scar tissue on her left eye had almost disappeared. She was pleased to see she had thick eyelashes on both her eyes. She began to smile then a frown spread across her brow. Her eyes looked different than she remembered; something about the irises! They seemed to fill her entire eye! The pupils even in the dim light seemed a strange shape. She stood up and made her way towards the window and pulled back the blinds. She held her breath as she watched her pupils narrow into long slits in the light! A scream rose in her throat as the mirror fell from her hands.

'What have you done to me?'

Suddenly the room was filled with noise and people. A stab of pain went through her arm and then she sank down into blackness.

It could have been minutes or hours when she opened her eyes again. Angus, Takir, Dr Neilson and a man and a woman stood around her bed. Zig's hands flew to her eyes.

'Take it easy!' The woman pulled her hands away.

'Well, Zig! Let me introduce my colleagues, Shana and Willis, friends from the United States. We've been working together since you and Angus left Edinburgh.' Takir smiled, 'You're in the honoured position of being involved in our research.'

'What have you done to me?' Zig whispered.

'As you are aware; your vision has improved greatly since your operation. And you are now also aware that your new eyes are not that of a mere human. No, they are in fact those of a cat – a wildcat, actually,' Takir continued.

'No!' Zig's face crumpled. 'How could you let them do this to me, Angus?' He remained silent as he looked at her coldly.

'I think it's time she moved in with the others,' Shana said.

'I'm not staying here! Just let me go!' Zig screamed.

Still struggling, she was taken from the room and down a long corridor. The hospital decor gave way to stone walls and a thick grey carpet. They stopped outside a high metal door and waited for a few moments until it was unlocked from inside. Two young men Zig recognised as acquaintances of Angus were there. Zig glared at them.

'Still feel tough, Zig?' one grinned. 'It will soon wear off!'

Zig lashed out, making the man's expression change to pain as her foot caught his groin.

'You'll soon buckle under, if you know what's good for you!' Takir pulled her arm roughly.

Another door was opened and Zig was pushed into a small bedroom and the door locked behind her.

After banging on the door and shouting fruitlessly Zig finally slipped to the floor. Only the sound of her own sobs filled the air until there was a light tap and a voice called quietly, 'Are you OK?'

Zig tensed as she heard the door being unlocked and a girl of about her own age came into the room. She waited by the open door. 'It's OK. I'm not one of them. I'm Jez.'

Zig looked at her silently, 'How do I know you're not one of them?'

'You're one of the Eyes; I'm one of the Ears.' Jez pushed back her hair. Zig watched in amazement as her ears twitched back and forth like those of an animal.

'I've got owl ear implants; you can't see them on the outside, though.'

'What is this place?' Zig asked.

'A research place. We're some sort of experiment for the Radicals,' Jez replied.

'Radicals?'

'That's what they call themselves. They're an American branch of Labs, from what I can gather,' the other girl smiled. 'They give me these super hearing ears, then talk around me as if I'm deaf sometimes!'

'Are there others here?'

'Yeah. Why don't you come and meet them?' Jez led her down a short corridor. 'That's Cam's room on the left, Brit and Lynne are in those two rooms over on the right, that's mine, Otis is next door to me and Simpson opposite Brit. Rhys and Tyler share the large room over there. Tony is in the last room. That's all of us at the moment. They're all in the lounge waiting to meet the new girl!'

Heads turned in their direction as they entered a large, comfortably furnished lounge. The boys were sprawled on a long leather sofa. Two girls sat in separate armchairs. All the young people were dressed the same in navy coloured tracksuits.

'Eyes!' A boy jumped up and came towards them, 'Hi, I'm Otis! I'm Eyes, too! Eagle!'

'Zig,' she replied, shaking his outstretched hand.

'Cat's eyes! Wow! Cool pupils!'

One of the girls looked up from the magazine she was reading, her nose twitching, 'I'm Brit, pleased to meet you. You smell like the hospital! Bet you can't wait to lose that smell!'

'She doesn't smell that bad, Brit!' a young boy said. 'I'm Cam.'

'Only 'cos you can't smell anything these days, Cam!' Brit raised her eyebrows.

'Lay off him, Brit,' Jez said. Turning to Zig she added, 'Brit and Cam are Noses.'

'Yeah, Cam's wonky dog nose,' Brit continued.

'And what are you then?' Cam stood up. 'You're dog, the

128

same as me!'

'But mine works!' Brit riposted.

'Don't you two start arguing again!' the third boy said, standing up and holding out his hand in a formal manner. 'I'm Simpson, pleased to meet you, Zig.'

'But he prefers to be called Bart!' Cam gave a loud laugh as Simpson gave him a withering look.

'You are *so* juvenile!'

'Simpson is Ears!' Jez continued. 'And so is Lynne.' The girl in the second armchair looked up from a book and gave a little wave.

'I'm Tony, Nose!' the last boy said.

'Are Rhys and Tyler outside?' Jez asked.

'Of course! They never sit still for long!' Cam replied.

'They had some new stuff pumped into them this morning!' Brit added.

'Rhys and Tyler are the Muscles. They put something into their muscles to make them stronger and faster,' Jez explained. 'So, Zig – welcome to the Zoo! That's what the staff here call us!'

'The Zoo?' Zig repeated in amazement.

'Yeah, we've all got some kind of animal implants – ears, eyes, smelling organs, and muscle stuff. Enhancements, they call them. Anyway, come and see the rest of the place.'

Jez showed her around a comfortable, well-furnished apartment. 'We all have our own rooms with a TV, DVD and CD players and computers – with very limited internet access, unfortunately. There's a big-screen TV in the lounge, if you're feeling sociable. Most evenings we go there. Not Simpson so much these days – don't get too attached to him!' She gave a knowing look.

'What do you mean?' Zig asked.

'The operation, didn't really take. I heard them talking about it. He'll be gone in a week.'

Zig stopped and grabbed Jez's arm. 'You mean because the operation hasn't worked, he's going free?'

Jez gave a short laugh. 'As if! That's what they tell them. Clean their memories and leave them near where they picked them up. Of course that doesn't happen!'

She met Zig's questioning look and shrugged her shoulders.

'And here's the kitchen!' Jez said. 'Washing machine, tumble dryer, iron, water cooler. Cleaning stuff in that cupboard. Oh and the closet next to the bathroom has sheets, towels, toothbrushes etc. You just help yourself. The next closet has a load of tracksuits; just pick out your size.'

Zig peered into the cupboards in the kitchen, 'Where's the food?'

'Delivered. We get our own breakfast rations and a snack each morning. Then we play for the evening meal. Except for Sundays. Evening meal is delivered then, too. I hope you're good or you'll be going hungry!'

Zig listened in shock as the other girl explained the rules.

'They keep us on our toes and monitor our abilities!' Jez said.

'How long do we have to stay here?' Zig asked.

'No one leaves!' Jez laughed, 'Except the defective ones.'

'It's like being in prison!' Zig gasped.

'Have you been in prison? Thought not! This is *nothing* like prison! In fact, here it's better than living on the street. We're all cleaned up here; we have rules, we have each other. I don't think anyone misses what they had outside. None of us has anybody that will even notice we're not around any more!' Jez told her.

'Well *I* do! I had friends, a job, a place to live …'

Jez looked surprised. 'Someone will miss you? So maybe they're looking for you now?'

A sudden thought came to Zig. She put her hands to her face and shook her head, 'No. I bet Angus has told them I cleared off. They'll just think I let them down. Even Ruby and Ginny!'

Jez put her hand on her arm, 'Were they your friends?'

Zig nodded, her lip trembling as she described her recent life at the Compound.

'It was like a dream! A proper life! And I blew it all because of Angus …'

She wiped her eyes roughly, 'I'm going to get out of here! I'm going back there, Jez!'

'Some of us felt that at first, too. You'll soon settle down.' Jez put her arm around the newcomer's shoulders. 'It's not so bad here, you know, and you have us now, Zig!'

She glanced at her watch. 'Sunday, so we'll get our evening meal delivered soon. We all eat in the lounge on Sundays, even Simpson. It'll give you a chance to get to know us a bit better!'

An hour later Zig watched as Brit and Jez spread out an assortment of Chinese takeaway containers on the table. Brit slapped Cam's hand, 'Just wait 'til you have a plate, will you? For once just try and use your manners!'

'Manners? He doesn't have any!' Simpson raised his eyebrows as he carefully spread a napkin on his lap.

'Oh, yeah? And you're so posh, are you, Bart?' Cam countered. 'So how come you ended up sleeping rough just like the rest of us?'

'Circumstances made it impossible for me to remain under the same roof as my stepfather,' he answered tersely.

'Come on, boys, this isn't a nice welcome for Zig, is it?' Jez intervened.

Zig watched as the others spooned food from the different containers onto their plates. Two boys, who must be Tyler and Rhys, Zig decided, held their plates and walked up and down behind the sofa. Both moved with long, fluid strides.

Jez handed her an empty plate, 'Better eat up before Cam has emptied all the containers.'

'So where did they find you, Zig?' Brit asked.

'I was tricked and brought here,' she answered.

'So you're not homeless?' Simpson looked surprised. Tyler or Rhys stopped pacing for a moment to look at her.

Jez noticed how Zig was biting her lip, 'Hey, let's tell Zig a bit about us. Most of us were picked up sleeping rough on the street. Tyler, the blond guy, and Rhys, the other Muscle, came from Nottingham, Cam was in Manchester, and Brit, Otis, and me in London, though we didn't know each other before coming here. From your accent you must have come from Scotland.'

'Yes, Edinburgh,' Zig nodded. 'That's where I met Angus. Then later we moved to Hambleton, to the Compound.'

'The Compound? Where the Labs live?' Simpson asked her.

She nodded, 'Yeah, some Non ... ordinary people live there, too. They're great people!'

'From what I've seen, Labs aren't great people at all!' Cam murmured.

'Come on, Cam, if these Labs hadn't picked you up you'd probably have died of an overdose by now! Or be back in prison!'

'I'm in prison now. We all are!' he replied.

'But a five-star one!' Jez quipped. 'I've been in worse!'

Cam glared at her and continued to stuff food into his mouth.

'I agree with Jez,' Brit said. 'We're actually better off here. OK, we've got their silly games and tests to do, but for the first time in five years, I've got a place to sleep and food to eat without having to turn tricks for it!'

Zig thought she must be about fifteen. She was a slight build, with a heart-shaped face framed by pale blonde hair. But her eyes seemed like those of someone much older.

Brit shuddered, 'I don't want to go back to that, ever! You think the Labs are bad? You should have met some of my punters!'

'I can see your point, Brit, but I can see Cam's point of view too, man,' Otis raised his fork. 'No one wants to lose their freedom.'

'Freedom to go to prison?' Brit smirked.

'I'm fine with this place,' Tony said. 'I wouldn't like to be out on the streets again.'

'None of us want to go back to the place we came from, for sure,' Otis nodded. 'Except Zig, of course.'

'A year or so ago I was pretty much in the same place as most of you are now,' Zig said. 'But I got through it somehow. And now you've been cleaned up you're different people than you were when you came here. Surely you'd have a better life outside now? Don't tell me you'd rather be locked up here than be free?'

'Yeah, maybe you're right, Zig,' Otis looked around for support from the others. 'Maybe she's right.'

'Well, I'm not prepared to lose what we have here – the best place I've ever been – and risk ending up in the same place I came from, or even worse! So don't you go spoiling things for the rest of us!' Brit narrowed her eyes at Zig. 'Look, they've spent a lot of money on us and we've got a great future with them if we keep on improving our skills. They told me.'

'How can you believe anything they say?' Zig countered.

The others looked away uncomfortably.

The silence was broken only by the movements of the two boys standing up.

'Hey, I feel like a run. Ready, Rhys?' Tyler, the tall blond boy, asked, arching his back and sending a ripple of muscles down the length of his body.

Rhys nodded, flexing his legs and twitching his upper body, 'Yeah. I can't relax with this stuff going through me!'

'What enhancements have you guys got?' Zig asked them.

'Not actual enhancements. We've got muscle conditioning,' Tyler replied.

'Makes it hard to keep still!' Rhys added.

They left through the French windows and the others could hear their shouts and yells as they raced off down the garden.

Zig tried to persuade the others to come around to her way of thinking over the next few days, but found little support. They all seemed either too resigned or too afraid to think of standing up to their captors. She spent the next few days examining every inch of her new home, determined to find a way out. Every room was covered by a CCTV camera.

The walls of the building were thick and solid. The only doorway to the main part of the building was electronically controlled and guarded at all times. The outside area was bordered by a high, dense hedge. When she tried to push a way through the branches her arms were quickly covered in scratches.

Chapter Twenty-four

Ruby sat in the office with Celia and Isaac.

'I just don't believe Angus's story! I don't believe Zig suddenly decided to go off with some of her old friends!'

Celia shook her head. 'Well, we don't really know much about Zig, do we? Or Angus for that matter.'

'I know she's only been here a few weeks, but I felt I was getting to know her. And I don't trust Angus! She'd have rung or something. She wouldn't have left without saying goodbye to us and Ginny, that's for sure!'

'I agree with you, Ruby,' Isaac nodded. 'I suppose you've tried ringing her?'

'Her number is unavailable,' Ruby sighed. 'Everything was working out for her: a home, a job, she was even talking about college!'

'Angus did say she wasn't really the studying type, didn't he?' Celia pointed out. 'And if she was enjoying herself with her old friends, she could very well have decided this life wasn't for her.'

'Did Angus say which friends she was supposed to have joined and where they went?' Isaac asked.

'He was very vague, a Maggie and Tess – no last names – and they were heading for Devon. No address!'

'Where would we start to look for her?' Isaac spread his hands. 'Report her as a missing person?'

'The police would not be interested, especially if Angus says she went of her own free will,' Celia pointed out.

'She doesn't have any close family, does she?' Ruby said. 'She's a bit of a loner.'

Celia frowned. She had come to realise how important

having a family was since she had met up with Vanessa. Although it would be quite a few months before they could meet up again, she valued the regular phone calls from both Vanessa and Vince.

'Well, we can be her family now,' she said determinedly. 'We could start with trying to contact any friends of hers that we can trace.'

'I don't think Angus is going to give us any names,' Ruby said. 'And I'm sure he *does* know where she is!'

'We'll start with her emails,' Celia turned towards the computer. 'I have her address here, I just have to work out the password!'

Chapter Twenty-five

Each morning Zig was taken to a room in the hospital wing and completed various tests.

Dr Neilson had beamed delightedly as he held up scans of her head.

'These are by far the most successful eye enhancements implemented!' he said as Takir came to study them.

'What about the darkroom tests?' Takir asked.

'They are timetabled for this morning. Shana is arranging things now,' the older man replied. He nodded at Zig, 'Come on then, we'll need you in the cubicle.'

Zig sat and looked straight ahead.

'Come on now,' he repeated.

Takir looked at Zig's set face.

'It's no use fighting us, you know. You won't win! I thought you might have worked out what happens to those who are no longer any use to us ...'

'OK! I'll cooperate if I can have a few minutes to talk to Angus!'

A moment later, she heard Angus coming up beside her.

'How could you let them do this to me, Angus?' he drew back as she spun around. 'You let them make me into a freak!'

He stood silently.

'What did you tell them at the Compound? You let them think I'd just gone off, left without a goodbye, didn't you?'

'It's what you would have done in the end, Zig. We all know that,' he shrugged, his face a cold mask.

'For the first time I had friends, a home, a good job. I was going to go to college ...'

Angus gave a short laugh and shook his head, 'It was never going to happen! You are not the studying type, Zig! You're more useful here!'

She jumped out of the chair and faced him, 'I'm going to get out of here and I'm going to prove you wrong, Angus. And I swear I'll get you back for this!'

He recoiled as her pupils narrowed into slits.

As Takir appeared in the doorway, Zig punched Angus in the chest and strode out.

Chapter Twenty-six

Jez and some of the others were sitting in the lounge watching television that evening. Cam watched hungrily as Tony tucked into a plate of pasta.

'You shouldn't be such a loser, should you?' Tony taunted.

'Hey, I don't want this.' Zig offered him her plate of fruit salad.

Cam looked as if he wanted to refuse, but instead he grabbed the plate and tucked in noisily.

'Where are Rhys and Tyler?' Zig asked.

'Those lucky sods are getting extra muscle-building supplements over in the main building,' Brit replied.

'And where's Simpson?' Zig continued. 'He wasn't in either team tonight was he?'

'Bart's gone!' Cam said. 'He told me they were finished with testing him and once they'd cleared his memory he'd be outside again. Lucky guy!'

Jez met Zig's questioning look with a slight raise of her eyebrows.

Later that evening Zig found Jez doing some hand washing in the kitchen.

'Is it true, about Simpson?'

The other girl nodded, turning the taps on so Zig could hardly hear her next sentence, 'And I heard them say that Cam is on the way out, too.'

'No! We have …' Zig began, but stopped as Jez's expression reminded her that all their conversations could be overheard.

'That's the way it is,' Jez said simply as she turned off

the tap. 'Come to my room. There's a good film on at eight. The others will be watching the football.'

The two girls sat in Jez's room later that evening.

'Help me do this crossword,' Zig said, opening a puzzle book on her knee.

'Oh, I'm not really that good at ...' Jez began, then glanced at the page, 'OK, I'll give it a go!'

She watched as Zig carefully wrote 'WE MUST DO SOMETHING ABOUT CAM' across the top blank squares.

'I've got one!' She snatched the pencil. 'IT'S IMPOSSIBLE'.

'NO WE WILL FIND A WAY OUT' Zig continued.

'I don't think that can be right. Not here,' Jez shook her head. She grabbed the pencil and wrote:

'CAMERAS EVERYWHERE!'

Zig responded. 'THEY MOVE AROUND?'

Jez shook her head. 'PRETTY QUICK'

'Me and Cam were getting pretty quick on the assault wall today!' Zig told her. 'How long do you think he'll have to get really good? Days? Weeks?'

'Does Thursday fit in there?' Jez asked.

Yes, and look what else I can fill in!' Zig smiled.

'THERES 1 PLACE WHERE THE CAMERAS DON'T GET A FULL PICTURE AT THE BOTTOM CORNER OF THE HEDGE'

'R U SURE IT WILL WORK?' Jez responded.

Zig wrote down the ideas she had for their escape.

'It's the closest match we've got. Worth going for!' Zig lowered her voice. 'Time to find out what Cam thinks.'

'You mean you think that the Irish girl and Weird Davey and Bart are dead?' Cam whispered in disbelief. 'They just killed them?'

'Shhh!' Zig pushed her lips close to his face, 'I'm going to pretend to kiss you! They mustn't hear us!'

She snuggled against him and pulled his face down onto

her shoulder. He stiffened.

'Don't worry, Cam; this is just an act!' she whispered fiercely.

'Just think about things. How do they treat us here? We are only useful for their experiments! Why would they let anyone go free? We know too much!'

'But they wiped Bart's memory clean, he can't tell anyone anything!' was Cam's muffled protest.

'Why would they waste money doing that, on a bunch of nobodies?' Zig whispered. She felt Cam slump, then his shoulders trembled.

'So that's what's going to happen to me, too, is it?'

'No! We're getting out! You and me! Then we're getting help to come back for the others! Come on! Once more around the assault course, I'll explain as we go!'

Every free moment they had, Zig pushed Cam to complete the assault course with her, always ending on the wall and insisting they timed it.

Angus, Shana, and Takir watched them through the window.

'Zig seems to have settled in here. She often walks around the gardens in the dark, making use of her new vision. And she spends most of the day on that assault course with that kid,' Takir observed.

'Pity he won't be around for much longer,' Shana said. 'We have a couple of new ones detoxing. One should be ready by Monday. Have you the olfactory enhancements ready?'

'They will be ready by then,' Takir told her. 'Sanjit is preparing them.'

They all looked up as a loud shout came from the garden. Zig was hugging Cam and dancing around, 'We did it! Less than one minute!'

'We're ready!' Cam shouted.

'Ready to wipe the floor with all of them!' Zig added quickly.

Angus shook his head. 'She doesn't realise it's not his speed, it's Cam's defect that holds them back! He's failed too many tests!'

That evening Zig started on her plan of escape.

'Just let us ladies clean, will you boys!' she said as she knocked and walked into Tony's room and grabbed all the sheets. 'These really need a good wash!'

'But they were new yesterday!' he protested.

Jez wrinkled her nose, 'Zig is right, you know. Here are some fresh ones.'

They continued around the apartment until all the rooms had fresh sheets and the kitchen floor was piled high.

'If you insist on washing our stuff you can take my socks, too!' Otis called.

Zig gave an exaggerated shudder. 'We'll start with the sheets, thanks!'

Glancing outside at the darkening sky Zig crouched on the floor with her back to the camera. As she heard a low whistle from outside she began to feed some sheets into the washer and others through the ventilation grid that led outside. Finally the floor was cleared and she stood up and started the washing machine.

Casually she walked out into the garden and glanced at the area outside the kitchen. She was pleased to see that Cam had covered the sheets over with a stack of outdoor chairs. She continued to walk leisurely to the end of the garden and looked up at the set of cameras that scanned the tall hedge. She counted as they switched to another area, then continued their circuit until they were back in the first position – one minute twenty seconds!

For the next two hours Zig, Jez, and Cam tried to act as normal in the lounge with the others.

'God, Cam, that's the second time you've knocked my coffee over!' Brit complained.

'Sorry, Brit!' he jumped up and sped to the kitchen, 'I'll get you another one!'

'What's up with him?' she frowned, 'He usually makes out it's my fault!'

'Well, I think I'll get off to bed. See you,' Zig stood up and stretched.

She opened her window as she had been doing for the past few nights and lay on the bed still fully clothed, pulling the blanket up over her. She forced herself to breathe slowly and to lie still. She hoped Cam would be able to do the same. When it seemed she was asleep, the CCTV camera would be turned off and they would only be checked on intermittently during the night. At last she heard a click. She pushed herself off the bed slowly, pulling the pillow down under the blankets to give the impression someone was still in the bed. Then she slid across the floor, her heart thumping in her chest. She waited for a moment when she reached the window before slipping silently outside. Watching each camera carefully, she made her way to the pile of sheets they'd stacked up earlier. As Zig knotted them together she saw a shadow approach her. It was Cam.

He helped her to knot the final sheets then, watching the cameras all the time, they made their way to the end of the garden at an agonisingly slow pace.

Crouching in the corner of the garden Zig and Cam watched as one particular camera turned to focus on each of its allotted places. Zig felt Cam squeeze her hand and could hear the tense wheeze of his breath as the camera clicked to its new position.

Zig scrambled up the hedge first, dragging the sheet rope in her hand. She stopped and threw the rope as high as she could then began to climb again, hoping it had caught on to something. At the top she made it secure, then lowered the rest over to the other side and let herself down. It seemed like an age before she caught sight of Cam's head at the top of the hedge, then finally he was beside her.

She grabbed his hand and pulled him behind her through an open field towards the road.

'Ouch!' he protested, 'It's all right for you, but I can't see a thing! It's too dark!'

'Just keep behind me,' she whispered back, 'We're nearly at the road!'

Zig stopped briefly as they reached the road and glanced around her.

'This way! There are some houses over there!'

Crouching near the hedge, they ran towards them. There was a terrace of about ten houses, a side road, and a group of three larger detached houses. Lights were on in four of the terraced houses and they could hear a television on in one of the larger homes. Zig stopped and pulled Cam closer to her at the side road and nodded towards a car parked nearby.

'We can take that. No one from the houses can see us here.'

She ran forward and pulled a hair grip from her hair. Her expression was intent as she forced it into the lock and moved it around. She smiled as she was rewarded with a click.

'Get in!' she whispered, 'duck down and release the bonnet!'

Cam was into the driver's seat before she had finished speaking. As soon as she had the engine started he pushed open the passenger door for her.

'Come on!' he urged, pressing down on the accelerator before she had closed the door.

As the car sped along the narrow road Zig grinned at him.

'I didn't know you could drive!'

'Since I was seven,' he replied cockily, 'Me and my mates used to pick up a motor most Saturday evenings.'

As they left the village behind them, Cam flicked the headlights on.

'Where to?'

'Let's see where we are at the next main road. We need to be heading south. Stop at the next town. We need to ditch this car as soon as possible to be on the safe side.'

She began to rummage around in the glove compartment and pulled out a pair of sunglasses and a mobile phone.

'Look at this! I've struck gold! I can ring Ruby!' Her face lit up.

'Wait till we know where we are, then try and ring her,' Cam suggested. 'Look: a signpost. Islingham, three miles.'

As soon as they reached the outskirts of the town, Cam pulled into a quiet side street and they left the car. Making their way to the main street, they mingled with other people heading home after a night out. Zig pulled the mobile out of her pocket and punched in Ruby's number and gave a gasp as she heard her voice.

'Ruby! It's me Zig! We're in a place called Islingham! We need help!'

'What? Zig? Where are you? Abel! It's Zig!'

'We got out of the place, but they could be after us already!' Zig continued. 'And this battery's nearly flat!'

'Who? Oh, never mind explaining now! Abel says we can be there in an hour. Where will you be?'

Zig looked around, 'There's a sort of clock tower thing, near a big shop ... it's called Watsons. We'll be there. See you in an hour.'

'Ok. Can you stay somewhere safe?' Ruby sounded anxious. 'We'll come as quickly as we can!'

Cam put his arm around Zig. 'I can see a place where we can stay. This is like the good old, bad old days!'

They sat huddled together in a deep shop doorway with their eyes on Watsons opposite.

'Do you think they've missed us yet? Do you think your friends will get here soon?' Cam asked nervously.

Zig squeezed his hand. 'We'll be fine. We're well out of the way here. And I'll spot Ruby and Abel easily.'

She looked at him as he raised his head and sniffed, his nose twitching.

'Can you smell things again, Cam?'

'It comes and goes. Sometimes I can smell everything,

then other times I can't smell anything at all. I tried to hide it, but they always knew when they gave me those tests,' he replied. 'What were your eyes like before?'

Zig grinned and pulled her old patch out of her pocket, 'I only had my right eye. I lost the left one in a fight! I wore this to hide the mess. I used to feel a bit of a freak but now I'd give anything to have my one normal eye back!'

'It's not so bad. You'll get used to your eyes looking like that,' Cam shrugged. 'You were in a fight?'

'Yeah, a girl from school really hated me! I was selling stuff her boyfriend was nicking and she said I was taking too much profit. The truth was she thought I fancied her boyfriend. As if!' Zig eyes narrowed. 'She challenged me to a fight, but she didn't tell me she was carrying a knife! I ended up in hospital and then in a children's home. I *hate* that bitch!'

'Children's homes! I've been in a few of those, when my mum would disappear. Some of them were really nice. I'd wish I could stay there; then she'd get chucked out by her latest boyfriend and get me and we'd move somewhere else again!' Cam sighed.

'Things are going to get better now!' Zig squeezed his hand. She jumped up. 'That's Ruby, getting out of that car over there!'

She grabbed his hand and pulled him across the road, ignoring the blare of a horn from a taxi.

'Hey! Slow down!' a young man said as she collided with him, her sunglasses falling to the floor. He reached down to pick them up. 'Don't know why you're wearing shades at this hour!'

Zig looked up as the light from the streetlamp fell across her face and saw his horrified expression. Quickly dropping the sunglasses, he ran. Zig pushed the sunglasses into place as she heard her name called.

'Ruby!' she flung herself into her arms. 'I'm so glad to see you!'

'Zig! Zig! I knew you wouldn't have just left like that!'
Ruby hugged her tightly.

'Hey, into the car quickly, we'd better make a move!'
Abel patted their shoulders. 'And this young man is …?'

'Cam,' he said.

They quickly climbed into the car and sped out of the
town.

On the journey home, Zig and Cam told them about
Bramways Abbey and the research taking place there.

'And you say Angus and Takir are involved in running
this place?'

'Takir was involved earlier, with Sanjit, his twin, and a
couple of other English men and women and an American
couple,' Cam told him. 'Angus came just before Zig did.'

'Jez heard them say it was run by the Radicals, a group of
Labs from America,' Zig added.

'And how many more of you people were there?' Abel
asked.

'Eight others – no, seven, Simpson went recently,' Zig
told him. 'That's why we knew we had to get Cam out
quickly!'

She explained what Jez had overheard their captors
saying about the defective ones.

'My God, that's awful!'! Ruby said. 'They're treating
human beings as guinea pigs! We have to do something,
Abel!'

He nodded. 'I'll get on to Reuben once we get home.'

A short while later the car swung through the gates of the
Compound. Abel pulled up outside their house as Celia and
Isaac appeared in the doorway.

Zig and Cam were soon seated with hot drinks in their
hands. Cam sniffed his drink, his nose twitching.

'Your nose is working pretty well tonight,' Zig observed.

'Yeah, it comes and goes.' Cam felt his nose.

'Which animal organ did they implant, Cam?' Abel asked
him.

'Bloodhound. Great when it works! Brit had the same as me; hers works really well, doesn't it?' He looked across at Zig who was still wearing the sunglasses.

She nodded. 'And the great thing about it is that you don't look like an absolute freak! Your nose twitches a bit, that's all.' She sighed, 'Even Otis's owl eyes were less noticeable than mine!'

'Yeah, but you could see so much better than him! Especially when it's dark' Cam pointed out. 'And, anyway, you get used to them, Zig. I hardly notice now!'

Zig started to laugh, 'One, you never saw me normal – or rather one-eyed – and two, we lived in a place known as the Zoo!'

Cam smiled, 'Well I think you're just brill!'

'Our medical Labs would like to take a close look at both of you over the next few days, to find out how they did this,' Celia said.

'Can they help me look normal again?' Zig asked anxiously.

'I'm sure they'll do all they can to help both of you,' she smiled.

'And what about the others?' Zig continued. 'Can we get them out, too?'

'If they want to come out,' Cam reminded her that most of them had found their new life a great improvement on their former way of living. He turned back to Celia. 'Our house was pretty cool, all mod cons. OK, we had to do stupid tests and things to get food, but it did keep us fit. And we all came from the streets. We hadn't had anything like that before.'

'That still doesn't give anybody the right to use you like they have done,' Isaac commented.

Abel had listened in silence for several minutes. A dark look passed across his face. 'No one deserves to be kept prisoner and experimented on, then discarded when they are no longer any use! No one – Non-Lab or Lab! We will find a way to free the rest of these people. Reuben is coming over first thing in the morning. He is a Lab who works in a special police department that deals with Lab matters. He may be able to help us get into Bramways discreetly. And Celia, we need to step up our investigations into Independent Lab groups. There may be more centres like these!'

'I can work on that with you, Celia,' Isaac offered. 'I'm due a few days leave, so we can start straight away.'

'It's two o'clock. Let's get some sleep now,' Ruby suggested. 'Zig, your old room is still there for you, and perhaps Cam could sleep on the sofa for tonight? Your roommates are away at the moment, in London, so you won't be disturbing anyone. You must both be exhausted.'

Zig opened her eyes the next morning to find Cam standing beside the bed with a cup of tea. She smiled.

'We're really free! It wasn't a dream!'

'Ruby phoned. She asked us to go to her house for breakfast.'

'I'll be ready in a minute,' she replied.

Soon they were seated in Ruby's kitchen. Ness and Zac were delighted to see Zig again and soon warmed to Cam.

'Where have you been, Zig? Why are you wearing sunglasses?' Ness asked her. 'Can we help you work in the garden this morning?'

Ruby smiled. 'Zig and Cam will be busy today.'

'There'll be other days!' Zig told her. She frowned, 'Unless Bailey has found someone else to do my job?'

Ruby shook her head. 'None of us gave up on you, despite Angus's message. He's disappeared, by the way. Celia phoned Adam just after you went to bed. Angus's room was empty. He packed a bag and left some time in the night!'

'Did Adam know about Bramways?' Zig asked her.

'If he did, he's not admitting anything. Celia said he sounded really angry to find Angus had gone!'

'Has Abel any plans to get the others out?' Zig continued.

'He's heading out there now with Reuben.' Ruby looked at both of them, 'If you're feeling up to it, some of the Compound Lab medical researchers would like to speak to you this morning.'

Zig glanced at Cam and said, 'That would be fine. I hope they can do something about my eyes!' The two children had left the room and could be heard playing in the lounge. With trembling hands she took off her sunglasses and watched as Ruby took a deep breath. 'Pretty scary, hey?'

Ruby stood up and wiped a tear from Zig's cheek. 'Hey, you're back with us, you're safe! That's what matters! And … they're not *that* bad, really …'

'They'll all get used to them!' Cam nodded in agreement as he ate another piece of toast.

'I'll keep these sunglasses on. Can I phone Ginny, Ruby? I know she won't be here until Monday, but I'd like to let her know I'm back. I worried about you and Ginny most of all when I was at Bramways.'

Ruby hugged her and nodded.

Chapter Twenty-seven

'Well, your eyes are functioning perfectly! It's amazing! The things you can see, even in almost total darkness!' Dr Schultz exclaimed.

'Yeah! I really enjoy being able to see so well, especially after managing on one normal eye for so long,' Zig agreed. 'But I hate looking like a freak! Even when I had an eye patch I didn't look like such a monster!'

Dr Schultz patted her shoulder, 'Don't worry. My colleague whom you saw earlier, Dr Nazir, and his team have come up with the perfect solution! Contact lenses!'

'But contact lenses will only cover half of my eyes! The white parts of my eyes hardly show anymore!' She frowned into the mirror.

'He has taken that into account. These will be a special kind of contact lenses! I'm sure he can explain it better than I can.'

Dr Nazir came into the room and opened a laptop on the desk in front of them. A 3D image appeared on the screen.

'This is what I have planned, Zig. We'll make you some special contact lenses, a bit like the coloured contacts you can find today, but larger, so that they cover more of the front surface of your eyes. They'll be coloured to represent the white, iris, and pupil. You can choose your iris colour!'

'And I'll look normal!' Zig cried. 'Will I be able to see through them easily?'

'Yes, though maybe not as clearly as you can without them. You won't be able to wear them all the time, though, as their size may mean they may cause some discomfort, so your eyes will need a rest quite frequently.'

'When will they be ready?'

'In two days' time. We hope you'll let us continue to study your eyes, Zig. If we can understand how they performed this transplant successfully, we may be able to use their ideas to help other people with sight difficulties,' Dr Shultz added. 'It will mean X-rays, further tests …'

'Operations?' Zig looked worried.

'No operations!' Dr Schultz smiled.

'OK,' she agreed.

'If you could just turn once more to the left, Cam and hold still,' said LuWin, a young Lab, 'we're nearly finished. Two more images and we'll be there.'

'Then we can have a snack break, you said,' Cam reminded her.

'Certainly!' she smiled. 'Our third snack break! Where do you put it all?'

'It's just so good not having to play for it! I was such a loser with this wonky nose!' Cam grinned as he sat down with a plate of sandwiches.

'Well, while you get your strength back, I'll upload these images and we can take a closer look at how your nose works,' LuWin said.

As she left the room, Zig appeared and sat down with him.

'You OK?' she asked.

'Mmm!' Cam mumbled through a mouthful of food.

'I'm getting some special contacts to make me look normal!' she smiled.

'That's great, Zig!' Cam said.

'I'll be glad when they've finished all this medical stuff, won't you?' she continued.

'No, I'm fine. I trust these guys here; more than Takir and his friends,' Cam said, 'You were right; the people here at the Compound are great, Labs and Non-Labs!'

LuWin reappeared in the doorway and turned to the

laptop on the desk.

'Hi, Zig, are they finished with you for today? We're nearly finished here, too, Cam. I've uploaded the images and we think we know what the problem is. If you take a look at these first three pictures it shows that the implanted organ just here at the top of your nasal passages actually moves slightly, only up to two millimetres, but that is what causes you to lose your sense of smell at times. Then in the next two images it moves back again. Your slightest movement, even the level of your breathing, can affect it.'

'So that's why I couldn't really smell anything much when we were running?' Cam said.

'Yes, that's very likely.'

'Why does it move?' Zig asked.

LuWin shrugged. 'We think that the organ chosen is actually too small for your nasal cavity.'

'But Brit never had any trouble,' Cam pointed out.

'Is she of a smaller build than you?'

Cam thought. 'Yes, she is quite small.'

'So what next?' Zig asked.

'We can solve the problem by strengthening the tissue holding the implanted organ in place.'

'Would you have to operate?' Zig raised her eyebrows.

'Yes, but we can perform keyhole surgery. That is if you are willing to go ahead with this, Cam?' LuWin looked at him.

He nodded. 'No problem, especially if you give me more of these cakes!'

'I think that can be arranged! Dr Schultz, the team and I can go ahead with the operation the day after tomorrow, if that's OK?' LuWin said.

Zig and Cam were making their way back to Ruby's house when they met Abel He stopped, shaking his head.

'I don't know how they managed things so quickly, but the place was virtually empty except for a few maintenance workers.'

154

'No sign of Angus or Takir or any of our friends?' Zig sounded astonished.

'Nothing at all. A Non-Lab security guard let us in and showed us around an empty building that was supposedly being renovated. He told us that it is due to open as a state of the art care home later this year. There was a partly furnished medical room, but the wing you described where you stayed was completely empty. A team of Non-Lab workers were fitting new carpets and hanging new curtains. There was no sign that anyone had lived there! Everything seemed brand new.'

'How could they have packed up and got out so quickly?' Cam asked.

'How can we find them?' Zig added.

Abel spread his hands. 'Come to our house this evening. I have asked a few other people who are interested. We can discuss things then.'

Just then there was a loud shout.

'Zig! Zig!'

Ginny came racing down the path and flung herself into the older girl's arms.

'Hey!' Zig hugged her tightly, 'I didn't think I'd get to see you until Monday!'

'I made Daddy bring me here today!' Ginny squeezed her face against Zig's, 'I *knew y*ou would come back! I told *everyone*! Mummy said you wouldn't – that you were a fly-by-night! But she wouldn't tell me what one was. And Daddy said it was for the best. What's the best about losing your friend? I *told* them you would come back! And you did!'

'I missed you, Ginny!' Zig smiled.

'I missed you, too!' she replied, 'Hey, you've got two eyes now! But why are you wearing sunglasses?' Ginny continued, 'And who is he, why is his nose twitching?'

Zig introduced her to Cam and told her he sometimes had trouble with his nose and that she still had trouble with her new eye and needed to wear the sunglasses for a while.

'So you got a new eye and he got a new nose? Wow! I bet it was a Lab doctor, wasn't it?' Ginny looked at Cam. 'Aren't Labs great? But lots of Non-Labs are great, too!'

Zig laughed, 'You're still a chatterbox, aren't you, Ginny? I want to know all your news! What have you been doing this last month? Let's see if Ness and Zac want to join us, then we can all go down to the play area.'

Soon they were heading for the park where they met other young children living in the Compound. Zig pushed the youngsters on the swings and watched as Cam kicked a ball around with the older ones. Ginny stood beside her most of the time, frequently reminding the others that she had always known Zig would be back.

Adam appeared, ready to take her home as dusk started to fall.

He glared at Zig, 'I hear you've been involved in research with Angus and some of his old friends.'

'Reluctantly!' she retorted.

'Where is he now?'

'I don't know; but I *do* know I'm going to find him!' Zig pushed out her chin.

'Or maybe you already know and you both have some other plan up your sleeve?'

'Don't think *I* wanted anything to do with their weird experiments!' Zig sprang up to face him.

'Daddy! Zig!' Ginny looked at them with a worried expression.

'Hey,' Cam walked up to them, and put his arm around Zig, 'Hey! Calm down. Come on, it's about time we got these kids home, anyway.'

Adam scowled over his daughter's head as she hugged Zig.

'You're not going to go away again, are you, Zig?' Ginny asked anxiously.

Zig kissed her forehead, 'No, Gin. I'm not going

anywhere. See you tomorrow.'

Ruby smiled and invited them both for a meal when they dropped the children off.

'Abel has invited a few people over later,' she told them.

'I'm not really hungry at the moment,' Zig replied. 'I think I'll take a walk around the Compound for half an hour.'

Lights flickered on as she walked past the groups of houses. A mother called her son to get ready for bed; a teenager stood on a balcony laughing and chatting on a mobile phone.

Zig wondered where the others from the Zoo could be. Were they safe? Had their escape put the others in danger?

She found herself near the garden area. It was quiet there; everyone had left for the day. The gate creaked as she pushed it open. Glancing around her, she slipped off her sunglasses and bent down to look closely at the first group of plants. The scent of the ripening tomatoes filled her nostrils. She fingered the downy leaves and idly began pulling weeds out from between the plants; tying up a loose stake here and there. She was so engrossed in her work that it was a moment before she became aware of people close by. Celia, Isaac, Bailey and another young man stood there.

'Zig! Bailey said he was sure you'd be here!' Celia said.

'We were worried – you've been gone for nearly two hours! I had an idea that you might be here, but it's so dark, how can you ...' Bailey's voice faltered as a beam of torchlight caught her eyes. Zig saw the look of astonishment on all the faces looking at her.

Fumbling in her pocket, Zig quickly pushed her sunglasses onto her face.

'I know ... I look like a monster!'

Isaac quickly stepped forward, 'No, Zig, it ... it just took us by surprise, that's all.' He pushed the sunglasses up and gently touched her cheek. 'You'll never be a monster!'

'You can see in the dark?' Celia said.

'Yes, as long as it's not pitch black. I've cat's eyes. Wildcat.' Zig gave a shy smile.

'Wildcat?' the young man whistled.

'This is Keith,' Celia said.

Keith held out his hand and shook Zig's. 'Pleased to meet you. Your eyes are pretty amazing.'

'Yeah, OK, for a comic book hero maybe! I can't wait for the Labs in the Medical Centre to fit me out with some new contact lenses!' Zig replied.

Bailey walked forward, shining his torch around the vegetable bed. 'You've been busy! We've been meaning to weed and sort out the tomatoes for weeks!'

He gave her a hug, 'We've really missed you, Zig!'

Another sound made them all turn around as Cam appeared, his nose twitching, 'I followed your scent as soon as I felt my nose was working again!' He stopped, 'Damn, it's gone again! I can't smell anything! It's so frustrating! I can't wait until I get it fixed!' He looked around at the others and smiled, 'I told you, everyone would soon get used to your eyes, Zig!'

Isaac hooked her arm through his, 'That's right, Cam. She's still our Zig! And what about you? What's special about your nose?'

'Inside it's bloodhound, but it's not really working properly at the moment. The medical guys here said they can fix me up!' Cam explained as they walked back to Ruby's house.

Abel sighed as he finished describing his visit to Bramways, 'You left everyone there less than twelve hours after we got there, yet there was no trace of them! Nothing at all!'

'How did they do it?' Isaac asked. 'How could they cover their tracks so quickly without leaving a trace?'

'They *must* have left some kind of traces,' Zig ventured. 'If I went back with you, maybe I could spot something. My eyes could come in useful.'

'Wait until I get my nose fixed, then between us we'd be sure to find something!' Cam said eagerly.

'That could be our best bet,' Isaac nodded.

'The sooner we go the better!' Zig added. 'I hope nothing has happened to any of our friends.'

'Abel has given me a list of all cars and registration numbers at Bramways today. I'll do a search on them and see if I can find out their owners,' Celia said.

'I'll help you with that, Celia. I could check up on the addresses you come up with,' Isaac offered.

'I'd like to help,' Keith said. 'Any way I can.'

Chapter Twenty-eight

'I'll meet you when school finishes this afternoon, if my eyes are OK,' Zig promised Ginny two days later. 'I feel a bit silly wearing these sunglasses all the time!'

'OK. I hope they can fix your eyes today!' Ginny hugged her and jumped up.

Zig watched her as she ran down the path then turned to Ruby. 'My new contacts should be ready today. I can't wait to get them on and look normal again!'

Ruby smiled and hugged Zig. 'We don't mind what you look like, but it will be easier for you, Zig. Here's Cam, are you ready to go?'

'I've been ready since five o'clock this morning!' Cam said as they stepped outside.

Zig looked at him as they made their way to the medical unit.

'Hey, you're quiet today,' she said. 'Are you worried about the operation?'

'No,' he shook his head, 'Just thinking about the others. I even miss Brit! I hope they're OK. It doesn't seem fair that here we are all safe and everything and they ... well, who knows what has happened to them.'

Two hours later Zig sat outside the operating room where Cam was, when a voice made her look up.

'Zig, have you had ...' Celia gave her a smile, 'Well, you *have* had your new contact lenses fitted! Are they comfortable?'

Zig gave her a grin splitting her face from ear to ear, 'Not too bad! But I don't care! I can face people again!'

Celia hugged her. 'We were getting used to it, but I know

it would be hard for you to keep hiding your eyes from everyone else.'

They both looked up as a young Lab medic came out of the room.

'The operation went very well. Cam just needs to rest for a few hours, and then he'll be fine.'

'Can I see him?' Zig asked.

'Just for a few minutes; then he really must rest,' she replied.

Cam looked up as she approached and his eyes widened. 'Hey, you look like a regular girl, Zig!'

Zig fingered her eyes, 'Yes! Isn't it great! Once you're OK we can start looking for the others.'

Cam nodded. 'The sooner the better!'

'Have a rest now, get your strength up!'

Zig and Celia made their way back to the Compound office. 'Did you find out anything from the number plates?'

'Isaac and I are going to take a look at some of the addresses that we came up with this afternoon when he's finished work,' she told her.

'I could come!' Zig suggested.

Celia shook her head. 'Stay here with Cam for the moment. When he's feeling better you could both come.'

Zig spent the next few hours with Ruby and her children.

'I think I'll go and meet Ginny from school,' she said, glancing at her watch, 'They'll be finishing now.'

The children were leaving the school building as she came around the corner.

'Zig!' Ginny's face lit up and she raced towards her friend, followed by a group of children.

'Zig! Ginny said you were back!' a little girl smiled shyly.

'And they've fixed your eyes!' Ginny cried.

'Two eyes, as good as new!' she smiled.

'Did the Compound Lab medics operate on you?' a boy asked her.

'Sort of,' she replied.

'Ginny, don't forget you have an extra ballet lesson this evening,' Amanda's voice rang out.

Ginny gave a sigh, '*Oh, Mum*, I want to stay and talk to Zig just for a while today …'

'We both want a first class pass at your next exam, don't we, Ginny?' her mother countered. She pulled her car keys from her pocket and took her daughter's hand.

'Oh, you've dropped something,' Zig said. 'It fell out of your pocket.'

Amanda peered at the ground near her feet, 'I can't see anything …'

Zig bent down to pick up a minute object and placed it in her hand.

Amanda frowned. 'Is that mine? I don't even know what it is.'

'It must be one of the stones from your ring.' Zig peered at the older woman's hand, 'Yes, there's one missing from the centre of the cluster, right there, look!'

Amanda screwed her eyes up and ran her finger over her ring, 'You're right! How could you possibly see such a tiny thing? How did you see it fall?'

Zig became aware of the children all watching her with interest. 'Oh, I saw something sparkle. It must have caught the light!'

'They fixed your eyes *really* well, didn't they?' Ginny said.

'Well, thank you. We must be going now, Ginny.' Amanda gave a tight smile.

Zig chatted to the children for a while then explained she had to go and see how Cam was after his operation.

As the other children dispersed, Hugo turned to two of his friends, 'Did you see that?'

'She has incredible vision,' Mariella nodded.

'Well above what you would expect of even the sharpest sighted Non-Lab,' Ethan agreed.

'And from what Ginny said, she spent nearly a month with Angus, the Independent Lab, before she returned here,' Hugo continued.

'And came back with two eyes!' Mariella said.

'Two remarkable eyes!' Hugo added.

'Perhaps the Compound Labs gave her superior vision?' Ethan suggested.

Hugo shook his head, 'No. The Compound Labs would not carry out any extreme experiments. They follow the laws of the Non-Labs! I heard Abel tell Celia that he is worried about the Independent Labs. They refuse to be limited by the same laws!'

'What kind of medical knowledge do these Independent Labs have?' Mariella asked.

'We really must find out!' Hugo said. 'Let's go and speak to Zig and Cam.'

They soon spotted them walking from the medical unit. Zig had pulled Cam's arm through hers.

'Are you sure you're feeling OK now?' she asked.

'I'm fine, honestly. I walked up and down the corridor several times while I was waiting for you,' he answered. He stopped and closed his eyes and took a deep breath, 'Hugo, Mariella, and Ethan are coming up behind us. Am I right?'

Zig turned to see the three hurrying up to them, 'Exactly right! Hi there, I'm just taking Cam back for a rest after his operation.'

'I don't need a rest. I want to go to Abel's house. Let's make a start looking for the others. We don't need to waste any more time!' Cam insisted.

'Is your nose OK now?' Mariella asked him.

'Couldn't be better!' he grinned.

'Is your nose out of the ordinary, too?' Ethan said. 'Zig's vision is clearly extraordinary!'

Zig gave a nervous laugh. 'Oh, so many questions! We've got to go now.'

'No, wait!' Hugo grabbed her arm. 'We're young, yes,

but don't forget, we're Hybrids!'

'Sorry, we must go!' Zig pulled herself free and grabbed Cam's hand, 'See you guys!'

The three youngsters stood and watched them walk away.

Hugo scowled. 'We've got to find out about these Independent Labs.'

'We could go and ask Abel?' Ethan suggested.

'Do you think he will tell us anything?' Mariella asked as both boys shook their heads.

'Well, we could just go and listen outside the house. See what we pick up,' Hugo said.

Silently the three youngsters installed themselves at the side of the house under a window. They could hear the sound of voices inside.

'No, nothing at all unusual about any of them. We took some photos. Here take a look,' Celia said.

'None of them look familiar,' Zig said after a few minutes.

'Well, I have been doing some investigation into Bramways …' Celia began. 'What is it, Cam?'

Cam sniffed the air, then strode to the door and pulled it open, 'Mariella, Hugo, and Ethan!'

Abel and Isaac raced outside.

Soon the three children stood in the centre of the room.

'What are you doing out there?' Abel asked.

Ethan and Mariella looked sheepish but Hugo looked stubborn, 'We want to know more about the Independent Labs. About the group that Zig and Cam have been involved with. I heard you and Celia talking about them.'

Abel shook his head, 'This is of no concern of yours, you are children!'

'We are Hybrids!' Hugo insisted.

Celia shook her head, 'I know it must be frustrating for you being so young and yet so intellectually advanced, but this is not something you can get involved in. You must leave it to us adults.'

'But we could help!' Hugo continued.

Abel shook his head. 'In a few years' time we will welcome your help. For the moment you must concentrate on your studies and leave this to us adults. And I want a firm promise that you will do this.'

The three children exchanged looks.

'Unless you would like me to ask your parents to remove you from the Compound School, and from the Compound itself?' he continued.

'OK,' Mariella and Ethan murmured.

Giving a loud sigh, Hugo also agreed.

'Your parents must be wondering where you have got to. Come on I'll give you a lift home,' Ruby said leading the children out.

The others exchanged looks as the children climbed into the car.

'We are going to have to watch those three very carefully,' Celia said, 'especially Hugo.'

For the next two hours they continued to discuss the facts that Celia and Isaac had found out. They had traced the owner of Bramways, Arnold Warner, an American who also owned several other properties in the UK. Isaac had marked the larger ones on a map.

'These are the ones we want to investigate first,' he said. 'I found out some facts about the two largest ones. Plaid Pharmaceutical Group is a branch of Warner UK division. They are based at Grafton Hall just outside Glasgow. According to their website, they employ a team of thirty who produce homeopathic medicines at the premises. They export all over Europe. The second property is Fairview Mansion in South Wales. It's a health farm for the wealthy. Mainly older people. From the records, most clients make several trips to Fairview each year. There are three smaller places nearer to us. Etherton Hall, near Coventry, and Beeches Spa and Cranberries, both in the Peak District. The last three are also listed as health farms, again for wealthy clients.'

'I've done some research on Warner himself,' Keith said. 'Arnold Warner is one of today's modern entrepreneurs, a rags to riches story. He claims in one interview to have been brought up by a single mother in a poor suburb of New York. His mother is said to have died five years ago, but I couldn't find any records of her death. The school he said he attended has since been knocked down and the site developed. There don't seem to be any complete records of students attending it.'

'Any siblings?' Abel asked.

Keith shook his head. 'Arnold Warner seems to a bit of a mystery man.'

'Do you think he's a Lab?' Isaac asked.

'The thought did cross my mind,' he replied.' I also found out that he is expanding his businesses into Eastern Europe.'

'Where medical laws are often not as strict as in the UK and USA,' Abel frowned.

'They could even be planning another Centre, like the one we came from here on the Compound.' Celia shuddered.

'I remember hearing something about all that on the news. What exactly happened there?' Cam asked.

Zig and Cam were silent after listening to the description of the Labs' early life, created as spare parts for humans, and their struggle to obtain freedom and then recognition as a race with their own rights.

'We don't want anything like that happening again,' Zig said.

'To ordinary people or Labs!' Cam added. 'We've got to act quickly!'

'Agreed. So here's the plan for tomorrow,' Abel said. 'Zig, Cam, and I will take a look at the properties at the top of this list. I'll find out if there are any Labs there and these two can use their special talents.'

'We can continue research on the internet.' Celia pulled a page out of a folder. 'I've listed ten more properties and some of the people connected to Arnold Warner through his companies.'

'I'll make a few discrete enquiries amongst my reporter friends here and in the US to see if we can find out any further details on these people,' Isaac said.

'We'll meet up here tomorrow evening,' Abel said.

'Can you meet me after school today, Zig?' Ginny asked her the following morning.

'Sorry, love,' she replied. 'I'll be out all day with Cam. We've some work to do.'

'I'm going to Ruby's for tea today. Will you be there?' Ginny continued.

'I'm not sure what time we'll get back, Gin,' Zig said as she waved goodbye.

The three older Hybrids appeared at the school gate. Hugo frowned at Zig.

'They trust an uneducated Non-Lab before they trust us! I'm not going to let them get away with it. I'll show …'

'Trust who? What about?' Ginny began.

Mariella grabbed her hand. 'Oh, nothing. Hugo is feeling grumpy. Come on, classes are starting!'

Hugo stood for a few minutes gazing after Zig, then a smile replaced the scowl on his face. 'I know exactly what I can do. You can't leave me out!'

Later that afternoon, Abel slowed down the car as they passed by a large wrought iron gate.

'Our third place today, Isaac. Etherton Hall,' Abel said, 'A discreet rehabilitation centre for wealthy clients wanting to overcome alcohol and substance addiction, according to the data Celia was able to unearth.'

He rolled down the window and slowly drove along the road around the perimeter of the Hall, which was flanked by a high, dense hedge.

Cam suddenly sat upright, 'Go a bit further! Stop here!'

The others looked at him expectantly.

'I think … no … I'm sure! I can smell Brit! And Jez!'

Abel grabbed his hand as he reached for the door handle.

'Wait!' He looked at Zig. 'Any sign of security cameras?'

Zig peered along the length of the hedgerow. 'No, nothing.'

Cam opened the car door and jumped out followed by Zig.

'Yes, their scent is very strong, Zig! We've found them!'

They both rushed back to the car, 'What do we do now, Abel? How do we get in? How can we get them out?'

Abel raised his hands. 'Wait a moment! First of all we'd better get out of here, we don't want to raise any suspicions.'

They climbed back into the car and Abel sped down the road. Soon they were on their way back to the Compound.

'How can we get in?' Zig asked.

'Well, I'll get in touch with Reuben as soon as we get back. He has contacts who can get the necessary permits to enter the premises.'

'How long will that take?' Cam asked.

'With his influence, we could be in there tomorrow morning!'

It was nearly dark as they drew up at the Compound. Celia appeared at the door as they got out of the car at Abel's house.

Soon Zig and Cam were seated around the table sharing the day's findings with the others. Celia had opened her laptop and brought up a map of Etherton Hall and the surrounding areas.

'That's funny, the internet is playing up. It doesn't usually happen on this laptop,' she remarked. 'Oh, it seems OK now.'

Abel appeared in the doorway and gave a curt nod. 'All set for tomorrow! Reuben and his friend will join us at eight o'clock and we will go straight to Etherton Hall.'

'You said there were seven of you at Bramways, didn't you, Zig? 'Ruby said. 'We could house them in the large apartment alongside the medical block initially, couldn't we,

Abel? I'll get it ready tomorrow morning.'

Keith was looking at a map with Etherton Hall highlighted on Celia's laptop when Cam joined him.

He looked up. 'So this is where your friends are being held now. It's quite a large property.'

Cam nodded and pointed. 'The scent was strongest at a hedge here, off the side road.'

Abel stood up. 'We want to keep things low-profile. I have discussed the matter of Independent Labs with Reuben and we have both decided it would better for the moment to keep any new findings to ourselves until we know where these new groups will fit in, or even if they want to fit in with normal Non-Lab society. We don't want any bad publicity which will impact on Compound Labs and Hybrid children.'

'You can't make yourself responsible for the actions of Independent Labs, Abel!' Ruby protested.

'I know that, but our own acceptance in society is still very precarious. We don't want those who are still prejudiced against Labs to have any more ammunition!'

'Unfortunately, you're right, Abel,' Isaac said. 'That is one of the reasons many Independent Lab groups don't want to make themselves known.'

'There may be other more sinister reasons, too!' Celia added. 'None of the groups we have been able to make contact with have shown any interest in becoming involved with us Compound Labs. Three of them actually admitted they did not want to be restricted by UK or Western laws.'

'OK,' said Abel. 'Once we have rescued these youngsters from Angus and his friends, we can concentrate on making contact with further Independent Lab groups and establishing ground rules.'

Chapter Twenty-nine

'Oh, Hugo! It's very late! Why are you still on your laptop?' his mother said as she pushed open his bedroom door.

'I was just finishing off something, Mum' he replied, minimizing the screen. 'I'll get myself a drink then get off to bed. Goodnight, Mum.'

'Goodnight, love.' She sighed. 'I know you're a bright boy, Hugo, but you are only nine and you do need your sleep!'

He watched as his mother made her way to her room and closed the door behind her.

'You're not the only one who's a whizkid on computers, Celia!' He smiled as he looked at the map that he had copied from her screen. 'Now why would you be interested in Etherton Hall? Just a quick search.'

He picked up his mobile and punched in a number. 'Etherton Hall? I need to talk to Angus. Urgently.'

'I think you have the wrong number,' a woman's voice replied.

'I'm Hugo, a Hybrid, from the Compound school,' he replied. 'I must speak to Angus! It's really important!'

'I don't know who you are talking about,' the voice continued.

'I *must* speak to one of the Labs there!' Hugo insisted. 'You are all in danger!'

There was a pause then a man's voice came on the line. 'Hugo? How did you get this number?'

'Angus! You must listen to me! They're on to you. They're heading out there tomorrow morning!'

There was silence for what seemed like several minutes,

then Angus's voice was cold.

'Why would you want to warn us, Hugo?'There was a murmuring of voices in the background.

'I don't know exactly what you have done to Zig and Cam but I want to be involved in your research!'

'If this is some sort of trap …' a second voice spoke into the phone. 'We have a way of getting our revenge!'

'I swear it's not!'

'We'll be in touch, either way!' The line went dead.

Hugo's hand was shaking as he switched off his phone.

Takir sighed. 'Whether he's telling the truth or not, we need to move. Sanjit, arrange for the residents to be moved as planned.'

The older man nodded and left the room.

Reuben and Abel pulled up at the wrought iron gates at eight o'clock the following morning. Reuben showed his ID card to one of the security guards.

'I'm from the Home Office. I'd like to speak to the Managing Director, please.'

The guard looked at the ID card and back at Reuben's face.

'I'll just phone through, sir.'

A few minutes later, Abel and Reuben drove up to the main entrance. A man and woman were descending the steps to the car.

'A Non-Lab guard at the gate, and these are Non-Lab, too,' Abel noted.

'Good morning, Mr Steiner. And your friend here is …?' the smartly dressed woman held out her hand.

'Abel,' he held out his hand, 'Miss Davidson.' He read the name on her badge.

'Ah, from the Compound,' the man nodded. 'I'm Jake Bould. Well, what can we do for you today?'

'We'd like to take a look around the premises,' Reuben said, opening a folder, 'Just a government routine monitoring check. In your prospectus you describe Etherton Hall as a rehabilitation centre.'

'Yes,' the man nodded, 'our clients are recommended by word of mouth and we assess each prospective client on a personal basis.'

'Our clients are not used to having their privacy disturbed.' The woman's face reddened slightly. 'They come here to escape from the public eye!'

'So the sooner we start, the sooner we can get out of your way,' Abel smiled.

Half an hour later they had seen a comfortably furnished lounge and dining room, a gym, and two massage rooms.

'Down this corridor we have the consultancy rooms, where our clients can speak to psychologists and medical advisors either in a group or on a one to one session,' the woman explained. 'It's probably best if we don't …'

'I'm sorry, Miss Davidson, but we do have to make a thorough check,' Reuben insisted. 'Since the work at the Compound …'

She sighed, 'Well, please be discreet!'

They walked along a thickly carpeted corridor. Despite the number of rooms, there were not many people visible.

'You're not very busy, are you?' Abel asked.

'To achieve our outstanding results and preserve clients' privacy there is always a restricted number of clients on the premises at any time,' Miss Davidson replied.

She turned as they came to the end of the corridor.

'What is there through that door ahead?' Reuben asked.

'Oh, we are planning on extending the premises over the next six months; these are just empty rooms at present,' Mr Bould told them.

'Can we take a look?' Reuben asked.

'Well, there's nothing to see!' he replied. 'Oh, OK, let's go.' He turned a key in the lock and they entered a long dark uncarpeted corridor with rooms leading off on each side. Abel glanced at Reuben, who led their two guides forward while he made a quick investigation of the first two rooms. He had picked up a small scrap of material and pushed it into his pocket when he heard Miss Davidson behind him.

'Have you seen all you need to see here?' she asked.

Abel nodded. 'Perhaps we could take a look around the medical rooms now?'

An hour later they were escorted back to their car.

'They've done it again!' Abel said in frustration. 'Not a sign of the youngsters or any Labs!'

'Are you sure Cam did scent the youngsters here?' Reuben asked him. 'It does appear to be a fully functioning rehabilitation centre, although there were very few clients to be seen.'

'I don't think Cam would have made a mistake!' Abel shook his head.

They were surrounded by disappointed faces when they sat down with the others that evening.

Reuben explained what they had seen on their visit.

'I did find this in one of the empty rooms,' Abel pulled the scrap of material from his pocket and handed it to Cam, who held it to his nose.

'It's Brit's!' he announced excitedly. 'They *must* be there!'

'Or they were there yesterday,' Zig added.

'How did they know we were coming?' Abel said. 'Someone must have warned them. They couldn't have moved the youngsters out while we were there!'

'Perhaps they've got this place bugged!' Isaac suggested.

'You may have a point there, Isaac,' Celia's eyes narrowed as she looked around the room. 'I'll arrange a complete check with some of the IT staff.'

Hugo smiled to himself as he climbed into bed that night. He had received a text from Angus asking him to download specific data from the computers at Adam's house and he was already planning on how he could accomplish this.

'So which university course do you think would be the best?' he asked Adam after school the next day.

Adam looked at the two prospectuses Hugo had shown him, 'Well, it really depends on what career you're planning on following.'

'I picture myself in the future being involved in designing and creating the perfect person!' Hugo gave an embarrassed laugh, 'I expect that sounds a bit juvenile to you!'

Adam looked at Hugo, a serious expression on his face, 'No. That doesn't sound juvenile at all. We've seen the intelligence levels of Labs and Hybrids, it doesn't sound far-fetched at all. You keep working towards that ideal!'

Hugo looked at the prospectuses, 'I don't really know if a Non-Lab course of study is really going to be enough. Could I ask you for help, Adam?'

'I'd be absolutely delighted to help in any way I can, though we are quite restricted in our research fields, I'm afraid. But I'll see what Abel thinks about you coming over to my house to take a look at the data we have collected so far.'

The next day he sat opposite Abel at the Compound office.

'Well, he is a Hybrid, and he's really keen on researching the possibilities of future developments of the human or Hybrid brain.'

Abel sat silently his fingers tented in front of him.

'I'm not sure it is a good idea to let him explore these ideas at such a young age. He may end up following the paths of some of the Independents, like the Radicals!'

'And that's why it is better that he does his research with us, under our watchful eye!' Adam pointed out. 'Left to his own device, who knows which path he may end up following.'

Abel sighed, 'You are right. But we will make sure his research is carefully monitored.'

Ginny was smiling delightedly as they all climbed out of

the car the following Saturday morning.

'I can't wait to show you Daddy's house!'

'I can't wait to see the research your father's been involved in!' Hugo replied.

Ginny was disappointed that he was not impressed by the advanced technological features of the house.

'Is this the way to the research wing?' he asked hurrying on ahead. He stopped when he reached the laboratory.

Celia appeared. 'Hello you two. Do you want to have a swim before we get you down to work?'

'Wait until you see the swimming pool, Hugo!' Ginny beamed.

'Oh, maybe later. I'd really like to have a look at some of the research you have been doing here,' he said.

Several hours later, Ginny was swimming in the pool alone. Her face was sullen as she recalled the lunchtime meal. All the others had talked about was the Independents and the work done by the Compound Labs. It reminded her of earlier discussions between Angus and her father, but at least she'd had Zig to talk to then. She sighed. Even Zig seemed very serious these days. She pulled herself from the water and began to dry herself. She decided she would go to the research wing and continue on her own work. If her father saw her working hard he would let her watch a DVD later. She wondered if she could tempt Hugo with an action movie.

Neither her father nor Hugo noticed her enter the room and turn on her computer. Two Compound Labs gave her a smile and Celia stopped behind her desk.

'How is your research coming along, Ginny?' she asked. She looked suitably impressed when Ginny showed her the 3D image on the screen and rotated it to show areas highlighted in different colours.

'Each colour shows which part of the brain controls which function,' Ginny explained. 'This is a typical adult Non-Lab brain ...' she clicked through several more slides, 'and these are images of the developing Non-Lab brain.'

'You certainly have been working hard, Ginny,' Celia said. 'Your parents must be proud of you.'

Celia sat with Adam and Hugo and discussed the research they had been doing.

'One of the Hybrid children broke her arm two weeks ago. The quick healing abilities of Labs and Hybrids is usually a good thing, but not always when there is a break like this. The bone began to knit together before it was properly aligned. Our medical Labs found a way to soften and readjust the broken bone without causing any pain or distress to the girl,' Adam explained.

'That's amazing!'

'Yes, they are now working on a method to apply similar techniques to Non-Labs. This could be a great help in developing countries where bone breakages are not always attended to quickly. Sometimes years elapse before any attention is given to the patient,' Celia continued.

They looked at several other projects the Labs were working on. Occasionally Hugo would ask a question or make a comment. Finally Celia looked at her watch and stretched.

'Well, we're going to have to get back to the Compound soon. Vanessa is calling at eight o'clock this evening. They want to make another trip to Europe later this year. We'd like to meet up in Paris. Can you save and download a copy of your work, Adam?'

'Can't we continue this evening?' Hugo turned to the older man.

Adam looked abashed, 'I'm afraid not. Once the Compound Labs leave, there is limited access to Lab research. For security reasons.'

'But, what if you want to continue a research project?' Hugo asked.

'It can wait until Monday.' Adam gave a tight smile.

Hugo masked his feelings as he watched Celia key in a

password and turn the machines off.

'Have you found this interesting, Hugo?' she asked.

'Absolutely!' he nodded.

'He has a clear insight into much of the work we have covered, Celia,' Adam added.

She agreed, 'Perhaps we could arrange for you to spend some of your school hours here, Hugo, if you are interested? You could ask your mother what she thinks about it.'

'I would like that very much. I know my mother will agree,' he said.

'It's such a pity we can't continue our research!' Hugo complained as they watched Celia and the two other Labs leave.

'The Compound is very strict on security,' Adam replied simply. 'So, as Celia suggested, let's enjoy the weekend! What have you organized for the evening, Ginny? No, let me guess … Pizza followed by mind-numbing DVDs!'

Ginny clapped her hands, 'Three different kinds of pizza. And we can watch *Pirates of the Caribbean* or …'

'James Bond!' Adam laughed.

Hugo sat eating a slice of pizza, his mind wandering as the film played out before him. Once Ginny seemed engrossed by the storyline he turned to Adam.

'The work the Compound Labs have done is amazing,' he said, 'Only …'

Adam raised an eyebrow.

'Well, they seem to be as concerned with Non-Labs as with Labs and Hybrids!'

'But your mother is a Non-Lab,' Adam pointed out.

'Non-Labs have their place, but … the future is with Labs, and Hybrids!' Hugo's eyes shone. 'We are the intelligent ones!'

He stopped and looked down. 'Sorry, I sound selfish. I know it's not right to dismiss Non-Labs as if …'

'As if they are inferior to us,' Adam said. He took a deep breath. 'But we all know they are, don't we?'

A slow smile spread over Hugo's face.

Ginny looked around at them with a frown. 'We are cleverer than they are, but there are a lot of really nice Non-Labs, like Ruby and Zig and Mummy, aren't there, Daddy?'

'Of course, love. We wouldn't have Hybrids without Non-Labs, would we?' he ruffled her hair.

It was two days later before Hugo was able to access the data Angus wanted. Adam had left him in front of the computer while he went to collect some printing. The two Labs who had accompanied him to the house were engrossed in a conversation about one of the investigations they were setting up.

With a beating heart, Hugo opened an icon and plugged a memory stick into the computer. He quickly copied and pasted the items he wanted onto the stick. Hearing Adam's voice, he pulled the stick from the machine and opened a new window.

'What were you looking at?' Adam asked.

'The work done on the Hybrid girl's bones that Celia told us about the other day. I was wondering would it be possible to make a person's bones even stronger by modifying this method,' Hugo said looking at the screen.

'That might be a good point to start your own research,' said Adam.

Chapter Thirty

The following evening, as Hugo made his way home from Adam's house he saw a message on his phone. He was to wait at a certain place at seven o'clock that evening. He flung his rucksack down in the hallway as his mother appeared from the kitchen.

'Hugo,' she put her arm around him and kissed the top of his head, 'I've just put a lasagne in the oven. It'll be ready in about half an hour. How about we have a night in together, it's been such a long time since we've done that.'

'Sorry, Mum, I've got to go and meet someone. I won't be back late,' he said as he made his way upstairs.

'But, Hugo, you can't just go out on your own at your age …' his mother protested.

He sighed, 'I'm fine. I'm with the Labs.'

'I sometimes wonder if going to the Compound School is really that good for you …' she began.

'So you'd rather I just sat back and wasted my intelligence, would you? Be some dumb layabout?'

'Of course not, it's just …'

'See you, Mum,' Hugo said as he closed the door behind him.

She leaned against the wall and sighed, a worried frown on her face. She would have to speak to the people at the Compound School.

Hugo's heart skipped a beat as he saw a BMW sports car draw up beside him. Angus leaned over from the driver's seat.

'Get in.'

They drove to a large detached house in a small village in

the Peak District. He was led to a comfortable lounge where he was introduced to Takir, an older man, Sanjit, and Liz and Jackie, who Hugo judged to be in their twenties. He placed the memory stick in Angus's hand.

'There is more data I'm sure you would be interested in, but it is hard to find the moment to download it. They are really tight on security at Adam's house. I don't know why, but they don't seem to trust him.'

'There is a reason, but I don't know the whole story. I think Adam is more like an Independent than a Compound Lab.' Angus shrugged, but smiled as he plugged the memory stick into his computer. 'Well done, Hugo! Takir, this is what I had started with Adam before we went to the Compound. He showed me some of the work they carried out before they produced the Compound Labs. They had a way of eliminating defects from the donor. It would have made a great difference to my early years!'

'And they were aware of the problems of cloning from a clone!' Sanjit gave a wry smile. 'I wish we had known that earlier, and then I would still look like your twin, not your older brother, Takir!'

Hugo gaped in astonishment. 'You're a clone of Takir?'

Sanjit nodded. 'But now I am rapidly ageing! I am affected by our donor's defects at a greatly accelerated rate, unfortunately!'

'Perhaps the Compound Labs could find a way to help you?' Hugo frowned. 'Celia told me about the work they have done on tackling the problems with a Hybrid's broken arm.'

He explained in detail what he had found out. Sanjit leaned forward eagerly.

'I'd like to know more! We could use this!'

Hugo nodded, 'I'll see what I can download. Who knows what we'll be capable of doing if we put the Compound Labs' research with yours! Can I see more of what you have done?'

181

The others in the room exchanged glances. Finally Takir spoke, 'We need to go back to Etherton Hall to show you what we've achieved so far.'

'Etherton Hall … didn't you move everything out of there?' Hugo asked.

'Yes, and back again shortly afterwards. Working on the theory that they wouldn't look in the same place twice. Though we have moved our little Zoo into more cramped quarters for the moment, as a precaution,' Takir told him. 'Our next move will be out of the UK. Our Benefactor feels that it is probably unwise to remain for much longer here with the Compound Labs taking such an interest in us.'

Chapter Thirty-one

'Angus must know where they are!' Zig said bitterly. 'We've *got* to find him! We need to go back to Etherton Hall, see what clues we can pick up.'

'Or look around some of the other properties owned by Warner,' Cam continued. 'They could be in one of those places by now.'

'Or they could have another place that isn't listed in his name,' Isaac pointed out.

'They could be anywhere!' Ruby said.

'I think Cam is right. We take a look at the remaining properties then we start to look further afield,' Celia said. 'I've started to list possible places against the size and facilities they would need to take into account. When Abel returns with helpers from Reuben's team we can make a start.'

'I think it would be a good idea if Cam and me look around Etherton Hall – with back-up close by,' Zig added hastily, seeing the look Ruby and Celia exchanged.

'Perhaps we could think about that when Abel comes back. He'll be here at the end of the week,' Ruby suggested.

Zig gave an impatient sigh.

'I know how frustrating it must be for you, but it's for your own safety, Zig,' Ruby squeezed her arm.

As they walked back to home that evening, Cam turned to Zig and sighed. 'Finding the others is like looking for a needle in a haystack.'

She shook her head, 'And the more time we waste sitting around the less chance we have of finding them safe. You know what I think we should do?'

He looked at her.

'Go back to Etherton Hall. I still think they're there. Or that's where we'll find clues to lead us to where they are now.'

'What? Just you and me?' Cam said.

Zig nodded eagerly.

'How will we get in?' he looked doubtful.

'Well, we managed to break out of the Zoo. I'm sure we can find a way to break in!' she replied.

Adam looked through the file again, nothing. He was sure he had saved it in folder B112. He exited and looked through several other files and gave a sigh of relief as he found it in a different folder.

Celia walked in and gave a cheery 'good morning'.

'You looked worried there for a moment.'

He smiled, 'Yes, without reason, thankfully!'

He explained about the misplaced file. 'I must have moved it from D32 when I was classifying yesterday's data.'

'Hmm, I've found some of the data misfiled lately. I don't think anyone from outside can access our data, but I'll step up the security system, anyway.' Celia said.

'No Hugo today?' Adam asked.

'No. He's going somewhere with his mother, Yvonne, today. He doesn't seem so keen to study here lately. He works here for an hour or two then he leaves. Have you noticed how preoccupied he seems these days, Adam?'

He looked up. 'Hmm? Oh, maybe he prefers to spend more time with the youngsters at the Compound.'

'No. Amanda was complaining about his poor attendance there. She thought he was spending all his time here,' she replied.

'Are those the results of Annalee's latest test results on her broken arm?' Adam said as Celia opened a file on her computer.

'Yes, she met with her doctor yesterday and he is very

pleased with her progress. We might have a blueprint for future cases. Dr Schultz says they'll be a great deal of interest in several African countries if we can use the same method on Non-Lab fractures.'

'Well, let's get down to saving the world!' Adam quipped.

At Etherton Hall, Hugo sat in front of a computer screen with Takir, Sanjit, and the two girls looking at the same data.

'It's incredible!' Sanjit said. 'The bone is perfect. No sign of any fracture whatsoever!'

'Yes, and using the data inputting method Adam and Takir were working on, I think we could apply this to bones in their developing stages so they are programmed to self-repair,' Hugo said.

'What age range?' Sanjit asked.

'I was thinking up to early teens in any Non-Lab trials,' he said.

'And the youngest would be …?' Takir asked.

Hugo spread his hands. 'Eventually, during pregnancy. Of course it's only ideas at the moment. I'd need to make a few trials and make a few tweaks.'

'Our Benefactor won't allow us to use any traceable Non-Labs. The youngest we have used so far has been fourteen years old. Untraceable younger ones could be more difficult to obtain.' Liz pointed out.

'In Western countries, yes. It depends on where we relocate to,' Sanjit added.

'This line of research is certainly worth continuing, Hugo! You are already a valued member of our team,' Takir slapped his shoulder. 'Make out a detailed plan and be ready to start your research when we relocate. It all goes towards our ultimate aim – to produce the perfect person!' They all nodded in agreement.

'Well, let's get to work. Liz, you're continuing with the enhancement adjustments with Helen, aren't you? I am going to assess our new intake with Angus, see how they can be used. Sanjit, have you got the latest test results of our current Zoo inmates? How are they managing in such cramped conditions, especially the Muscles?'

As he walked to the door, Hugo came up beside him.

'Can I have a word for a moment?'

The older man stopped and faced him.

'I've an idea, it's only an idea at the moment, about our ultimate aim,' Hugo began. 'It's just that, when we begin to create the perfect human, what will we start with? A Hybrid, an Independent Lab, an original clone?'

Takir frowned. 'Yes, I see what you mean. Originally we had planned to clone one of our team, one judged by their physical and mental attributes, but since we have seen the degeneration of Sanjit and others like him we haven't really given it much thought at this stage of our research. It is something that we will need to consider in the foreseeable future. Have you any thoughts on the subject, Hugo?'

He nodded. 'Actually, I have. We know for a fact that Labs, because of their programming, have a much higher IQ than their Non-Lab donors, and also that Hybrids so far have shown an even higher IQ levels in certain fields than their Lab parents. I was wondering what the offspring of a Hybrid and Lab would be like. And if it is possible.'

Takir's eyebrows rose. 'But the oldest Hybrid, Frankie, is only about a year older than you, isn't he? Hardly old enough to be thinking of producing young!'

'Of course, not yet,' Hugo continued, 'but as you say, we do have time. We need to set out the attributes we want with for our ideal being. I've started a database of possible male and female candidates based on my own criteria. Would you like to take a look at it?'

'You're right, Hugo, we do need to give this careful consideration now. Email me your ideas so I can take a look at them.'

Chapter Thirty-two

Zig and Cam drove the hire car past the main entrance to the Hall and parked in a layby nearby. They walked back towards the hall, ducking into a field as a silver BMW sped past. The tinted windows hid the occupants from view. They waited until the taillights disappeared, then stepped back out onto the narrow lane.

Cam closed his eyes, sniffed the air, and shook his head. Zig walked forwards, scanning the hedgerow for a possible entrance. Finally she stopped and crouched down in front of a small gap made by a fox or rabbit. Pulling on a pair of gloves, she broke several more branches until she had a glimpse of the grounds.

'There aren't any guards this side, just two near the front door,' she told Cam. 'We could make our way around the back of the building and see if we can get in there.'

'Don't you think we should tell someone before we go in?' Cam asked her.

She shook her head. 'They'll say no! I've got my mobile if we need to get in touch, and anyway, we're both armed.'

'Two metal pipes against we don't know what!' Cam raised his eyebrows. He used his pipe to push back some of the thick brambles. 'There! That should do it.'

Zig pushed through the narrow gap and peered about her. 'No sign of anyone!' she whispered, helping Cam struggle through after her.

They both made their way silently towards the house, then slowly around the grey stone walls. As they crouched under a large bay window there was the sound of voices.

'Angus!' Zig mouthed.

'... for a youngster, he has pretty sound ideas,' he was saying.

'Who has he in mind for the Hybrid?' a female voice questioned.

'It could be a female Hybrid and a male Lab,' a second female voice joined the conversation.

'It might be an idea to have a selection to choose from,' a second male spoke up.

'That's true.' Angus's voice sounded louder as he neared the window. 'We could set up a few trials for compatibility.' With a clatter the blinds were drawn and only a low hum of conversation could be heard.

'I wonder what that was all about!' Zig said.

She peered into the darkness and, taking Cam's hand, led him around to a small back door. Rubbing at the layer of grime on a glass pane in the top half of the doorway, she peered in.

'It looks like a storeroom,' she said. 'I can't see signs of anyone.'

Cam sniffed the air near the door. 'I can't smell anyone, either.'

Zig unwound the scarf from her neck and wrapped it around her hand. With a sharp blow she shattered a small pane of glass. They stood and waited for a moment, then, hearing nothing, she put her hand through the glass and opened the door.

Trembling, they both stepped inside and took a few tentative steps forward. They were in a low-ceilinged storeroom. A narrow strip of light shone from under a door which opened onto the main part of the house. Cam sniffed the air near the door and signalled Zig to stay still. Soon they heard the sound of approaching voices. Both stood back against the wall until the sound faded into the distance.

Zig looked at Cam, who nodded as she slowly turned the handle of the door and gently pulled it open. A glance up and down revealed an empty corridor. They turned to the left where the voices had originated and walked along a narrow corridor with white painted plaster walls. The narrow strip of coir carpet on the grey tiled floor deadened the sound of their feet. Cam stopped suddenly and pushed open a small wooden door and pulled Zig in behind him, just closing the door as the sound of footsteps went by. Looking around, they found themselves at the foot of a small stone staircase that wound its way up above them. Exchanging glances, they were soon creeping quietly upwards. Cam felt Zig pull his sleeve as they came to a small landing with a large wooden door. She leaned down and peered through a large old-fashioned keyhole. On the other side of the door was a wide, well-furnished reception area. Two white-coated women chatted as they crossed in front of the door and walked along a corridor leading off to one side. A man appeared from another corridor and stopped to read a notice board on the wall opposite. He then left. Zig gave Cam a questioning look, pointing to the door and then up the staircase.

'Up,' he whispered, leading the way.

After climbing the stairway for a further five minutes, Cam suddenly stopped and clutched Zig's arm. He sniffed the air and spluttered, 'Brit, Jez, Rhys!' He hurried up the staircase to another door which had two large boards nailed over it. He was grabbing the side of one of the boards when Zig pushed in front of him, shaking her head.

'Wait!' she whispered. She leant down and peered through the keyhole. She smiled as she saw their old friends sitting around a shabby lounge. There were two new faces; they could be brother and sister. They were both dark-skinned. The girl was tall and slim and was striding up and down with Tyler and Rhys behind a long chintz-covered settee. She looked about sixteen. Sitting next to Jez on the settee was a scared-looking boy of about twelve or thirteen. Zig smiled as she watched Cam's expression brighten as he took in the scene.

'There's no staff around, let's go in!' he whispered.

'There are probably cameras,' she replied.

'How long do you think we'll have to stay in this place?' Brit grumbled. 'It's ages since the Compound Labs paid a visit. They didn't find anything, so why are we still stuck up here?'

'Yeah, it's too cramped!' Rhys complained as Tyler nodded.

'At least we could get out and run in the other bit,' the new girl added.

'They must be worried about the Compound Labs coming back,' Lynne said.

'I wish they would!' Tony commented. 'It's as if they've given up on us!'

'Yeah, so much for "we'll be back for you"! Some friends Zig and Cam turned out to be!' Otis said.

'Wait!' Lynne said, her ears twitching. She stood up and walked near the door, beckoning Jez to join her.

As they reached the door, Zig put her mouth to the keyhole, 'It's us! Zig and Cam. Are you being watched?'

Jez leaned down and smiled as she saw her friends. 'No. This is a temporary arrangement, there are no cameras. We're all alone until morning!'

Cam explained how the doorway was nailed up. 'But don't you worry; we'll get you out!' he said.

Using the metal pipe as a lever, he eventually managed to prise the boards from the door. Soon they were inside, Jez and Zig hugging each other, Cam standing with a grin on his face as Otis slapped his shoulder.

'Hey, man!' he spluttered, 'You came back for us! Hey! They came back!'

'Meet Shiva, the new Muscles, and her brother Zane, new Ears,' Jez said.

'I'm Zig, I'm Eyes,' she held out her hand to Shiva.

'And I'm Nose – in working order, Brit!' Cam smiled at her.

'We'd better get out of here before anyone finds out

about us!' Zig said. 'I'll call Abel first; let him know what's happening.'

The others could hear Abel's reaction as she explained where they were.

'What were you thinking, the pair of you? Just stay out of sight! We'll be there as soon as we can!'

Zig explained where they had made their way through the hedge and the route to the attic room.

'OK, just stay there! We're on our way!' Abel shouted.

'If we could get out of the building and the grounds we'd be a lot safer,' Zig suggested to the others. 'Otis, Jez, Tyler, and Lynne, follow Cam; the others, follow me. We have enough enhancements between us to notice anyone coming.'

Brit sat trembling on the sofa as the others made for the open door.

'Come on, Brit,' Cam walked towards her and held out his hand.

'No! I'm not going!' she cried, hugging her knees.

'What? Don't be afraid. We'll look after you,' Cam continued.

'Yeah, we all will, Brit. Come on!' Tony added.

'No! No! I'm not going! Why did you come here and wreck everything?' she shouted at Zig. 'We had a great home at the other place until you came along!'

'Hey, she's trying to help you, help all of us!' Lynne said. 'We're all going back to the real world.'

'Yeah, out of this prison!' Otis muttered.

'Well I don't want to be helped!' Brit sobbed. 'I don't want to go back to my real world. What you call a prison is a hundred times better than any place I've ever been in!'

'Brit, we've talked about this loads over the last weeks,' Jez said gently. 'They're nervous. They're talking about moving to Eastern Europe any day now …'

'But they'll take us! After all the time and money they've spent on us, they're not going to leave us behind, are they?' Brit looked around her with wild eyes.

Tony shook his head. 'They'll just get replacements. We've served our purpose. We're the first step on the ladder. Look at Shiva.' He turned towards the tall girl who moved restlessly between Tyler and Rhys. 'She can outrun and outjump both the boys by miles. And Zane, he can hear better than the other Ears! They're the next step up and there will be more steps after them, until they get what they're aiming for.'

'Yeah, we've got to get out while we can,' Lynne agreed.

Jez stepped forward but Brit drew back. 'I'm not going! And if you try and make me I'll scream the place down! I'll have the guards up here!'

Tyler stepped forward and gave her a sudden jab on the back of her neck.

'Old army trick! She'll be out for a while. Hope I don't have to do it again.' He slung her lifeless form over his shoulder. 'Let's go!'

Zig and Jez led the way down the staircase. As they arrived at the small landing, Brit began to come around. She groaned and pushed out her hand, knocking against the door. They all looked at each other with bated breath as they heard a woman's voice say, 'What was that?'

A second woman replied, 'I'm not sure. It came from behind the door.'

'Get on to security, quickly! They said don't take any risks after last week!' the first woman ordered.

'Run, quickly!' Zig screamed as they heard the sound of an alarm going off. 'We'll stand a better chance if we get out of the building!'

Takir stood stern-faced in the reception hall as Angus appeared. 'The guards are going for the kids. We're just taking the two new ones. Our priority is saving the data! Destroy the computers once you've downloaded. There's a helicopter on its way. It should be here in any minute. They've arranged to have a plane scheduled to leave from a private airport in twenty minutes,' Takir issued several more instructions to the people around him. Angus reappeared at his side carrying a large holdall followed by Liz and Jackie.

'We already backed up the data this evening. Only Sanjit has added anything new since then, so he's taking care of that now.'

There was a loud shout followed by a scream. Angus pushed the holdall into the girls' hands and set off with Takir to follow the sounds. Two guards were pulling Shiva along with them, while a third was carrying a screaming and kicking Zane. Behind them, Zig and Cam appeared followed by some of the others.

'You're not taking them!' Zig shouted. She lunged at one of the guards, clawing at his arm. He knocked her aside, but she leapt up again and continued her attack. Cam and Jez were trying to wrestle Zane from the arms of the third guard.

Angus stopped and pulled a gun from his pocket. He glared at Zig. 'Don't make me use this! Back away, all of you!'

The sound of rotor blades was heard, getting louder as a bright light neared them.

'I mean it! Move back!' Angus shouted again as the helicopter began to land.

They all stood still and watched as Liz, Jackie, Sanjit, and Takir climbed on to the helicopter.

Zig looked Angus in the eye as he gave a slow smile of victory. He stepped onto the helicopter and signalled for the guard to hand up Zane and Shiva. In a flash, Zig pulled out the metal bar and threw it with all her might at him. He clutched his arm, screaming with pain as the gun fell from his hand. As Cam dived down and grabbed it, Jez and Zig ran forward and grabbed the two siblings, pulling them to safety as the rotor blades began to move. In the distance the sound of police sirens could be heard.

'Come on! Let's get out of here!' Takir shouted. 'Leave them!'

Zig and the others threw themselves flat on the ground as

the roar of the rotors and the turbulence whipped the air around them. When she could finally raise her head Zig could make out a police car screeching to a halt on the nearby drive way, a figure jumping from it before it had actually stopped.

'What were you both thinking of?' Abel shouted as he reached the children.

Reuben ran up beside him, 'Let's just get everyone safely out of here first! Where are all the youngsters, Zig?'

Zig stood up and looked around her, 'There's Jez, Shiva, Zane … and Rhys …'

'Tony and Otis are coming over. And there's Lynne,' Cam added, pointing to the muddied figures approaching them. 'Where are Brit and Tyler?'

He breathed a sigh of relief as Tyler appeared, carrying the sobbing girl, 'We're all here!'

'Get them all back to the Compound while I see who's left here, Lab and Non-Lab,' Abel said to one of the policemen.

'Three of our cars are after the guards. They left in two 4X4s going in different directions,' Reuben said as he joined them. 'Let's hope they catch them and can give us some answers.'

Later that night the youngsters sat together in an apartment in the Compound. Ruby smiled as she passed around cups of hot chocolate and a plate of biscuits. She went to ruffle Zane's hair, but his sister pulled him under her arm protectively.

'It's OK, you're safe here,' Ruby said quietly.

Celia nodded in agreement. 'No one can harm you now.'

'What is going to happen to us?' Otis said in a quiet voice. 'Are you going to send us back where we came from?'

Zane froze and dug deeper into his sister's side. Brit whimpered quietly.

Cam stood up, shaking his head. 'No, no! Don't worry!

No one's going back to danger, or anything horrible! We didn't rescue you for that!'

Otis let out a long breath. 'You mean … we can give this new life a real go? Like you said when you first joined us, Zig?'

She nodded.

He rubbed his face with shaking hands. 'Freedom! Man, I'd forgotten how good it could feel!'

Brit bit her lip and sobbed into her sleeve.

Ruby stood up, looking around at the frightened faces. She felt a shiver run down her spine as memories of her own past came into her mind. Her voice shook as she said, 'Cam's right. You're free and you're all safe now! This will be your home until we sort out what you can do next.'

They had all fallen into an exhausted sleep by the time Abel and Isaac returned to the Compound.

'They caught some of the guards, the men are been questioned at Reuben's headquarters,' he told the women. 'The other car was found abandoned with no sign of anyone. They'll continue the search when it gets light.'

'I think we all need some sleep,' Isaac yawned, running his hands over his face. 'I have to be in London at nine o'clock tomorrow morning.'

Celia rubbed his shoulders. 'You are so good, Isaac. You do so much for us!'

'You give me great news stories,' he grinned. 'Most of which I'm unable to print!'

'Maybe someday in the future!' she said as she walked with him to the door.

'And what are we going to do with all our newcomers?' Abel said to Ruby as they made their way to bed.

'It'll be like the old days! Finding a way to make them fit into normal Non-Lab life without looking conspicuous!' she smiled.

'Reuben suggested maybe Zig and Cam or some of the others could use their enhancements to help him with locating the guards,' Abel said. 'I said as long as they are not in any danger it could be a possibility.'

'We repeated everything you said,' Zig told Ruby the next morning. 'That they can all stay here until we can sort out the best thing for them. And that they are not to worry about anything. They all agreed they would keep their enhancements a secret from everybody else as they will be safer. But Shiva and Zane won't tell me where their aunt lives. They are afraid you will send them back to her. Shiva said their aunt was a terrible woman who beat and half-starved them. That's why they ran away. Brit is afraid of ending up on the streets again. She says she doesn't know any other way to make a living because she thinks she's too stupid.'

Ruby shook her head. 'Poor young things! I'll speak to them with Celia; we'll reassure them.'

'We will not let you go to anyone who mistreats you,' Celia told the brother and sister.

'We came to the country as visitors, years ago. We don't have papers to stay here,' Shiva told her, her eyes cast downwards. 'My aunt said we would be put in prison if anyone finds out. Can you just let us go? We can look after ourselves!'

Ruby patted her arm. 'You're very brave, Shiva, but you can't look after yourself and your brother. You need help, and we can help you.'

'But how can we repay you? How can we make a living here?' Shiva continued.

'There are lots of things you can do to help around the Compound,' Ruby smiled. 'You too, Brit.'

Brit sat with a solemn face. 'We would have been better off if Zig had left us in the first house!' she protested.

'We had to escape! Cam was next on the list to disappear!' Zig replied. 'We were just part of their experiments. We were all disposable! Surely you see that now? Last night they were only taking Shiva and Zane because they have the most up-to-date enhancements.'

'Look, you're not going back to your old life, Brit.' Ruby sat beside the girl and put a hand on her arm. 'You can stay here and decide what you want to do. The house you are all sharing is your home.'

'And if you are willing, our Compound medical staff would like to find out more about your enhancements. They could use some of these developments to help other people,' Celia added.

Over the next few weeks, life settled into a new pattern on the Compound. While Shiva, Zane, and Brit kept to their new home, Cam, Otis, and Jez used their enhancements to help Reuben locate the guards. They were soon asked to use their talents in other investigations.

'I never thought I'd be helping the police with their enquiries in this way!' Otis joked over an evening meal.

'There is no chance of any of you getting involved with drugs again, is there?' Abel asked him.

Otis shook his head. 'Never! I'm way past that! This life is too good to screw up!'

'Well, Celia has sorted out your ID and National Insurance numbers, so you're official citizens now,' Isaac said.

'Sometimes it's difficult to remember to act like a normal person out there now,' Cam said. 'It's OK here on the Compound, 'cos most people are sort of ... well ... not *as* normal as other people are, so we don't stand out too much!'

Ruby smiled. 'It reminds me of the early days of the Labs, trying to get them used to living with Non-Labs, normal humans. Abel found it quite difficult!'

Abel chuckled. 'I made things quite hard for you, didn't I? After life in the Caves, Non-Lab life was so hard to get accustomed to!'

'What were the Caves?' Tony asked. Otis leaned forward.

'It's a long story!' Celia laughed. 'I'll get some tea and

Chapter Thirty-three

Zig pushed the new plant into the soil and watched as Ginny patted the earth around it.

'That's great, Gin! You're getting good at this! Will your mum be cross with you for getting dirty again? '

'Daddy's is picking me up today. I'm staying with him until Sunday afternoon,' the young girl said, brushing the mud off her T-shirt with an even muddier hand. 'He doesn't mind. He'll be too busy talking to Hugo about bone structure and other important Lab things to even notice! I wish you would come to Daddy's house again sometimes. You're more fun than they are!'

Zig smiled. 'Me and your dad don't really get on! Anyway, I thought you were interested in those things, too. Are you still doing your research on the brain?'

Ginny smiled. 'Yes! Celia was really impressed with my computer 3D images. I've scanned my mum's brain and mine, that's a Non-Lab and a Hybrid, and next I'm going to scan a Lab. I'm going to ask Celia if I can scan hers when I see her today. Then I want to scan the same kinds, but male. And compare the differences.'

'That sounds really interesting, Gin. You'll have to tell me the differences between them all,' Zig told her. 'You're so clever!'

'With brains, but not with plants!' she replied, as Zig leaned over to help her rearrange a lopsided beanstalk.

The next morning, Ginny carefully resized the image on the computer and rotated it. She opened the tool menu and selected a colour. She colour-coded the new image to match the three other images she had in the file. Then she typed up notes comparing the different sizes of different lobes in each example.

'Hey, is that me?' Celia asked, coming to stand behind her.

'No, that's Mum. This is you,' she replied bringing up another image. 'Your frontal lobes are 3% smaller than my mum's and 20% larger than mine. The frontal lobes are linked with behaviour; they can take 20 to 25 years to reach maturity.'

Celia pulled up a chair and sat down beside her. 'This looks really interesting, Ginny.'

Hugo glanced at the screen as he walked past and stopped.

'Who do the images belong to, Ginny?'

She explained who she had chosen as her examples of Non-Lab, Hybrid, and Lab.

'Hey, could you scan my brain image in too?' he asked excitedly.

Soon they were all peering at the images on the screen.

'My frontal lobe development is only 13% below yours, Celia!' Hugo grinned. 'And my hippocampus is almost on a par with your mother's, Ginny. How does yours compare? Oh, 75% of mine. That shows how quickly we develop long term memory and spatial navigation ahead of Non-Labs!'

'It would be great if you could compare the brain image of a young Non-Lab of your age with your own development. I know the Compound scientists have information on this,' Celia added.

'The bigger the database you have the more useful the information will be to us, Ginny,' Hugo continued. 'Do you think I could have a copy of this, please?'

'Of course you can have a copy, and any new stuff I come up with, too!' Ginny beamed with pleasure. 'I wonder if Daddy wants to see my research!'

Some time later Celia looked at the clock. 'I'd better get back to the Compound. Do you want a lift home, Hugo?'

'Yes please, Celia,' he replied. 'Here, I'll back this data up, Ginny. You go and help your dad pack up before Celia disables the computers.'

Ginny jumped up from her chair and headed off to find her father, 'I wonder if he wants to watch *Skyfall* again?'

Hugo backed up the data onto a memory stick for Celia, and then quickly repeated the procedure on to his own stick.

'That was an interesting day's work,' Celia remarked to Ginny and Hugo as they headed for the main door of the building. She stopped. 'Oh, I've left a folder in the kitchen. Here are the keys, wait for me in the car.'

She emerged a few minutes later and was startled to hear the crunch of gravel as the car drew up by the front door with Hugo grinning at the wheel.'

'You can drive!' Ginny exclaimed. 'You must teach me how to do it!'

'When you're bigger,' Hugo smiled as he slid into the passenger seat.

'Who taught you?' Celia asked him.

He shrugged. 'No one; I just watched you, my mum, other people drive. There's not much to it really, is there?'

She smiled as she slipped into the driver's seat, 'You surprise me every day!'

Over the next few nights Hugo examined the images copied from Ginny in great detail on his laptop at home. He carefully studied each female Lab and noted that Celia's development in most areas was higher than other female Labs. He smiled with satisfaction and typed up notes and comments on each of her strengths. He needed to collect more data on other female Labs, but he was beginning to think that maybe he had found the perfect Lab. He wanted to discuss with Takir and Angus how they could go about creating the perfect embryo. They had suggested using a Hybrid female and a Lab male, but the oldest female Hybrid was only eight years old, so it would be some time before they could trial this. In the meantime he would collect data

Chapter Thirty-four

Abel listened to the voice on the phone, grim-faced. 'I agree, it is better to keep things under wraps for the moment. Reuben has suggested meeting with some of the Labs working in your police department, Simon, to share information on how we can handle these new developments. Most of the Independent Lab groups we have been able to contact here in the UK have been quite hostile towards us. Somehow the Radicals are persuading them that the Compound Labs have given in to the Non-Labs and their laws. They are afraid that they will not be treated fairly.'

'We have found the same thing over here. The Radicals are often mentioned as the way forward for Independent Labs. They seem pretty persuasive. I wish I knew what they were planning!'

Abel nodded. 'If this becomes public it could make things very unpleasant for recognised Labs in all countries. Parliament has already passed a Bill to allow the setting up of a government-controlled Centre to produce Labs for childless couples. It won't be long before the US will be thinking along similar lines. So that will be another group of Labs that could be vulnerable to Radical persuasion. The sooner we can arrange a meeting with your Lab investigation team the better it will be. Reuben has suggested that two of our youngsters with special enhancements work with your team. They've proved very useful over here.'

They talked for a few more minutes before he said, 'OK, we'll email the details tomorrow morning. Here's Ruby to speak to Sakura, Simon.'

Ruby took the handset from him and sat down, 'Oh, dear.

I don't suppose this is making things any easier between you and Simon's parents, is it, Sakura?'

Sakura's voice sounded shaky. 'No, not at all. Simon's mother won't even look at Simone, never mind hold her! She even told me she wished Simon had never met me the other day!'

'Why don't you come here for a break? You must be tired out with having a new baby. Come and have a rest here and let everyone spoil you both for a few days before Leon and Johnny's engagement party!' Ruby suggested. 'Their fiancées are great, so easy to get on with. And Dette will be here a few days early, too.'

'Simon is too busy to get away at the moment,' Sakura answered. 'He said he'll probably only be there for a couple of days for the party.'

'Well, you come on ahead anyway. Once you feel more rested you'll be more use to him and the baby!'

Sakura was finally persuaded and put down the phone in a much better frame of mind.

Ruby turned to Abel, who was staring out of the window. She put her arms around him with her head on his chest.

'You can't be responsible for all the Labs, you know, Abel! You already do so much for the Compound Labs.'

'I know,' he sighed, 'I just find it so frustrating! Why can't all the different Labs sit down and talk about things together? We don't have any idea of where the Radical research is leading.'

'Some of them may be at the early stages where they don't trust Compound Labs or Non-Labs,' she said. 'Many Compound Labs felt that way about Non-Labs at first. You didn't trust Non-Labs for a long time, Abel.'

'But in the end we wanted to become part of society and live and work together. Let's hope the Independent Labs do, too,' he looked into Ruby's eyes. 'I wouldn't say this to anyone but you, but I am afraid of what these new Labs are planning for the future!'

Ruby saw the fear in his eyes and pulled him closer to her.

Chapter Thirty-five

Zig looked up as she heard her name called, her pupils narrowing into long slits in the strong sunshine.

'Oh, great, just what I need! Coffee!'

She stood up and smiled as Bailey held it out to her.

'You have been working here for nearly three hours without a break!' he admonished her. 'You promised me you would slow down today, and not make me feel too bad about taking the afternoon off!'

'I didn't notice the time. I wanted to get this bed sorted out and maybe get a new line sown over by the fence. You could take that box of salad stuff over there with you to the hall. Are you sure you won't need any help?' she asked.

Bailey shook his head. 'Most of the people who live on the Compound are helping set up the hall for tonight's party. Even the newcomers! Brit and Lynne are setting out the tables with Rachel and some of the others. Tyler, Rhys, and Shiva are decorating the actual hall. The stamina of those three! Zane is entertaining Simone while Sakura has a rest.'

'Fancy being invited to the engagement party of two of the biggest celebs! I still can't believe it!' Zig smiled.

'I still can't think of Leon and Johnny as big celebrities even though they've played for England!' Bailey chuckled. 'And their fiancées are lovely, too. Don't get too carried away here this afternoon. We need to be there by seven thirty, Zig.'

'I'll be ready,' she replied.

She was humming to herself when she heard someone clearing his throat behind her. ''I know, I know, Bailey! I should be getting changed by now! Oh, it's you, Keith!'

'Sorry to startle you, Zig. I wondered if I could ask you something.' He coughed, 'I don't mean to upset you or anything, but I wondered if you'd mind, erm …'

'What is it, Keith?' Zig frowned.

'Has he asked you, Zig?' a lean, olive-skinned young man appeared at Keith's side.

'I was just going to, Pellier,' he said.

Pellier had been one of the first Labs to live anonymously among the Non-Labs as a music student. With his laid-back attitude, he had quickly fit in to student life. Now he was working with Keith as sound and special effects technicians for Zorro and his band.

'We want you to appear in the video trailer for Zorro's new single,' Pellier interrupted. 'It's called 'She-Devil'. Your eyes would be just perfect!'

'What? You want everyone to know what a freak I am?' Zig stood up dropping the trowel she was holding onto the ground. 'No way!'

'No, Zig, please don't be offended!' Keith began. 'We'd never put you in that position …'

'Zig, you'd be performing a dance routine. Everyone will think your eyes are done by special effects, 'Pellier explained.

'What if someone found out? Anyway, I can't dance. No, this is not for me, no way!' She shook her head.

'No offence taken?' Keith held out his hand. Zig squeezed it and smiled.

'You could always sleep on it, let us know tomorrow?' Pellier patted her shoulder.

Leon and Johnny beamed as they walked into the hall that evening hand in hand with their fiancées, Fern and Violet.

'Hey, man, this is even better than the do we had on Monday evening!' Leon said.

'Yes, that was the official one. This is introducing the girls to our family!' Johnny added, as several people came up to shake their hands and wish them well.

Ruby smiled and nudged Abel as Sakura and Simon came up to talk to the newly engaged couples. Johnny held out his arms as Sakura passed him the tiny baby she was holding in her arms.

'They'll have their own little ones to think about soon,' she whispered to him. 'And I think it might be twins!'

Abel raised his eyebrows questioningly.

'It's not women's intuition!' Ruby laughed. 'Fern told me they're both expecting, and twins are quite common in their family!'

Isaac and Celia joined them as they went to speak to the couples.

'The place looks really wonderful!' Fern said to them looking around at the heart and flower decorations festooning the hall.

'You must have all worked so hard!' her sister added.

'And we really appreciate it,' Fern said.

'It was a joint effort!' Celia smiled. 'Everyone wants to celebrate the good news!'

'Look at Leon with Simone!' Ruby grinned. 'He's getting in training!'

'The boys have another six months to prepare themselves!' Violet laughed, rubbing her stomach.

'And yes, it *is* twins, for both of us!' Fern added with her hands on her own stomach. She groaned as her fiancé approached. 'No, Johnny, put away that name book!'

'The longest girl's name I can find is Alexandria,' he opened a well-thumbed paperback.

'She'd be called Alex,' said Dette. 'Or maybe Lexi.'

'Or even Lex,' added Violet.

'That would not be allowed!' Johnny continued, 'As for boy's names, the longest I have found so far is Dionysius.'

'His friends would call him Dion,' Violet said.

'I am also going to have a say in our children's names, and I'm not so hung up on the number of syllables, Johnny!' Fern pointed out.

'You've got one girl's name and one boy's name. What if you have two girls or two boys?' Dette mentioned.

'Oh, I never thought of that!' Johnny groaned, 'I'm going to need at least two more books!'

Leon looked at Abel. 'And how is life here on the Compound, Abel? Are the Labs still keeping you busy?'

'You could say that,' he said, smiling. Simon caught his eye and looked away.

'Tonight there is no talk of work, we are celebrating.' Sakura caught her husband's arm, 'Come and dance with me!'

Isaac offered his hand to Celia and they joined them on the dance floor. They danced for a while and then she looked up at him. 'You are such a good friend, Isaac. You spend so much time doing things for us Labs.'

'I enjoy being with you. There's never a dull moment with you lot! Really, you all mean a lot to me. Especially ... I really admire you, Celia ... Anyway, what plans do you have for the future?'

'Oh, I don't know. Continue working here on the Compound, I suppose,' she shrugged.

'I meant your personal life. I mean ... do you see yourself with your own family one day?'

Celia was silent for a while.

'Hey, sorry, sorry! Tell me to mind my own business!' Isaac stuttered.

'No, it's fine,' Celia said. 'It's just with all this talk of the Radical Labs, I wonder what the future holds for us all. What about you, Isaac? Do you picture yourself as a family man?'

'I know we can't guarantee the future, but, yes, with the right person I can.' He took a deep breath. 'Oh, Celia, you must know how I feel about you!'

She smiled. 'I had hoped. I don't know what I would have done without you on so many occasions, Isaac. I can't see my life without you now.'

Isaac moved closer, clasping both her hands in his.

'You'll never have to.'

Zig smiled and looked across at Cam and Zane who were hanging on to every word Leon and Johnny were saying.

'They can't believe they are meeting their heroes in the flesh!' she smiled. 'And you were right, they are so down to earth. Their girlfriends, too.'

'Yes,' Bailey replied. 'They have done a lot to get Labs the recognition and acceptance we have now.'

'Sakura hoped Simon's mother would come to accept her, especially now they have a baby; but things aren't going too well for them,' Zig said.

'No, we've come a long way; but there's still a long way to go,' Bailey agreed.

Zig brushed her fingers over her eyes, 'I really understand how it feels to be different now. Thank God for these contact lenses. All of us from the Zoo know what it is like to be outsiders!'

'The Independent Labs haven't made your life, or life for any Labs, easier, that's for sure.' Bailey's lips narrowed. 'The only thing to do is face up to people. Don't run away. We've done nothing wrong. Why should we hide?'

'You're right! I'm here at the Compound with good friends now, so I suppose in a way, Angus and his gang sort of did me a good turn. Though I'm glad I broke his arm!'

Bailey frowned. 'How did you know that?'

'Someone – yes, it was Hugo – said he'd be nursing a broken arm for a few days.'

'Hugo? He wasn't even there, was he?' Bailey looked puzzled.

'No. He must have heard one of the others say something. I really threw that metal bar at him. He let go of Zane straight away! Anyway, let's forget about the bad guys for the moment and enjoy ourselves. Come on! Let's dance!' Zig laughed as she pulled him on to the floor.

Ruby and Abel were dancing too. Ruby caught the

expression in his eyes. 'No, you're not going to corner Simon and start on Lab business tonight, Abel!'

He smiled ruefully. 'OK, it can wait until tomorrow!' He pulled her closer to him. 'You know, seeing that little baby, and the news of more babies on the way made me think ... how about *three* of our own?'

Ruby drew her eyebrows together. 'Oh, Abel, three never works, it's an odd number ...But maybe *four* would be OK ...'

Abel smiled and pulled her closer to him. 'We must talk about this later ...'

Towards the end of the evening Zig made her way to the sound system where Keith was sitting with Celia and Isaac.

'A song from your past. Isaac!' Keith smiled as he leaned over the equipment and adjusted the volume slightly.

'This takes me back to my uni days!' Isaac sprang up, pulling Celia behind him. 'Come on, we've got to dance to this!'

Keith smiled at Zig as she slid into the seat beside him. 'I hope you have forgiven us. We certainly didn't mean to upset you, Zig.'

She squeezed his arm, 'You haven't. I'd ... I'd like to do it. But I don't want anyone to know about these,' she pointed to her eyes.

'As Pellier said, everyone will be made to think they are special effects, even contact lenses,' Keith reassured her.

'And I'm no dancer, I'll tell you that now!'

'It's not so much dancing we have in mind, more strutting and looking mean!' he replied. 'And we have a great choreographer, you'll get on really well with him!'

'Well, I've had plenty of experience strutting and looking mean!' Zig grinned.

Johnny and Leon and the two girls looked up from the breakfast table as Dette and Celia came in the next morning.

Abel came in carrying two chairs. 'Sit yourselves down,

ladies! Ruby and Isaac have cooked enough bacon and eggs to feed most of the Compound!'

'And I made the toast, Daddy!' Ness said, placing an overflowing plate in the centre of the table.

Abel smiled and ruffled her hair. 'Thanks, love. Give a piece to your brother, would you?'

Johnny looked around, beaming. 'It's just like the old days!'

'With lots of extra people!' Leon pointed out. 'It's good to get together again. We haven't seen much of anyone these past few months.'

'We hope it will be easier once the season ends next month,' Johnny added.

'The next big get-together will be the wedding,' Violet said.

'If we ever get it organized!' her sister joked. 'You boys will have to make time for a suit fitting next week.'

'There's no point in us having our dresses altered again until the last minute!' Violet said. 'We're growing by the day!'

'Hybrid babies do grow quickly!' Ruby smiled.

Sakura sighed as her daughter closed her eyes, 'At last! I can get myself some breakfast. I'll put her down in her pram in the other room.'

'How is your work going, Dette?' asked Ruby. 'Are you still working on the sustainable fuel project in Scotland?'

'At the moment. A new team of Labs and Non-Labs are taking over at the end of this month. Now we've proved that the first station had very little effect on the environment, we're hoping we don't have so much opposition against the second station we want to set up in Cornwall.' she said.

'So, what is the news on the Independent Labs here in the UK?' Simon asked Abel. 'Have you managed to track them down yet?'

'We have some leads that we are following up. The youngsters we rescued have been able to help us to trace most of the guards from Etherton Hall.'

Dette leaned forward, 'Celia was telling me about this group. They sound as if they can be very dangerous!'

Violet put her hands protectively over her stomach, 'What do you mean, Independent Labs? We haven't heard anything on the news about them!'

Abel shook his head, 'No, you won't have. It's being kept under wraps at the moment. The government doesn't want a panic situation and the Compound Labs don't want bad publicity. We're working with Reuben, the head of the police force in charge of Lab matters.'

'Who exactly are they? Are they a threat to us?' Fern asked.

'It's the same group that Takir and Angus are involved with,' Abel answered. He went on to explain how Zig had become involved with them through Angus, and about the other youngsters who were now living on the Compound.

'They are ruthless in pursuit of their aims!'.

'Which are what exactly?' Johnny asked.

'From what Zig and her friends have told us, we believe they are trying to produce a perfect being,' Abel said.

'And from what you have said, it is difficult to stop them! They just disappear when you get close,' Dette said. 'Do they have inside knowledge? Is there someone here who is keeping them informed of your moves?'

'We have checked that there are no bugs planted here. I can't think of anyone here who would be in touch with them,' Celia shrugged. 'There's just us, the youngsters, and a few of the Hybrid children who became aware of Zig and Cam's talents who even know of the existence of Independent Labs.'

'Hybrids?' Dette pursed her lips. 'These children may seem the same as Non-Lab children, but even at a young age their IQ levels are well above those of most adults. It might be worth keeping a careful eye on them.'

Ruby shook her head. 'Dette! We have two Hybrid

children, and so do Beth and Frank! We have perfectly normal but very bright children.'

'Yes, I accept your point – but are all the Hybrid children cared for as much as your children are?' Dette continued. 'I suppose you can get delinquent Hybrids just like you can get delinquent Non-Labs and Labs!'

Ruby frowned. 'I suppose you could be right, Dette.'

There was a loud wail and Ness appeared in the doorway, carrying a red-faced Simone.

'She smells a bit! I'm not very good with nappies!'

Celia got up and motioned Sakura to sit down. 'You finish your breakfast, I'll take care of her!'

Isaac followed her into the other room and watched as she quickly changed the tiny baby.

'Hey, you're pretty good at that,' he laughed.

'There seems to be plenty of opportunity to develop skills at this job around the Compound!' Celia joked.

Isaac watched the tender look that passed over Celia's face as she gazed at the child in her arms, and felt a stab of longing in his own heart.

Chapter Thirty-six

Pellier let out a low whistle of approval as Zig entered the studio. 'You look good, Zig.'

'I should do, it's taken nearly an hour and a half in Make-up!' she quipped, then drew a sharp breath as she looked in a full length mirror. 'Hey, that doesn't look like me!'

She turned around, viewing the skintight leather jumpsuit and the six-inch stilettos. 'What do you think, Keith?'

He blushed and ran his fingers through his hair, 'Yes, you look, erm, very nice, Zig. Just what we had in mind. Shall we run through the track again and talk you through it?'

The first half hour went well, but Zig found it hard to look mean when Keith took close ups of her face and eyes.

'Hey, I don't think she-devils laugh like that you know. You're supposed to be feeling mean!' he grinned.

'How can I stop laughing with that camera stuck in my face and you shining lights in my eyes?' she giggled.

'We need the close up of your pupils narrowing in the light. When we edit this shot we'll slow it down. Why don't you think about someone or something that really annoyed you?' Keith suggested.

Zig closed her eyes and the image of herself standing confronting Angus on his betrayal of her at Bramways came into her mind.

'How could you let them do this to me, Angus?' she'd said. *'You let them make me into a freak!'*

He'd stood there silently.

'What did you tell them at the Compound? You let them think I'd just gone off, left without a goodbye, didn't you?'

'It's what you would have done in the end, Zig. We all

know that.'

'For the first time I had friends, a home, a good job. I was going to go to college ...'

Angus had laughed at her but she had punched him in the chest and promised to prove him wrong. She remembered how he had recoiled as her eyes bored into his.

'Wow!' Keith's voice recalled her to the present. 'That's it! I pity the poor person you were thinking of!'

Two hours later Pellier stood up and clapped his hands. 'That's it! Exactly what we wanted. You were brilliant, Zig. Zorro is going to be really pleased with this! Take a break while we finish off the editing.'

Later that afternoon Zig's mouth fell open as she watched herself strut around the stage in time to the music, pouting and posturing; scowling into the camera as her pupils narrowed to slits.

'They won't guess about my eyes, will they?' she said.

'No, they just look like part of the special effects,' Keith assured her.

'I bet you once the video is out there will be a rush to buy wildcat contact lenses,' Pellier added.

'But they don't make them, do they?' Zig asked.

'Not at the moment, but I think I'll exchange a few ideas with Ramsey from Materials,' Pellier added, slipping off his chair. 'Now if we could get something up and running before the album launch concert ...'

'There goes the great entrepreneur,' Keith smiled. 'How about having a bite to eat before we head back to the Compound?'

'Great idea! All that strutting and pouting has made me hungry!' Zig grinned.

'I never thought I'd be saying this, but that was really good fun!' she said a short while later as she spooned rice and vegetables on to her plate at a nearby Chinese restaurant.

'You were a natural!' Keith complimented her. 'You really looked the part. A girl of many talents!'

'Hardly. It doesn't take much talent to strut around to some music, even good music!' Zig laughed.

'You'd be surprised at how few really good dancers there are out there.' Keith told her. 'Sometimes we spend more time editing than shooting. We rarely get it finished as quickly as we did today.'

'How did you get involved with Zorro?' Zig asked him.

Keith told here about his earlier life and how Zorro had been a great supporter of the Labs when the Centre had first been in the news.

They talked for several hours about their lives, as a Lab and as a 'Special', as the Zoo members had decided to rename themselves. Finally Zig looked at her watch.

'It's nearly midnight! We'd better be making a move.'

It was quiet when they arrived back at the Compound and Keith walked Zig to her door.

'Goodnight, Zig. Thank you for all your hard work, and for a most enjoyable evening,' he said.

'I've enjoyed it, too,' she replied.

'Perhaps if you're free on another evening … unless there's someone else …'

She shook her head. 'There's no one. I'd really like that, Keith.'

He leaned forward and kissed her cheek. 'Goodnight, Zig.'

Chapter Thirty-seven

'Leon promised they would be back here as soon as the season finishes and they would teach us some of the moves and tricks they use on the football field!' Frankie said excitedly to Hugo after school a few days later.

Hugo shrugged. 'If you like that sort of thing!'

'Oh, I would love to be such a good player!' Frankie stood up and kicked an imaginary ball, then jumped in the air. 'He's done it! He's scored! Frankie scores the winning goal for England!'

He stood in front of Hugo. 'What about you, Hugo, what do you want to do in the future?'

'Something a bit more worthwhile than kicking a ball about,' Hugo looked at his companion. 'I want people to remember me for ever!'

'Well, I suppose if you go on to be a famous scientist, they will,' Ginny remarked.

'Yes! The leader of the Rad ... revolution!' Hugo stood up. 'Well, I'd better be going.'

'Aren't you going to work with Daddy?' Ginny asked him.

'No, I'm busy this afternoon.' He waved and left.

'He doesn't go to Ruby's house or work with Daddy as much as he used to lately. I wonder what he does,' Ginny frowned as he walked away.

'Probably stays at home studying how to be a great scientist!' Frankie said.

'No, he isn't at home much. I heard his mum talking to my mum on the phone the other day. She says he's never at home and won't even tell her where he spends his time,' she continued.

'What did your mum say?' Frankie asked her.

'She told her to take her son in hand as she should hold herself accountable for his well-being.'

'And how did Yvonne take that?'

'She cried, and then my mum ended the conversation and told me she couldn't be doing with weepy women who had no backbone and that she could understand exactly why Hugo spent such little time at home!'

'She's such a comfort, isn't she, your mum? What does she do if you hurt yourself, give you a plaster and tell you to get over it?' Frankie grinned.

'No,' Ginny shrugged. 'She tells me that I know where the plasters are kept!'

Chapter Thirty-eight

'So you see, Takir, I'd be a valuable team player over in Romania. I could really help to get things moving. You said yourself you were expecting things to move on quicker than they have done under Sanjit.'

Takir looked at the boy's earnest expression and smiled, 'Hugo, I'm sorry. You are too young. I know you are much more mature mentally than your chronological age, but the Radicals won't consider letting you work over there until you are older.'

Hugo bit his lip. 'The Compound Labs don't appreciate me and neither do the Radicals! Perhaps I should just form my own Lab group!'

Takir sighed. 'OK, look, how about I see if I can arrange a trip for you to Romania, just a short visit for a week or two?'

The boy's face lit up. 'Oh, Takir! That would be great! When can I go?'

'Slow down. We'll need to arrange ID and also a story that will convince your mother to let you go.' Takir frowned. 'I'll be in touch later this week. Don't say anything to anyone else.'

Hugo could hardly contain his excitement as he sat in Takir's office the following week.

'So, the story is I'm going away for a fortnight's holiday in Devon with my new friend, Geoff, and his parents,' he repeated.

Takir nodded. 'Yes. Next Wednesday, Geoff will spend the evening at your house. His parents will drop him off and pick him up, so they can meet your mother. You will spend Thursday and Friday at his house. In two weeks' time his parents will suggest the holiday to your mother. As long as this goes to plan, everything has been arranged for the actual trip at the end of the month.'

'Everything *will* go to plan!' Hugo said firmly.

His mother had been pleased and relieved to see her son spending time with someone of his own age who obviously shared his interests. Though Geoff's parents had seemed rather cold, Hugo was very keen to join the family on holiday and she had willingly agreed after a chat with them.

Three weeks later, Hugo smiled at Takir as the private plane prepared for take-off.

Chapter Thirty-nine

Takir and Hugo climbed out of the airport taxi in front of a tall, old-fashioned stone building. Hugo gazed up at the ornate carvings over the wide, wooden doorway. A large plaque on one side of the doorway read 'Hudson Institute'.

Sanjit appeared with a beaming smile and embraced Takir. 'Good to see you, brother!' He turned to the young boy. 'Hugo, how are you? It's so good to get the chance to show you around our latest centre! We've used so many of the ideas you gathered from the Compound Labs.'

'I can't wait to see it all for myself,' Hugo replied. He followed the two men down a long corridor through the main building and out in to a courtyard.

'We've put you into two rooms in the annexe,' Sanjit said as they reached a small one-storey building. 'If you'd like to settle yourselves in, we'll all be eating in the main dining room in about an hour.'

Hugo threw his rucksack onto the bed in his room and turned to Sanjit. 'Can't I have a look around now?'

The older man gave a chuckle. 'Still as impatient as ever! OK, I'll give you a brief tour before dinner.' As he led him back to the main corridor he told him about the company. 'The Hudson Institute produces chemicals for different types of vaccines, mainly those used against tropical diseases. Much of it is exported to the rest of Europe, and Africa, but the company makes them available to the local city hospital at a heavily subsidised price. The production lines are in the two front rooms. Down this corridor we have the research laboratories where new vaccines are developed and trialled on mice and rats.'

They entered a long room with two rows of benches where several people were working. Sanjit stopped at the first bench where a woman wearing protective glasses was measuring a white powder onto a delicate balance.

'Lucy here is a team manager. Her team are working to perfect a vaccine to protect young children from water-borne diseases.' He stood back as a young man put a cage of white mice on the bench. 'What are the results so far, Lucy?'

'Very pleasing,' she replied in accented English. 'This is the third dosage administered. We will introduce type one disease after six hours. We are confident that the rats will be immune to it.'

Sanjit smiled and nodded. 'Well done. I look forward to seeing the results tomorrow morning.'

He led Hugo from the room and further along the corridor. 'The Hudson Institute also sponsors the city orphanage nearby. Hudson's is a well-respected name around here.'

'Do you use children from the orphanage in trials?' Hugo asked.

'No, our Benefactor has stipulated that trial subjects must not be under fourteen or over twenty-five,' Sanjit replied. 'So we obtain youngsters in the same way we did in the UK. We go up to the city centres late at the weekends and there's never a shortage. Another group the Non-Labs have failed, eh? Still, it's to our advantage.'

They had reached the end of the corridor and stood in front of a wide frosted glass door. Sanjit used a fob to open it then stood back and waved Hugo through.

'This is where the real work is done,' he smiled.

Two Labs that Hugo recognized as Darcey and Mike from the UK branch were waiting for them as the door opened.

'Hello, Sanjit, Hugo.' Mike held out his hand. 'Takir called through to tell me you were on your way. Let's go to the dressing area and get you fitted out in the non-contam room before we go any further.'

Hugo zipped up a soft white hooded all-in-one suit and pulled on close-fitting shoes and gloves. Darcey checked his glasses and face mask then led him from the room.

'You'll be amazed at how much progress we have made in the last six months!' the young woman said as she led them into the first room. 'These first two benches are Eyes.' She signalled for him to sit beside her at a computer screen and scrolled through images of eyes. 'We have selected this particular species of wildcat as being the most suitable for adaptation to human types. We are very pleased with the actual sight performance. What we are working on now is appearance. We are hoping to develop something similar to the contacts the Compound Labs have made for Zig, but have them attached to the actual eyeball before the enhancements are transplanted.'

Swivelling her chair away from the screen, Darcey stood up and led him to the second bench where three young Labs were working.

'These are some of the fabrics created so far.' She handed a thin, pale grey membrane to Hugo. 'This is the latest one, isn't it, Mike?'

'That's right. We hope we can fuse it successfully and that it won't have adverse effects on the actual vision. We haven't quite achieved that yet but we're hopeful the next Non-Lab trial will be more successful.'

'When will that be?' Hugo asked and was disappointed to hear it would not be during his trip.

'Don't worry,' Sanjit told him. 'There are several other trials scheduled for this week.'

'Where are the actual eyes that are used?' Hugo asked.

'They're kept in a separate wing. Only authorized personnel are allowed to enter,' Darcey told him. 'But we can take a close look at them from here. Come with me.'

They entered a small, dark room containing a long bench and several large screens. They sat in front of one of the screens and she keyed in a password.

'From here we can view any of the rooms in the high security wing. This is the eye block.' The screen displayed several white clad people working on an assortment of tasks in a small room. 'Now I can select a particular bench and take a closer look at what is happening. I can also communicate with the staff from here or read the updates on their department wall, here.' She entered a new password and a screen appeared with a list of text and numbers. 'Looks like everything is running to schedule. We can also oversee a transplant or view a previous operation.' A new image appeared on the screen and Darcey zoomed in on a surgeon standing over a still figure. 'Last week's Eyes. It went OK but the membrane is either too thick or the tint too dark to allow the level of vision we're looking for. That's why we need further work on the membrane before our next trial.'

She shut down the screen and stood up. 'Let's go back to the laboratory. Mike can show you some of the work his team has been doing in Nose and Ears.'

Mike was deep in discussion with Sanjit when they went back into the laboratory.

'We have fewer real discards as we make progress. The Zoo block is full. It makes sense to select some for reuse and dispose of the rest,' Mike said. 'The finance department is complaining about the increasing cost of upkeep.'

'I think that's false economy!' Sanjit replied. '*All* the Zoo kids are useful, not just the ones we reuse, because they show us the progression we are making in our research. Anyway, I have drawn up plans of different work these kids can do to pay for their keep, as it were, basic cleaning and laundering tasks.'

Mike glanced up as Hugo and Darcey approached. 'We'll talk about this at the next budget meeting.'

He smiled, 'What do you think of the viewing room? Now come and see what we have been doing with Ears and Nose.'

He led Hugo to the third bench, 'We've made rapid progress here using the data you sent from the Compound on the repairs done to Cam's olfactory organ. The organ was too small and moved slightly, causing him to lose his sense of smell when he moved. We are using the Compound Labs idea of packing materials around each organ so that we can now make the exact fit for each individual. And we're using the same technique for Ears. Our success rates with Nose and Ears is now 95%. Hence the excess of Zoo subjects.' As Hugo scrolled through the results on the computer, Mike exchanged a look with Darcey and said quietly, 'We'll have to start disposing of some of them. Sanjit's argument doesn't hold water. I think he's just getting attached to some of them. He actually spends time talking to them when he collects their results! He's getting soft in his old age! Maybe it's time for him to move to a new department.'

Over the next ten days Hugo was shown around the rest of the centre. He was particularly impressed with the blueprints to introduce a new method of implementing muscle enhancements.

'Up to now we have used injections to stimulate muscle development very similar to the use of steroids that athletic Non-Labs used previously but without the harmful side effects. The biggest setback was the length of time the effects of one injection lasted. We had managed a maximum of five years. Now our team is working on a device that can be attached to the heart. It pumps the set dosage of muscle enhancer through the blood stream to reach all the muscles. But instead of the drug been dispersed and released as waste, the residue is directed back to the device where it is filtered and released as enhancer once again. And the cycle continues!'

'Wow!' Hugo's eyes grew wide as he viewed images of the tiny device on the screen. 'How long would this last for?'

'Once we have perfected the device, it will last indefinitely,' Mike told him. 'The only hurdle we face now is attaching it without damaging the heart. We've lost two Non-Labs so far through heart attacks during the operation. We've another one scheduled for tomorrow if you'd like to view it, but we're not one hundred per cent confident of success yet. Still, we can learn by our mistakes.'

Takir noticed Hugo's glum mood on the last day of his visit.

'I know it's difficult for you to go back Hugo, but you have seen how valuable the information you collect from the Compound is to our research here. I will see if we can arrange similar visits for you in the future.'

Hugo sighed, 'We're getting so close to producing the perfect being, I just want to be a bigger part of it!'

'You're right, we are getting close, and like you said before, we need to think carefully of the embryos we can use. You can be directly involved by gathering as much background information on suitable donors, male and female and preparing a full database on suitable candidates. Keep me up to date with your findings, won't you.?'

Hugo nodded solemnly, 'I certainly will.'

Chapter Forty

'Are you sure you don't want to live in halls at university, Hugo?' his mother asked him one morning as they ate breakfast together. 'It's quite a long train journey from here to Oxford, even though you're only going three days a week. And you might make some new friends there. There are lots of bright students at Oxford, some of them twelve-year-old Hybrids like yourself. The accommodation officer said they usually team up their younger students so they don't feel lonely or out of place with the older ones.'

'No, I'm better off living at home. It's easier to get to the Compound and Adam's house from here,' Hugo replied, buttering a slice of toast. 'The research I do with them is more important than the degree work, which is pretty basic, but I suppose I might be able to pick up some useful knowledge while I'm studying for my MA.'

'I'm sure you will, Hugo, and it'll help you to get a good job later,' his mother said. 'I'm really pleased you put your name forward to work with the Hybrids at the Compound summer school.'

'I agree with Ms Harrison, it's criminal the way the Non-Labs just abandon their children's education for six weeks every summer!' he said. 'She was interested in an idea of mine, to assess the development of Hybrids and compare the results with those of Non-Labs. The summer school will give me a chance to try it out.' He drained his coffee cup and grabbed his laptop from the floor. 'See you later.'

He arrived at the Compound to see Ness and Ginny sitting outside the school.

'Are you tutoring, Hugo?' Ness sounded surprised.

'Not exactly.' He explained his idea for assessing the development of the two different types of schoolchildren. 'As well as carrying out case studies here, your mother has agreed to let me look through the records of achievement of the Hybrids that have attended the Compound School. And I have arranged to look at similar records of Non-Labs at a high-performing primary school in London so that I can compare them.'

'Hey, that would be really interesting, Hugo,' Ginny said. 'What will you do with the results?'

'Not quite sure yet,' he looked down, scuffing the ground with his shoe as he thought about the impact it could have on his database of possible donors for the Radical's ideal person. 'But I'm sure it will come in useful somewhere. As a Hybrid, how do you think we compare developmentally with Non-Labs?'

'Mmm, well, a Non-Lab child can walk at about one to one and a half years old, whereas a Hybrid can walk at about ten months. A Hybrid two-year-old seems more like a five-year-old Non-Lab when you look around the play groups. Do you think a Hybrid child develops at maybe twice the rate of a Non-Lab?' Ness suggested.

'No, I don't think so. Five-year-old Hybrids are not like ten-year-old Non-Labs, are they,' Ginny said. 'And, except for IQ levels, we aren't like eighteen-year-old Non-Labs, are we?'

'You're right, and Frankie is thirteen with a very high IQ, but he definitely isn't equivalent to a mature Non-Lab!' Ness laughed.

'Well, that's Frankie for you!' Ginny grinned. 'Seriously, though, I think most Hybrids will mature at about fourteen.'

'We could use our own experiences and that of the Hybrids we know well to make a more accurate assessment of the maturity of Hybrids,' Hugo nodded. 'This should be an interesting study.'

'Yes. I'd like to see what you find out,' Ness said.

'And what about mature Labs and Non-Labs?' Ginny looked thoughtful. 'The Labs were awakened at maturity, that's always taken to be eighteen years old. My Dad and your Dad, Ness, have been awakened for at least fifteen years – so they'd be in their mid-thirties. Which Non-Labs do we know of about the same age?'

'Isaac had his thirty-sixth birthday last month,' Ness said. 'He does look a bit older than our dads.'

'In what way?' Hugo asked.

'Well, our dads look fitter generally ...'

'So that's muscle tone, would you say?' Hugo suggested.

'Yes, definitely, although Isaac does go to the gym regularly,' Ness said. 'He keeps himself pretty fit.'

'And Labs seem to have quicker reactions,' Ginny added. 'Then there's the females. How do the Non-Labs – Ness's Mum and Zig, or my mum – compare to the Labs – Celia and Dette? But I don't suppose you'll be interested in this, if you're thinking about Hybrid education, will you, Hugo?'

'I don't know. I could start with Hybrids and Non-Labs, then expand my research to take in physical and mental development and deterioration of all the human groups. There's quite a wide scope here,' he said, standing up as Amanda Harrison neared the school.

Chapter Forty-one

Hugo rubbed the soft stubble on his chin as he looked at the folder on the screen in front of him. It was the final product of two years' research. He clicked on the folder and then opened the file marked 'Candidates'. The first page showed a list of characteristics – IQ, physical attractiveness, physical strength, independent, ambitious, ability to communicate ideas, adaptable, decisive, quick-thinking, patient, rational, versatile, reliable, leadership qualities. The second page gave details of the tests and evidence he had acquired to award a score in each of the characteristics.

Next he clicked on 'Females'. He scrolled down the list and added or subtracted from the scores in the characteristic columns next to some of the names. Selecting those with the highest scores, he copied and pasted them into a new page and sat back to view them. He leaned forward again and deleted two of the names, which left him with six on the list, two Labs and four Hybrids. He minimized the screen and opened 'Males' and once again cut the list to three names, one Lab and two Hybrids. Finally, he copied and pasted the edited female and male lists on to one page.

He rubbed his chin again as he read out the names in front of him. Two really stood out from the others: Celia (Mature Lab Female) and Hugo (Mature Hybrid Male). Saving all the documents he opened a new email. For several minutes he stared at the page, then finally he began to type.

Dear Takir,

On completing my research into desired characteristics and developmental traits for the Radical Project 'Leadership', I have enclosed the details of the two people I

237

have nominated as donors.

As you are aware, this decision was not made lightly, but is the culmination of two years investigation.

Although you were kept informed at each stage of the investigation over this period, I have attached a summary of tests, evidence and conclusions drawn over the two year period.

I would like to draw your attention to Document 5a to back my nomination of the male donor, highlighting evidence on the maturation age of Hybrids, and also to Document 5d highlighting evidence of delayed aging in mature Labs.

I would like to arrange an appointment with you and the other members of the Radical 'Leadership' committee at a suitable date.

Hugo

He took a deep breath as he reread the email then hit the send button. He was now fourteen years old, and the outcome of his two-year research hinged upon Takir and the committee's response. His future ambitions rested in their hands.

A week later he sat nervously in front of Takir.

'The committee were very impressed with your dedication to researching the ideal donors for the "Leadership" project,' he began. 'They also looked very carefully at your Hybrid developmental investigations and results. These findings will prove useful in many areas. You have been very thorough, Hugo.'

He paused and flicked through the documents that Hugo had emailed him.

'Your proposals have been accepted,' he continued. 'The committee recommended pre-trials to be set up as soon as possible.'

Hugo let out a long breath as a smile spread across his face.

Chapter Forty-two

Hugo, Takir, and Sanjit waited with bated breath as Liz placed the liquid in a glass container. She manoeuvred the container until it was under a microscope attached to a computer. A tiny flicker appeared on the screen.

Liz drew a loud breath. 'This could really be the start of something!'

She removed the container carefully and in turn placed two different ones under the microscope. They looked at the three tiny flickering dots on the screen altogether.

'We used eggs from three Independent Lab volunteers so that we can carry out a broader investigation. All investigations proved successful,' Jackie commented.

'Different female donors, but only one Hybrid donor!' Takir slapped Hugo's back. 'The first Hybrid/Lab foetuses!'

Hugo looked calm although his flushed face betrayed his excitement.

'How long did it take for the women's treatment and to harvest the eggs altogether?' Sanjit asked.

Liz flicked through the papers on her clipboard, 'Altogether three weeks and two days.'

'We must monitor their development carefully over the next month,' Jackie said, 'before we think of bringing her here.'

'How could we keep her here for three weeks?' Hugo asked.

'We have thought of that,' Sanjit replied. 'She will be kept in an induced coma.'

'So we have a few weeks to work out how to get her here without arousing any suspicion,' Takir said.

'I have a plan worked out that I think will work,' Hugo explained his ideas to the others.

Chapter Forty-three

'Have you seen the pictures of you and Keith at the "Wild Ones" launch?' Jez said waving the newspaper in the air at Zig. She put down the hosepipe and brushed the mud off her hands before taking it. 'What's it like being famous?'

Zig smiled as she looked at the picture of herself in the paper. She was wearing a tight, shiny red dress with red stilettoes to match. Her cat-like eyes were looking straight into the camera and she wore a look of cool indifference on her face. Inside she had been absolutely petrified and only kept upright by hanging on to Keith's arm.

'What's it like being famous?' Jez asked again.

'Hardly famous! An overnight wonder, that's all!' Zig grinned, handing the paper back and pulling two dead leaves off one of the plants, 'They'll have forgotten about me this time next month.'

'I don't think so!' Jez said. 'Zorro's hits usually stay at the top for ages. And those cat contact lenses are doing really well! Everyone is wearing them! Zorro's wife was wearing yellow lion ones last week!'

Zig laughed. 'Yes, I've got Pellier to thank for that! Now I leave off my contact lenses and pretend I'm wearing some.'

'How does Bailey feel about your new career?' Jez asked.

'He knows I'm not giving up my day job!' Zig sighed and looked around her, 'I don't want to leave the Compound. This is the best home I've had since my mum died.'

'And there's Bailey, too …'Jez raised her eyebrows.

'Bailey? There's nothing between us like that! He's like my big brother! Just a pal.' Zig laughed again.

'You're not still thinking about Angus, are you?' Gez

241

frowned.

'I'm way over him,' Zig shrugged and studied the plant in front of her, 'No, I'm not thinking of Angus anymore. What about you, Jez, what are your plans now?'

'Reuben has asked if I'd like to go to New York with Cam and Otis to work with Simon and his department out there for a while. As Specials – Eyes, Ears and Nose!'

'Nothing dangerous?' Zig asked.

'No. Abel was very strict on that one. He looks out for us as if we're Labs,' Jez smiled. 'But I'm a bit worried about the others, especially Brit and the two new ones.'

'Don't worry, they'll be fine. And I'll be here to keep an eye on them. It's a great opportunity for you but I'll miss you, we all will!'

'I'll only be gone a month or two. But I will miss you, too,' Jez hugged her friend.

Chapter Forty-four

'We have to know that everything is in place, and once everything is arranged she must be brought here the same day. We can't allow for any setbacks!' Sanjit said.

'We've checked and double-checked,' Takir told him as Hugo nodded.

'Let's run through the plan once more,' Liz joined in, 'and make sure we've covered everything.'

'Friday, at about quarter past seven,' Takir read from a pad, 'she'll be leaving Adam's house. Hugo will text me as soon as she's left. The car will be waiting on Field Way, near Greystone's Farm, off the road and out of view. Cora has arranged to hire the horsebox for the car and will pick it up at seven. Angus will be stationed further down the road on his motorbike to warn us if anyone is approaching. He'll detain them with a story of a breakdown to give us time to move. Once she's in our car we'll bring her straight here. Cora will load the car onto the trailer, wearing Hugo's jumper, jeans, gloves, and hat. Then she'll drive the trailer with Angus following.'

'Once you are here, we take over,' Jackie said. 'We have everything ready. We follow the same procedure as on the three trial female Labs.'

'And she'll be returned three weeks later, none the wiser!' Sanjit smiled.

Chapter Forty-five

'Hugo,' Celia's eyes widened as she looked at the screen,' this is amazing! Adam, have you seen the work Hugo has done on bone reconstruction?'

Adam left his seat and stood behind him. 'That is very impressive, Hugo! You've obviously been working hard on this. Have you shown this to Dr Schultz and his team yet?'

'Well, if you think they'd be interested …' Hugo began with a shy smile.

'Of course they will be! How did you manage to advance the basic theory so far without actual trials on bone matter?'

Hugo thought of the new Zoo members at the Radical's latest centre in Romania. He exchanged information by email and Skype at least once a week with Takir, who arranged the tests and forwarded him the results after each trial. 'I put forward a few hypotheses and ran the probabilities of different bone matter reactions and based my results on that. These ideas were for male and female nearing the end of their maturity. How could this be adapted for those older or much younger? I'd be really interested in finding out what Dr Schultz and his team think about this.'

'I'm going to get him to come over here one day next week! He'll be so excited when he sees this!' Celia patted Hugo's shoulder. 'You know, if I ever have a son, I hope he'll be like you!'

Hugo smiled broadly at her.

'Well, I had better get going,' she continued, glancing at her watch. 'Just after seven. Are you ready for me to back up everything, Hugo, before I disable the computers?'

A short while later she drove through the main gates,

waving to a Lab guard as she passed. She hummed as she sped down the narrow road wondering if Isaac would like to go to the cinema that evening as they were both finishing work quite early. As she drove around a bend she was forced to brake as a figure appeared in the centre of the road.

'Help! Please! You've got to help me!' the young man said.

His jacket was torn and his face was smeared with mud and blood.

'My car, it skidded off the road!' He headed for a gateway almost concealed by an overgrown hedgerow, 'She's still in the car! I can't get her out!'

Celia sprang out and ran after him, pulling her phone from her pocket. 'I'll call an ambulance!'

A moment later someone grabbed her from behind, covering her mouth with a cloth. There was a brief struggle then she fell limply into his arms.

'Are you sure no one saw you?' Liz asked for the third time as they wheeled her into a small sterile room on a stretcher.

'Positive. Cora stayed there for another half hour and no one, on foot or in a vehicle, passed the gateway,' Takir reassured her. 'I sent a text on her mobile to Abel to say something had come up and she'd be back late tonight, so she would see him tomorrow. No one will even be looking for her until at least tomorrow morning!'

Liz let out a sigh. 'Good. Then we can prepare her straight away. Sanjit is ready to start the pre-med. Jackie has the drip ready.'

Chapter Forty-six

'Did she give any idea of where she might have been planning to go? Apart from home?' Abel asked Adam and Hugo as they sat in the Compound office the next morning.

They both shook their heads.

'She said she expected to be back before eight,' Adam said.

'She texted me at quarter to eight to say something had come up and she'd be back late,' Abel said. 'She hasn't been in touch with anyone since then and her phone is switched off.'

'It's only eleven o'clock. Maybe she spent the night at a friend's house,' Hugo suggested.

'Celia would have let us know!' Ruby looked pale. 'I think we should get in touch with Reuben.'

Abel nodded and picked up the phone.

'Still no news?' Isaac asked that evening. His eyes were red rimmed and his face was unshaven.

'We've been in touch with all the Labs and any Non-Labs Celia knows through work or socially. Nothing,' Ruby told him.

'None of us Specials could find any trace of her on the road she would normally take,' Cam said.

'I hope she's not in the kind of place they put us!' Zig clenched her fists until her knuckles were white. 'I'm *sure* they're involved. We've got to find her!'

'We don't know if they headed abroad after we rescued the youngsters or if they're still in this country,' Ruby said.

'Jez said they were talking about relocating to an eastern European country, but they didn't say which one,' Zig looked at a map of the region on the computer screen.

'I've contacts in Bulgaria, Romania, and Croatia. I'll see if they can find out about any new medical centres in any of these places,' Isaac said, pulling his mobile phone from his pocket.

'Did you see the story about Celia on the news last night?' Ginny said as she sat down beside Hugo at school the next day.

'No, I don't watch television,' he replied, turning on the computer.

'Abel was on it, asking anyone with information to get in touch with the police or with him,' Ginny continued. 'Mariella thinks some mad Non-Lab has kidnapped her, do you think so, Hugo?'

'Sorry, what did you say?' he looked up. 'I want to print this off and take it to your father's house tomorrow.'

'Aren't you worried about Celia?' Ginny asked him as he stood up.

'I'm sure that Celia will be back soon,' he said.

'How do you know that?' Ginny asked.

He coughed, 'Oh, well, what could have happened to her? There's probably a logical explanation.'

'A complete success!' Dr Neilson beamed across the table. 'We now have five fertilized embryos. Three male and two female, all ready for the next stage.'

'Are we using the same speed development that my donor implemented in me?' Angus asked.

'Yes, with some modifications,' Neilson continued. 'From American trials, the Radicals' medical team have perfected a method of slowing some of the effects of the ageing process; so these young ones will be able to avoid the usual illnesses and physical problems that beset Non-Labs as they enter old age; such as arthritis, failing hearing, sight and such like.'

'And they will have selected programming during their

development, won't they?' said Hugo excitedly. 'With the enhancements they will be given when they are mature, they will be truly superior beings!'

'Yes,' Neilson smiled, 'they will be a force to be reckoned with!'

'And if they are placed in the right position,' Takir smiled, 'they will be a force that will be a great asset to us!'

Sanjit grimaced as he stood up, rubbing his back, 'You told me this research can help me with some of my problems. When can we start the treatment?'

Neilson shuffled his papers together. 'Not long now. Be patient. Some things can't be hurried! Well, I'm going to check up on our female donor. See how she is faring! We should be able to send her home in the next few days. Have you taken care of all the details for the move?'

Takir nodded, 'Liz and Cora have everything organized. The car has been cleaned and is in the carrier ready. Her clothes have also been cleaned.'

'No traces left?' Neilson asked.

'Nothing, apart from those of Hugo on both front seats, steering wheel, and doors.'

'It's a great car to drive! When I'm old enough, I'm getting myself a car like that!' Hugo said.

'You seem to share a lot of the same tastes,' Angus smiled.

'He shares a lot more with her than she'll ever know!' Takir added.

Hugo joined Neilson as he went to leave. 'Can I come with you, to see her?'

The two of them headed down the corridor and stopped at a white door. Looking through the glass top, Hugo could see a motionless figure on a bed and a young nurse checking a monitor and tapping data into a tablet. Neilson passed a security card over the lock and they entered the room. The nurse looked up and smiled.

'Dr Neilson! I've downloaded the latest progress report

just this minute.'

'Good!' Neilson looked at the screen in front of her, 'Hmm, all seems to be in order. No unexpected changes in vital organs, brain activity … good. We can start to bring her round tomorrow. And she can leave the next day.'

Hugo gazed down at the still figure, watching her chest gently rise and fall and smiled to himself.

Chapter Forty-seven

'Reuben sent a team to the new medical centre in Croatia that you had reports on,' Abel told Isaac the same evening. 'It seems to be authentic. The staff there told the team members that they are working with children suffering from childhood illnesses caused by malnutrition. There was nothing to suggest it was a cover for anything else. And none of the staff or children were Lab or Hybrid.'

'That leaves Romania,' Isaac sighed. 'And I have no leads at all on any medical centre new or old there. I could go there with Dette and see if we can find out anything.'

'Where would you start to look?' Ruby asked.

'We could follow a similar plan to the trip I made with my uncle to Laqaar, when we went to find the twins,' Isaac said. 'Just collect details of medical centres, hospitals, places like the ones Warner's people have here in the UK, and work through the list.' He stood up. 'I can't just sit here! I've got to do something! I've got to find her!'

Ruby put her arms around him. 'We know how you feel, Isaac. We all feel just as worried!'

Chapter Forty-eight

Celia opened her eyes slowly and looked around her. She was lying back against the driving seat of her car. Groaning softly, she pulled herself up straight and peered through the windows into the blackness.

'Where am I?'

She climbed out and looked around her. The car was parked at the side of a deserted country track.

'How did I get here?' she muttered, with a feeling of panic rising in her throat. She rummaged through her pockets and gave a sigh of relief as her hands closed over her mobile phone.

With trembling fingers she scrolled through her contacts until she came to Abel's number.

He answered on the second ring.

'Abel …' she began.

'Celia? Celia? Where are you? Where have you been?' he cried.

'Celia? Is she OK? Where is she?' she could hear Ruby in the background.

'I don't know where I am …' she mumbled.

'Are you safe? Did anyone harm you?' Abel continued. 'I will kill them!'

'I'm OK, just a bit dizzy. I'm alone. I'm in my car. I'm somewhere in the countryside. I don't know where,' she said.

'OK, Celia, stay on the phone so we can trace where you are.' Abel was making a great effort to calm himself down.

She heard a tapping of keys then he came back on the line. 'We've located you. We'll come and get you straight away; it'll be about an hour.'

It seemed longer to Celia before she saw the car draw up and Abel and Ruby hurrying towards her. She stepped out of the car and hugged Ruby, who took a deep breath. 'Oh, Celia! Where have you been? You've had us all so worried these last three weeks!'

Celia's eyes clouded over. 'Three weeks? Where have I been for three weeks?' She ran a hand over her face.

'Hey, let's get you home!' Abel stepped forward as Celia slumped in his arms.

'I'm a bit dizzy and my stomach hurts,' she muttered.

'Don't worry, you're safe, I've got you,' Abel told her as he guided her into their car.

Once they arrived back at the Compound, Celia was taken straight to the medical block.

Zig was waiting by the gate and hurriedly followed Ruby into the building and into a small waiting room.

'Is she ill? What have they done to her?' she began.

Ruby shook her head, 'She feels dizzy, and she has no idea where she has been for the past three weeks. She wasn't even aware she had been missing for so long. She's complaining of stomach pains, too. But she's back safely now. She's in good hands!'

After half an hour a Lab doctor appeared.

'Physically, she's going to be fine. She has been subjected to several weeks of a tranquillising drug which is why she has no recollection of recent events,' she began.

'You said physically …' Zig repeated.

The young woman raised her eyebrows. 'Celia is going to need a lot of help and support over the next few weeks or even months …'

Zig clenched her fists, 'What did they do to her?'

'Well … it would appear that a procedure was used to harvest eggs from Celia. This is why she is complaining of a tender feeling in her lower abdomen.'

'What … why … does that mean they have taken Celia's

eggs so someone else can have her baby?' Zig asked.

The doctor nodded, 'It is very possible. Or to carry out an experiment of some sort on a foetus created using Celia's eggs.'

Ruby looked solemn. 'Does this mean Celia won't have the chance to have children of her own later on?'

The doctor shook her head. 'No, a considerable percentage of eggs were taken, but she is still fertile.'

'Why would someone do this, and why Celia?' Ruby wondered.

'Can we see her?' Zig asked.

'She is still sleeping, but she will be pleased to see a familiar face when she wakes up. I don't think she realizes exactly what has happened. She is still getting over the effects of the drugs,' the doctor said, leading them to a small side room where Celia lay.

Abel appeared with Reuben and went with the doctor to her office. Ruby and Zig sat at the foot of Celia's bed.

Celia moaned softly and her eyelids fluttered, 'Where … Ruby, Zig! What …?'

Zig plumped up the pillows and helped her to sit up.

'You're OK now, Celia!'

Celia rubbed her temples, 'I came back here with you and Abel last night, didn't I?'

Ruby nodded. 'Then you came here for a check-up …'

Celia's eyes flew open, 'The doctor told me what … what had happened to me … oh, no!'

Zig put her arms around her, shaking shoulders, 'It's OK, Celia.'

She leaned back against the pillows and closed her eyes, 'No, it's not OK … but I'm so tired.'

'You need to sleep off the drugs they gave you, then you'll feel better,' Zig continued quietly. Soon Celia's breathing slowed as she slept once more.

'She's going to need all her strength to deal with this,' Ruby sighed.

Celia sat in the chair next to her hospital bed gazing straight ahead as Ruby, Zig and Abel entered the room.

'Celia, you're awake!' Ruby said. 'How are you feeling?'

Her expression was distant as she looked up at her, 'What have they done? Will there be a child out there, my child? What will he or she be like? There could be more than one child! Will I recognize them if I meet them?'

'Hey, we're going to sort this out!' Zig put her arms around Celia's trembling shoulders.

'Reuben and his team have taken some of the Specials to the place where your car was found. The car is back here on the Compound and they are having a look at it now. I'm going to see what they have found. When you feel up to it, if there is anything you can recall, anything at all, Celia, just let us know,' Abel squeezed her hand. As he left Ginny came hurrying into the room followed by her father.

'Celia! We're so glad to see you back!' she said.

Celia gave a slight smile as Ginny squeezed her hand.

Adam placed a bunch of flowers beside her, 'How are you feeling, Celia? Any recollection of where you have been?'

Celia shook her head. 'Nothing at all. How long was I gone for? What date is it today?'

'You were gone for three weeks,' Ruby reminded her. 'It's the twenty-third today.'

'Three weeks? Where is Isaac?' Celia looked around her.

'He's in Romania with Dette. They'll be here this evening. They send their love and can't wait to see you! In fact, you have a list of friends all wanting to come and see you. I told them we'd have to take it easy until you're back on your feet,' Ruby told her.

'Thank you, Ruby. I don't know if I want to see many people at the moment,' Celia wrung her hands. 'How will Vanessa react when she hears what has happened? She'll never forgive me!'

'She won't hold you responsible for what happened!'

Ruby said firmly. 'Nobody could!'

Celia shook her head. 'We have to find out who did this!'

'We'll help find them, won't we, Dad?' Ginny said indignantly.

'Of course. I think Celia needs a rest now. It's time for school anyway,' her father replied.

'I'd better get going, too,' Zig said. She kissed Celia goodbye. 'I'll call by later.'

'So is this is anything to do with Angus and his friends?' Adam asked as they left the building.

'You can't still think I have any contact, or want any contact with him!' Zig narrowed her eyes.

'Hugo wasn't worried about Celia when she was missing. He said she would be back soon. I didn't believe him, but he was right!' Ginny said as they neared the school building.

'How would Hugo know?' Zig frowned.

Ginny shrugged. 'He just said he was sure that Celia would be back very soon and that there was a logical explanation. Well, he was right thank goodness!'

'Mmm, How would he know, indeed?' Adam replied with a thoughtful expression.

Chapter Forty-nine

Two days later, Isaac sat with the others in Abel's lounge.

'Last time we were all together it was for a happier occasion.' He gave a wry smile at Johnny and Leon. Leon nodded sadly.

'Do you think Angus and the Radicals are behind Celia's kidnapping?' Johnny asked Abel.

'We have found no evidence at all from Celia's belongings or her car. There are only traces of Hugo and Celia herself in the car,' he replied.

'So we are no nearer to finding out who kidnapped me!' Celia sighed.

'I still think the Radicals are behind this!' Zig said. 'What did you discover on your trip, Dette?'

Dette pulled out a notebook, 'There was one place near Constanta that raised our suspicions.' 'What was the place like?' Abel asked.

'It was very similar to the Centre ...' she began, a shudder running down her spine. 'The main building is a simple two-storey unit, but one of the locals who was involved in the construction told us that The completed building was much bigger than that shown on the original plans.

'But he also told us that buildings didn't always match their planning details. Some people were able to work outside the law, mainly to avoid paying tax and planning fees,' Isaac added. 'Anyway, we decided not to enquire further so as not to raise any suspicions. If Warner's people are involved they would recognize me for sure, and they'd realize that Dette is a Lab. But the place definitely deserves further investigation.'

'Reuben will be here tomorrow morning,' Abel said. 'We can discuss the situation with him.'

'We have to find them,' Celia said looking around the room. 'None of us are safe until we do! Or our children!'

Leon and Johnny exchanged anxious glances, thinking of their families.

'We must!' Johnny breathed.

'And soon!' Leon agreed.

'Can I walk you home, Celia?' Isaac asked at the end of the evening. 'I have some news for you, good news, but I thought you'd want me to tell you while you are on your own.'

Celia led him into her kitchen, 'I could do with some good news.'

Isaac put on the kettle as she prepared two cups of coffee.

'I spoke to Vince just after we got back. He and Vanessa were very upset to hear about what had happened. He's taking a few months off work so he can spend some time with Abel and Reuben and try to find out who is behind this. He'll be here at the end of the week. Vanessa wants to come, too, for a few days. She's very anxious to see you and make sure you are all right.'

Celia stood holding the two cups, not moving for a few minutes and then she let out a long breath, 'She doesn't hate me? There might not be just me around now, there could be I don't know how many!'

Isaac put his hands on her shoulders, 'Of course not, Celia. Why would she hold you responsible for what happened?'

Slowly Celia turned around and put her head on his chest. 'When Vanessa finally agreed to meet me, I thought I might, just *might*, have a chance to move forward with my own life … the things I'd like …'

He put his hands on her shoulders. 'You can, Celia.

Whatever happens, you can live the life you choose.'

She looked up at him. 'Do you really think so? That I can carry on as normal knowing that I might have at least one child out there somewhere?'

'Giving up the life you really want won't change things, Celia,' Isaac said simply. 'And it won't make you a happier person.'

Celia pulled herself away and gave him a cup of coffee, 'Yes, well, it's all a bit too much to think about at the moment. Will they be staying on the Compound?'

'Yes, Ruby is arranging the same rooms they stayed in last time they visited,' Isaac said.

A few days later Celia was making breakfast when there was a knock on the door.

Isaac stood there. 'You've some visitors, Celia,'

Vanessa and Vince appeared behind him. The older woman rushed to Celia and hugged her tightly. 'Thank God you're back safely!'

'I was afraid that after what has happened you wouldn't want to see me again,' Celia whispered.

Vanessa shook her head, 'How could you think such a thing, Celia? I was so worried about you. We all were. Now I'm furious with them for what they've done to you. They've not only stolen your children; they've stolen our grandchildren!'

Vince nodded. 'We're going to look for those people and we won't give up until we find them, no matter how long it takes! And whatever we find out, we'll deal with it together!'

'Now, we've been talking and Bill and the boys agree – in fact it was Tom's idea originally. We think you could do with a holiday and we want you to come and stay with us in Florida for a few weeks,' Vanessa said. 'What do you say? Come and relax with your family?'

'Well, I …' Celia looked at Isaac.

'It sounds like a great idea to me, Celia,' he smiled.

Chapter Fifty

'See you later, Dad,' Ginny said as she climbed out of the car.

'Come on then, Hugo,' Adam said.

'Isn't Celia coming with us today?' Hugo looked around.

'No, she's having a break for a few weeks,' Adam told him. 'She's only just getting back on her feet, you know.'

'But she's not *ill*, is she?' he said curtly. 'I mean, she wasn't harmed in any way, was she?'

'Obviously the whole ordeal has affected her!' Adam replied.

'I would have expected her to be mentally capable of handling … different … situations. From what she has told us of life for the Labs earlier on, they were all resilient and adaptable.'

He noticed the look Adam gave him. 'Sorry, I'm being selfish. I really wanted to talk to her about my project. I need some advice and Celia is always so helpful.'

'Well, you'll have to manage with my advice, and we'll have Leonard with us today. He'll have some thoughts on the matter. Actually Dr Schultz suggested a trial on mice. We'll call by the medical block and pick up a cage they'll have ready.'

'Mice?' Hugo shook his head, 'Why can't we carry out some tests on some Non-Labs? There must be plenty of them with broken or problem bones!'

Adam gave a chuckle. 'If only it were that simple, Hugo! Medical research is thwarted at every corner by Health and Safety regulations!'

He saw the look of frustration cross the boy's face as he

followed him to the car. Hugo stared stonily out of the window as Adam stowed the cage of mice in the boot and climbed into the car again. He started up the engine and they headed away from the Compound. After ten minutes Hugo frowned as Adam pulled into a layby on a remote country road.

'I think you and I need a bit of a chat, young man,' Adam said as the car came to a halt. He turned to face the boy. 'I'd like you to give Angus a message from me next time you see him. No! Don't deny it! I've been watching you. You know far too much. I've covered for you several times when I found out you've been copying data. You're lucky Celia never caught you out! Anyway, you tell Angus I'd like to meet up with him very soon. I've some ideas he – and his friends – will be interested in. He's already seen some of it on the data you've handed over. They have to realise we're on the same side, all heading for the same goal. It's time we worked together. Make sure he gets this message, Hugo.'

'I don't know what you're talking about …' Hugo looked him in the eye.

'You know exactly what I'm talking about! Just make sure you pass on the message, Hugo,' Adam repeated quietly.

Without a word, he turned on the ignition and continued their journey.

Later the same day, Hugo sat nervously biting his fingernails as Takir paced the length of the room.

'How could you be so lax, Hugo? Who else knows about you?' Takir said angrily. 'Why did I ever let myself be persuaded to trust a child?'

The boy bristled and took a deep breath. 'I told you, he might just be bluffing. I denied everything! He has no proof of anything!'

'You hope! But why hasn't Adam gone to Abel yet?' Takir scowled. 'What does he want?'

'I'm sure Adam isn't like the other Compound Labs,'

Angus replied. 'I think what he said to Hugo is true, he's on our side.'

'And if it's a trap?' Sanjit looked up.

'I think we should meet him. We can decide what to do when we see him,' Angus said.

'And if he poses any kind of a threat, we get rid of him. We'll go and have a chat with him,' Takir turned to Hugo. 'Whatever happens, keep your head down and your mouth shut, boy!'

Hugo nodded his head silently.

A few days later Adam was making way to his flat when two men approached him.

'Angus!' he beamed holding out his hand, 'And you must be Takir? Or Sanjit?'

'Takir.' The second man gave him a cold smile as he shook his hand briefly, 'Care to join us for a ride, Adam?'

The three men got into a black sedan with tinted windows and the car sped away.

Takir looked around from the front passenger seat. 'So you wanted to meet us, Adam.'

'Yes, very much so. As I told Hugo, I believe we can work together. I've been very impressed with the research the boy is coming up with. I want to be involved!' Adam leaned forward.

'I thought you had settled in well with your Compound friends again, Adam,' Angus looked at him in the rear view mirror.

Adam sighed. 'I'm just biding my time. You know I've always found their ambitions to be limited. They sold their souls for a place in the Non-Lab society! Labs and Hybrids are capable of so much more!'

Angus glanced at Takir, whose face remained unreadable.

'So what exactly have you got to offer us, Adam? We are managing our research very well without you, though I was impressed with the work you started with Angus,' he said.

'From what I hear from Abel and Celia, I know the

Radicals have won over many of the Independent Lab groups …' Adam began.

'It's only a matter of time before we win over *all* the Independent Labs,' Takir stated.

'Except for the Compound Labs! And that's where I come in.'

Takir waited for him to continue.

'You need someone you can trust on the Compound, someone who can gradually plant the idea with the Labs there that Abel is selling them out to the Non-Labs, and to get them on our side! I've already looked around to see which groups will be more vulnerable. The younger scientists, for example; it wouldn't take much to sway their opinions.' he smiled. 'And someone mature who can make sure Hugo is a little more discreet.'

Takir looked thoughtful as he signalled for Angus to stop the car. 'We'll be in touch, Adam.'

Chapter Fifty-one

'You're looking a lot better today, Celia,' Adam commented as she walked into his house the next morning.

'Celia!' Hugo smiled. 'I'm so glad you're back! I've been working on the bone reconditioning and made some really interesting discoveries!'

'Hugo, that's incredible!' she leaned over his shoulder to look at the screen. 'How can you come up with these hypotheses without actual trials?'

'Now we've set up the trials on mice, I think things are going to get even more interesting!' Adam said.

'Do you want to take a look at this, Celia? Just sit down here,' Hugo pulled a chair over for her.

She ruffled his hair. 'I'm afraid I don't really have the time at the moment. I've just come to tell you both that I'm going to Florida for a few weeks to stay with my family there. Isaac is outside waiting to take me to the travel agency to pick up my ticket.' She saw a look of disappointment cross the boy's face. 'Look, if you email your findings to me, I'll take a look later in the week, I promise.'

He shrugged.

'I really need this break,' she said. 'Hugo, when was the last time you saw your dad? You know it might be an idea to get in touch with him. He'd be so impressed if he could see what you have achieved already!'

'He can't be bothered to keep in touch with me, so I'm not going looking for him until *I'm* ready!' He looked at her. 'He *will* be impressed, I'm sure!'

Celia hugged him. 'Oh, Hugo. Don't always work so hard. Take some time to just enjoy being a kid!'

Adam watched the look of anger cross his face as she ruffled his hair again.

'And she just treats me like a kid!' he complained to Ethan later that week.

'Well, you are to her,' his friend pointed out.

'I'm a Hybrid! I've already proved my superior intellectual level academically! And I've proved that ...' Hugo stopped.

Mariella looked at him, 'What?'

'Nothing!' he stood up, shoulders slumped and hands pushed into his pockets. 'You don't understand, none of you. But you will one day!'

He nearly bumped into Adam and Ginny as he walked away.

'Hey, Hugo, what's up?' Ginny called out.

'What's wrong with him?' Adam asked the others.

Ethan explained the conversation.

'Personally, I think he's got a bit of a crush on Celia,' Adam smiled indulgently. 'Young love!'

'No Hugo today?' Zig asked as she met Ginny after school at the end of the week. 'I was going to ask if he'd like to come and look at the work Bailey has been doing on the GMT crop, see if he'd like to make any comments.'

'No, he wasn't in school yesterday either. And he hasn't been to my Dad's house. Mum phoned his mum again because he keeps missing school; but she was rather vague. Mum says Yvonne probably doesn't even doesn't know where he is herself.'

'This isn't the first time he's taken a few days off, is it?' Zig frowned. 'Where does he go to when he just disappears?'

Swinging the huge office chair around away from the view of the Thames, Hugo gave Angus a sullen look. 'When can I move out there with the others?'

Angus smiled. 'Be patient. We have been through this before. You're not old enough to move over there permanently yet. And you are valuable to us on the Compound.'

'Oh, yes. So I can play with mice while all the important work is been done over there with real people! Anyway, you have Adam on the Compound now, you don't need me there,' Hugo spun the chair around, 'I'm sick of everyone treating me like a kid!'

'I hate to point out the obvious, Hugo, but you *are* still a minor; in the eyes of the law anyway,' Angus told him.

'Stupid Non-Lab laws! If Celia and Abel and those others only knew …' he began.

'They won't!' Angus snapped, making Hugo sit up. 'If you say anything about our research there won't be a Lab group that will go near you! The Radicals will make sure of that!'

'No, no, of course not,' he quickly replied. 'I'm just frustrated, not being able to get on with the work I really want to do!'

'I know. And you'll be a valuable worker with us in Romania. In the meantime, try to be patient and make yourself as useful as you can to us while you're still on the Compound. Have they got any further leads on Celia's disappearance?'

Hugo shook his head. 'But I heard Isaac tell Celia they're not going to give up.'

That evening Hugo sat stony-faced on his bed as his mother spoke to him.

'Try to understand, son,' she pleaded. 'You can't just disappear without telling anyone, not even me, where you are going. It's such a worry not knowing where you are.'

He sighed, 'I told you. I meet up with some friends. That's it.'

'Which friends? I want to meet them. They're not from

the Compound or school,' his mother continued. 'Dr Harrison was on the phone to me again, complaining about you missing too much school. She said maybe the Compound School isn't the right place for you to be. Perhaps you should be looking at attending university full time.'

'No. I'd prefer to stay where I am at the moment,' he answered. 'My friends won't be around for a while, so I'll make more effort at school, OK?'

His mother sighed as he turned back to his laptop screen.

'That was a brilliant idea, Zig, getting Brit and Shiva involved in the creative classes at the school!' Jez said the following week.

'Oh, I loved helping the little ones to bake cakes today!' Ginny enthused. 'They can't wait until next cookery lesson!'

'Yes,' Mariella said, 'It was fun. I'm going to have a go at making cupcakes myself tonight!

'Great!' Hugo sneered. 'Being able to make cupcakes is such a wonderful career opportunity!'

'Oh, come on, Hugo! You know what they say about all work and no fun!' Zig quipped.

'I have no interest in what *they* say and even less in who *they* are!'

The others exchanged looks as he stomped outside.

'He's really grumpy these days!' Ginny remarked.

'Oh, he just works too hard. I'll give him a lift home, Ginny, while you wait for your mother,' Adam said. 'He'll be fine tomorrow.'

Hugo was standing outside where Ethan was kicking a football around with Cam, Jez, and a few of the younger Hybrids as Adam joined him.

'Nope, no sign of intelligent life around here!' he muttered under his breath, 'Get me out of here, Angus, before I go mad!'

Adam noticed Jez freeze and the ball sailed past her into

the net. 'Come on, Hugo. I'll drop you off home.'

A cry went up from one of the young boys, 'We won!'

Throwing the ball to one of them, Jez nodded in agreement grabbing Cam's arm, 'You win! Game over for today!'

Inside the house she looked across at Zig. 'Fancy a stroll?'

She followed them outside and they headed towards the garden area.

'What is it, Jez?' she asked.

She looked around and satisfied herself that they were alone before she told them what she had overheard, 'Adam didn't seem to notice, but I'm pretty sure Hugo said Angus.'

'He's involved with Angus?' Zig let out a low whistle. 'We need to speak to Abel right away!'

They found Abel in the office and told him what Jez had heard.

'That would explain quite a lot,' he said.

'Dette said to keep an eye on the Hybrid children!' Ruby sighed. 'I had hoped she was wrong!'

'So through Hugo we can find Angus and the Radicals. And find out if they were involved with … my disappearance,' Celia said softly. Isaac moved over and put his arm around her.

'How are we going to handle this?' he asked Abel.

'Let's get Hugo in here straight away. Where is he now?' he looked at Jez.

'He left with Adam. He was going to drop him off home.' she replied as Abel picked up the phone.

Adam pulled up at his flat and both he and the boy got out. As he pulled the front door closed behind them he said, 'Jez heard what you said, Hugo. You could have put everyone in danger!'

'I didn't mean …' the boy began as Adam punched a number into his mobile.

'Angus, you need to get Hugo out of here now! I think they're on to him.' He explained what Hugo had said and how Jez had reacted.

Angus drew a sharp breath and swore. 'OK. I'll get on to Takir straight away. I've been pushing him to get Hugo over there as soon as possible, anyway. He was getting too impatient and becoming a danger to us here. Sanjit is due to fly out to our new centre this evening so Hugo can accompany him. Keep him with you until you hear from us.'

Adam turned to the boy as the line went dead and repeated the conversation. Hugo was filled with both trepidation and elation. He was going to work in the new Radical centre! Suddenly he bit his lip as his eyes were glazed with tears.

'I need to get some stuff from home,' his voice came out as barely a whisper.

'I don't know if that's such a good idea, Hugo,' Adam began. At that moment his phone rang. Adam glanced at the screen.

'Abel, hi. I don't often get calls from you,' he said, signalling Hugo to remain silent. 'Hugo, yes, I dropped him off near the bus station just ten minutes ago, said he was meeting up with a friend. I gather he was planning on going home in an hour or two as he promised to email me some websites he thought I'd be interested in later today.'

'How has he been acting lately, Adam? Have you noticed anything strange in his behaviour?' Abel asked.

Adam chuckled. 'No more moody and argumentative than usual. I assume Hybrids are affected by puberty just like Non-Labs are! I'm so glad we were awakened at maturity and didn't have to go through all of that!'

'Well if you hear from him, please give me a call, OK?' Abel continued.

'Hey, he's not in any trouble or anything, is he?' Adam sounded concerned.

'No, nothing like that, I'd just like to chat to him about

his school attendance and see how he's getting on.'

'I'll let him know if I see him, Abel,' Adam hung up and dialled a second number.

'Hello, Yvonne. It's Adam. Is Hugo home yet?'

'No,' his mother replied, 'In fact Abel was just around here looking for him himself less than ten minutes ago. I wasn't really expecting him back until this evening.'

'Thank you, Yvonne. I'll call back later. It's nothing urgent.'

He turned to Hugo. 'You have a couple of minutes to collect some belongings from home. But you'll need to be quick.'

Adam parked the car around the corner from the house and scanned the area, 'Remember, you must be quick. Abel could call back here, or one of the others from the Compound.'

Hugo nodded and hurried to his front door, struggling to get the key in the lock.

'Hugo, is that you? You're back early,' he heard his mother's voice from the lounge. Smiling, she looked up from the ironing board, 'What a nice surprise, I wasn't expecting you until this evening.'

'I'm not staying. I just called by to get something,' he replied. He walked up to her and put his arms around her waist. 'I love you, Mum.'

'Oh Hugo, it's not often I hear that from you! I love you, too, sweetheart.' She smoothed his hair back from his forehead. 'You may be one of the cleverest people in the country, but you'll always be my little boy.'

He moved away from her. 'I'd better get that file. See you.'

As he walked upstairs, his mother called to him, 'Adam's been on the phone and Abel has been around looking for you. You haven't been missing school again, have you, son?'

'No,' he replied. 'I just need to catch up on some work.'

He grabbed a bag in his bedroom and pushed a handful of

273

clothes into it. He packed papers and several memory sticks into his laptop bag, then with a quick look around he ran downstairs. His mother walked into the hall to see the door closing behind him.

'Hugo, what time will you …?' she began.

'Bye, Mum.' With a quick smile he pulled the door closed. He ran down the street and back to the waiting car. Adam glanced at the boy's white knuckles as he gripped his bag tightly.

'Are you OK?' He received a brief nod and a muffled reply. 'Takir is sending the car to my flat in fifteen minutes. You'll be flying out as Sanjit's grandson. He has all the paperwork sorted. They'll sort you out with clothes and anything else you need out there.'

A short while later he watched as Hugo climbed into the black sedan. He squeezed his shoulder.

'Take care of him, Takir.'

'Of course, he's a valuable member of the team. And he won't be able to jeopardise our research over there! We'll be in touch, Adam.'

With that the car sped away. Hugo hunched in the back seat, looking every bit a frightened boy. Then, closing his eyes, he took a deep breath and sat up straight. His face seemed to turn to stone as Takir met his eyes in the mirror.

'That's it, Hugo. There's no room for baggage if you're working with us.'

Waiting in the Shadows
Trish Moran

Perfect for fans of Veronica Roth's **Divergent** trilogy and Lois Lowry's *The Giver*.

Book One in the Shadows Series. Amidst the excitement of the advances in stem cell research, little thought has been given to the spare parts created at the world-famous Centre. But what happens when those 'spare parts' are revealed to be a lot more than that – to be living, breathing human beings? When teenage orphan Stella flees from a life in care homes, she encounters the 'Ferals'. The media portrays them as dangerous criminals, but Stella soon realises they're not so different from her. They call themselves Labs, and they're clones, products of a sinister research programme. Some of them managed to escape, where against all odds they survive under a fierce leader called Abel.

Faced with fear, hatred, and violence, the Labs – with Stella's help – fight for freedom, acceptance, and a place in a society that would rather not face up to some unpleasant truths about itself...

Other titles you may enjoy

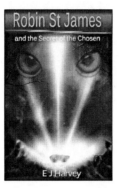

For more information about **Trish Moran**

and other **Accent Press** titles

please visit

www.accentpress.co.uk

Lightning Source UK Ltd.
Milton Keynes UK
UKOW04f0703291115

263741UK00001B/10/P

9 781783 759422